YEAR WRITTEN
1886

797,885 Books
are available to read at

Forgotten Books

www.ForgottenBooks.com

Forgotten Books' App
Available for mobile, tablet & eReader

ISBN 978-1-334-03350-6
PIBN 10750597

This book is a reproduction of an important historical work. Forgotten Books uses state-of-the-art technology to digitally reconstruct the work, preserving the original format whilst repairing imperfections present in the aged copy. In rare cases, an imperfection in the original, such as a blemish or missing page, may be replicated in our edition. We do, however, repair the vast majority of imperfections successfully; any imperfections that remain are intentionally left to preserve the state of such historical works.

Forgotten Books is a registered trademark of FB &c Ltd.
Copyright © 2015 FB &c Ltd.
FB &c Ltd, Dalton House, 60 Windsor Avenue, London, SW19 2RR.
Company number 08720141. Registered in England and Wales.

For support please visit www.forgottenbooks.com

1 MONTH OF FREE READING

at

www.ForgottenBooks.com

By purchasing this book you are eligible for one month membership to ForgottenBooks.com, giving you unlimited access to our entire collection of over 700,000 titles via our web site and mobile apps.

To claim your free month visit:

www.forgottenbooks.com/free750597

* Offer is valid for 45 days from date of purchase. Terms and conditions apply.

English
Français
Deutsche
Italiano
Español
Português

www.forgottenbooks.com

Mythology Photography **Fiction**
Fishing Christianity **Art** Cooking
Essays **Buddhism** Freemasonry
Medicine **Biology** Music **Ancient Egypt** Evolution Carpentry Physics
Dance Geology **Mathematics** Fitness
Shakespeare **Folklore** Yoga Marketing
Confidence Immortality Biographies
Poetry **Psychology** Witchcraft
Electronics Chemistry History **Law**
Accounting **Philosophy** Anthropology
Alchemy Drama Quantum Mechanics
Atheism Sexual Health **Ancient History**
Entrepreneurship Languages Sport
Paleontology Needlework Islam
Metaphysics Investment Archaeology
Parenting Statistics Criminology
Motivational

THE CRUISE OF THE S.S. ATALANTA ON THE RIVERS & CANALS OF HOLLAND & THE NORTH OF BELGIUM.

BY G. CHRISTOPHER DAVIES,

Author of "The Swan and Her Crew;" "Norfolk Broads and Rivers," etc.

London:

JARROLD AND SONS, 3, PATERNOSTER BUILDINGS.

CONTENTS.

CHAPTER		PAGE
I.	INTRODUCTORY ...	-
II.	ACROSS THE NORTH SEA TO YMUIDEN	12
III.	YMUIDEN: THE NORTH SEA CANAL ...	
IV.	YMUIDEN TO AMSTERDAM	
V.	AT AMSTERDAM ...	
VI.	THE ZUYDER ZEE AND HOORN ...	
VII.	HOORN TO ENKHUISEN	
VIII.	ENKHUISEN ...	
IX.	THE ISLAND OF URK	
X.	SCHOKLAND AND KAMPEN	
XI.	A CHANGE OF ROUTE—ZWOLLE	.
XII.	URK AGAIN—STAVOREN ...	
XIII.	HINDELOOPEN ...	.
XIV.	MEDEMBLIK ...	
XV.	TWISK ...	.
XVI.	TEXEL STREAM AND NIEUWE DIEP	

CHAPTER

XVII. NORTH HOLLAND CANAL, ALKMAAR

XVIII. PURMEREND TO HAARLEM

XIX. HAARLEM TO GOUWSLUIS

XX. BOSKOOP TO GOUDA

XXI. AT ROTTERDAM

XXII. THE HAGUE AND SCHEVENINGEN

XXIII. DORT AND WEMELDINGE

XXIV. TO ANTWERP

XXV. ANTWERP AND TERMONDE

XXVI. TERMONDE TO GHENT

XXVII. GHENT TO TERNEUZEN AND FLUSHING

XXVIII. A *KERMIS* AT SOUBERG

XXIX. MIDDLEBURG, VEERE, AND ZIERICKZEE

XXX. FLUSHING. THE END OF THE CRUISE

APPENDIX

ILLUSTRATIONS.

	PAGE
Entrance to Urk Harbour	*Frontispiece*
Sluices at Ymuiden	
Zaandam	
Group of Tjalks, Amsterdam	
At Amsterdam	
Yacht Harbour, Amsterdam	
The Port of Hoorn	
Hoorn Harbour	
Hoorn	
Schuyt on Zuyder Zee	
Urk Islanders	
Urk Harbour	
Kampen Bridge	
Gate at Kampen	
Our Pilot	
Stavoren	
Stavoren Lock	
Medemblik Harbour	
Medemblik	
Medemblik Church	
Farm at Twisk	
Villa, Twisk	

ILLUSTRATIONS.

Dogs and Cart
Tjalk on Canal
Purmerend   207,
Spaarndam Lock
Mill at Haarlem
Haarlem
Gate at Haarlem
At Rotterdam
Mill at Rotterdam
Fishing Boats—Scheveningen
Dordrecht   259,
Group at Wemeldinge
On the Schelde
Sas Du Gand
Schuyts at Sas Du Gand
At Terneuzen
Ships at Terneuzen
Souberg Village
Group at Souberg
Middleburg Town-Hall
At Middleburg
Quay at Middleburg
Veere Town-Hall
Town-Hall, Zierickzee
Water-Gate at Zierickzee
The Atalanta in Veere Lock

CHAPTER I.

INTRODUCTORY.

TAKE it that pleasure-loving Englishmen like to hear or read about the holiday experiences of their countrymen. If a man possessed of any hobby rides it hard, and derives enjoyment from it, he is almost sure of gaining a sympathetic audience. More particularly is this the case if the hobby is an out-of-door one—yachting, sporting, or natural history, leading a man into rural scenes, country life, or on sea, river, or lake. It matters not much whether the ground be new or old, or the subject-matter novel, or well-worn. Indeed, it is almost impossible to find new grounds for holiday exploration, or to do anything that has not been done before. But this is no reason for keeping silence if one has an enjoyable holiday experience to recount, and can tell one's tale with simplicity. At all events, I myself thoroughly enjoy books so written and with such an object, and I have excellent reason for supposing that other men are similarly constituted, since — if the personal allusion may be pardoned — I have written many books which have met with a friendly reception for no other reason, as far as I could see, than that they were simple records of very simple personal amusements.

I therefore feel no great fear of condemnation for the intrusion of another holiday history upon the public, nor, after a recent snub, shall I offer any apology for the egoism which necessarily attends the relation in the first person singular of one's own doings. It may point a moral if I relate how this snub occurred. I had been requested by the editor of a high-class periodical to write an article upon a certain congenial subject which I was anxious to treat well. So I said to myself, said I, I will condense into this article all the information I possess or can crib. I will polish up my sentences, round my periods, select my adjectives, and generally go in my level best for a superior style and a cultured article. So I did. But, alas! my article was, after much kindly consideration, rejected, on the ground that there was too little personal incident, that I had destroyed my individuality, and that, to speak plainly, it was stale fish, and not fresh. Thus ended all my aspirations after a nobler and a better style, and I come back perforce to a recital of the doings of myself, my friends, and our good ship, and "I," "we," "my," and "ours;" must often be written.

I shall not attempt to give any very valuable information, or essay any wise reflections, or do anything but give an account of the cruise of the good ship "Atalanta" on the waterways of Holland and the North of Belgium, during her hire by three friends bound on a well-earned holiday.

Now that foreign travel is so easy and cheap, few men, I think, attain the age of thirty-six without having been abroad, at all events, for a few days. That I was an exception is due partly to the exigencies of professional duties, and partly to an absorbing love for yachting and sailing, which confined me in my short holidays to home waters. But a year's ill-health necessitated a longer holiday and a greater change, and in casting about for a scheme which should have as little rail and hotel work, and as much water and change of scene as possible, I remembered an oft-projected cruise, talked over in winter evenings with kindred spirits, but abandoned when the summer's work interposed its difficulties. This was a cruise to that hollow land won from the waves by man's labour, and intersected by rivers and canals, and to which it was said our favourite Norfolk Broad district bore some resemblance on a small scale.

No country within easy reach of England is so foreign in its appearance, in its costumes, and in its manners. Its buildings are more quaint than those of most other countries. Its waterways are its chief highways, a matter of great interest to yachtsmen; its past history is of extreme interest, whether one looks to its physical struggle with the waves, or to its equally persistent and noble struggle against human tyranny. The saying that "God made the country, man made the town," is only partially true, even in the sense of the proverb, of a land where man has had to wrest the very land he lives on from the sea. As he built towns, so did he make his land, so did he gain a resting place for the sole of his foot. In the dry hollows—dry but by contrast—of this land, he lives, conscious all the while that he owes the safety of his house, his flocks and herds, and even his life, to the massive dykes which hold up the outer waters far above his head.

A very large portion of the country is out of the tourist route, and here the ancient, distinctive costumes are worn with as much pride as of yore, while the habits of the people are as primitive. There was thus every inducement to cruise in one's own floating hotel on the waterways of such a distinctive land, and our subsequent experience proved the pleasant wisdom of our choice.

It was not an easy thing, however, to obtain accurate information as to the best route to follow, the depth of water, size of locks, accessibility of interesting places, pilots, charts, and other matters necessary to be known. We found plenty of travelled friends who could tell us of the best hotels, or where they had badly cooked beef-steaks, or where the best *cafés chantants* were situate, but none who knew the waterways. The few books published by prior voyagers were not much help, as they did not descend to small details. Indeed, the most interesting of all—Havard's "Dead Cities of the Zuyder Zee"—was rather misleading, through his exaggerated idea of the perils of his voyage in one of the local smacks or *tjalks*, than which no safer vessel for the purpose could possibly be.

So we had pretty much to take our chance and trust to circumstances. In fact we sailed with a roving commission, having simply a general idea of the direction we intended to take.

The first thing to do was to get a suitable yacht. My first idea was to have one of our Norfolk pleasure wherries towed across. If this could be managed, it would be difficult to find a more comfortable craft for the purpose. They have great accommodation, are of light draught, are easily managed, and sail faster and closer to the wind than any Dutch vessel can. I found that a tug could tow a wherry across to Flushing, in fair summer weather, in nine or ten hours, and as in the early summer the east-coast tugs are not busy, and, in fact, lie idle for days and weeks at a time, I imagined that they would be glad to undertake the job for say twenty pounds there and back; but I have always found that yachtsmen are expected to pay heavily for their sport. As a shore loafer at Harwich once told me, gentlemen ought not to go yachting unless they can afford to pay for it; his idea of what I ought to pay being the modest sum of two pounds ten shillings for the loan of a rusty anchor, worth at the outside five shillings, for two days. He did not get it.

So when I was asked the sum of forty-five pounds for towing a wherry across to Flushing and back, I gave up the scheme, and looked out for a steam yacht. None were to be had on the other side, therefore we had to have one big enough to cross the North Sea in, yet of light draught to enable us to navigate the canals. The nearest approach to our requirements was the "Atalanta," of Lowestoft, a smart-looking, nearly new vessel of some sixty feet in length, by ten feet beam, and drawing five feet of water.

THE ATALANTA.

The draught was a trifle too great for the smaller canals and rivers, and, as will afterwards appear, we were stopped on two occasions for want of water. A foot less draught would have taken us everywhere, but, on the other hand, the sea passage would be more risky, unless the launch were taken, say from Dover to Calais or Ostend, a voyage which a very small steam yacht would do in safety in fine and settled weather.

The gross registered tonnage of the "Atalanta" was twenty-three tons, and at first, in the pride of our hearts, we proclaimed her as such, but when we found that the lock and other dues were calculated upon the tonnage, we sank our pride, and called her sixteen tons only, which was the net registered tonnage after deducting engineroom.

The accommodation on board consisted of—forward, the forecastle, in which two of the crew slept, and which was also the cooking galley; and the main saloon, twelve feet long, which was our dining and living room, and the bedroom of one of us at night. The engine and boiler were of course amidships; and aft of these were a lavatory, and a ladies' cabin, where two of us slept, and where the berths were a little too short for my length of limb; and an after cabin, where the engineer and the pilot slept.

There was good headroom everywhere, which was no

end of a comfort. At the age of twenty I did not mind living and dressing in a cabin the size of a cupboard, but now my back is not so supple, and I like to stand upright while putting on my garments. I do not glory in the discomfort of roughing it in small yachts as I used to do, although I can still go through a good deal, provided the yacht is a sailing one. The only apologies for the lack of sport about a steam yacht are its speed and comfort. If it lacks either of these it is an atrocity.

It was a stipulation in our hire of the "Atalanta," that she was to be surveyed by the Board of Trade, and her machinery be approved of before we started, a test which she satisfactorily passed. This is a precaution which hirers of steam yachts "bound foreign" should always adopt. If anything happens to the machinery on an English cruise it is sufficiently vexatious, but abroad it is much more serious, and it would be a sorry ending to a holiday to be hung up for the greater part of it in some out-of-the-way place waiting for repairs. As I mean this book to be of some use to those who may follow in our footsteps, it is necessary to say that the cost of hire for a month was £50, and that we had to pay insurance (which on £1,200, the value of the vessel, was £9 3s., the insurers always charging full rate on a hired boat, presuming no doubt that a hirer does not take so much care of the vessel as if she were his own).

Then we had to pay the wages of the men, which came to, weekly: skipper, 35s., engineer, 35s., and deck hand, 30s., the men finding themselves The pilots whom we had to engage from time to time cost us five shillings a day and their keep. We found it more convenient that the pilots should mess with the crew, to whom we allowed eighteenpence a day for their keep. Then there were some small items for oil and waste, harbour and lock dues, and of course the cost of our own keep, all of which, as it happened, we managed to estimate beforehand within a pound or two of the actual total.

There was room on the "Atalanta" for four passengers; three were easily found, but the fourth was not procured. Many a nice fellow would have liked to join us if considerations of cost or of time had not intervened, and as in a joint cruise like this it is absolutely necessary that each man should be thoroughly nice and obliging, we remained content with three—Blake, who by virtue of his having been at sea for some years was elected our captain; Dendy, a brother professional, who by virtue of his linguistic attainments was appointed the interpreter; and the writer, who had nothing to do but keep the log, take photographs, and look after the morals of the other two.

There are so many tourist photographers nowadays—

one sees the neat leather case and tripod on every railway platform, and in every hotel—that it will interest many to hear what my outfit consisted of. My camera was the half-plate size, most useful to tourists, made by McKellen, and was a model of lightness and compactness, having side and vertical swings, rising front, reversing back, turntable for tripod top, and a tripod very light, rigid and portable. For lenses, I had a Dallmeyer's single landscape lens, a Ross's portable symmetrical, and a Ross's rapid symmetrical, the latter fitted with an instantaneous shutter by Sands and Hunter. In addition I took a cheaper form of camera as a duplicate apparatus in case of accident. For plates, I took twelve dozen special instantaneous ones in grooved boxes, half of which turned out to be very good, and the rest anything but good. As a matter of course the best subjects were taken on the worst plates, to my subsequent grief when developing. This will be the place to explain that if any buildings out of the perpendicular are noticed in the illustrations to this book, it is not the fault of the artist, but of the buildings. It was the exception, not the rule, to find a perpendicular wall in that country of leaning towers and reeling houses. I took special care to keep my camera upright, and in cases where there were masts of vessels, it was best to take them as one's gauge of uprightness.

The troublesome process of provisioning need not be described, as every man will please himself with regard to what he takes. We filled all our tanks with Lowestoft water, knowing that none so good would be procurable in Holland; and we took an immense store of mineral waters which we need not have done, as these are better procurable abroad. More particularly would I recommend the Minerva water, which was palatable enough to drink solus with meals, and was very cheap. Indeed, one day I washed in a bottle of it, the fresh water in our tanks being at a low ebb.

CHAPTER II.

ACROSS THE NORTH SEA TO YMUIDEN.

IN accordance with a superstition of mine, that it is lucky to start for a sea cruise on a Sunday, we had fixed to start on the night of Sunday, the 23rd of May. We chose thus early in the season because of the fear (well founded, it afterwards appeared) that the canals being mostly stagnant, and receiving the drainage of the towns, would in their neighbourhoods, be odoriferous of anything but eau de Cologne; also because there is generally a greater depth of water in the earlier months of the year. With the fine weather we were subsequently favoured with, the long days of June were undeniably the pleasantest time at which to take a holiday in Holland waterways; but we find that an early vacation has this drawback, that it is over before the home year takes on its holiday aspect, and when August approaches, and the heat of confinement in offices in narrow streets is unendurable, when there are blue skies and cool breezes outside, one feels rather as if one had really had no holiday at all, and to want another one. Local considerations apart, it is better to take one's rest towards the end of the summer than at the beginning. But it is too bad to grumble. Although I write these lines on a hot, close August evening (because I have promised to get this book done by a certain time, and the night is my only time for such pleasurable work), and although outside in my garden there is a comfortable hammock where I should otherwise be reclining, watching the stars come faintly out as the glow of the sunset fades, yet I must ply my pen cheerfully and gratefully, for I am *well again*. Yes, that undesirable feeling of ill-health, which made life last year a burden for the first and only time, has gone, and in its place there is the buoyancy of one-and-twenty, and the strength of forty—in a word, my Dutch cruise has cured me.

But I must hark back to the start. As the time arrived, we anxiously regarded the weather, which for weeks had been in a most unsettled state. The glass had been going up and down "like a fiddler's elbow;" cyclones had been roaming on the loose about Europe and in England; and especially on the North Sea there had been very dirty weather, which seemed in no hurry to clear. Two or three days before the 23rd May, we were much in the dumps, for fairly fine weather was necessary for the crossing over to Ymuiden, 102 nautical miles over the turbulent North Sea. On the Saturday it was wild and stormy-looking, with the wind veering and backing half round the compass, and the spindrift clouds careering overhead across the sky at a great rate.

"We may be hung up in Lowestoft harbour for a fortnight," said the skipper by way of consolation, as he looked at a heavy bank of clouds to windward, from which smaller pieces detached themselves to scud away on the wings of the wind.

"But the sea is fining down, and the nights have been much finer than the days," we replied; "we shall get across to-morrow night;" and we went to look at the barometer, which, confound it! was still falling. We really felt we should like to tamper with it, like the sexton, whose rector had commanded that the thermometer in the church must on Sundays be maintained at a certain height, and found the easiest way to do so was to *warm the thermometer*, which thus contradicted the shiverings of the doubting parson.

Sunday morning woke fine and still, with a calm sea, but hazy with symptoms of a fog, which kept us uneasy during morning service at Kirkley Church. We spent a lazy but somewhat fidgetty afternoon, lounging on the yacht in the harbour.

Lowestoft is an interesting place even on a quiet Sunday. There is not overmuch quiet though, for there appear to be several detachments of the Salvation Army and Salvation Navy, which are powerful of lung and unmelodious of song. Then friends passing along the pier would stop and deliver themselves of uncomfortable sentiments, such as, "You don't mean to say that you are going to risk your lives in that thing. She is too long and narrow: too fine in the bows: she rolls tremendously. I shall be awfully anxious about you. Send me a post card if [not when] you get there safely," and so on. About five o'clock, however, Dendy hove in sight on the shore, and soon he and his traps were on board, so I had someone to talk to. Blake, the captain, was to come by a train a few minutes before eight, and we were to start at nine sharp. Presently, while Dendy and I went ashore to tea, the engineer came on board and lit the fires, so that we had the satisfaction of seeing the "black pennant" hoisted, or, in plain English, the trail of smoke from the funnel which indicates the approach of "getting under way."

We were all ready, steam was up, the train had arrived, but there was no captain. A glance at the time table showed that the Sunday train started a little earlier than on week days, and it needed no great effort of imagination to picture Blake unconscious of this, and, as the fact was, sipping another glass of port, waiting for a train which had gone. The telegraph office was not open, so there was nothing to do but to wait in patience until shortly before eleven, when Blake and the skipper, who was also his private henchman, tumbled on board in a great hurry, and a towering rage with themselves. A loud whistle announced to the small crowd of friends on the fishing pier, who had kindly come to see us off, that we were at last about to start, the ropes were thrown off; the lifeboat jolly hoisted on the davits (the little one, which belonged to my own yacht, being already on board), and we glided gently out of the harbour, followed by shouts of good wishes and fatherly advice, on to the calm and gently heaving sea.

"The night is made for us," said the captain, "and it will keep fine until the morning," a remark which shows how easy it is to prophesy what one wishes to happen. We ran for a mile or so to the southward, and then crossed the sands as soon as there was depth enough. Then the course was set straight for Egmont, according to the deviation card showing the variation of the compass due to the "Atalanta" being an iron ship.

The log, a patent revolving machine, which marked on a dial the number of knots we ran, was thrown overboard, and towed at the end of twenty fathoms of line, and the cruise was fairly begun. The lights of Lowestoft town, doubled in the smooth sea, were the first to disappear, then the high and more powerful lights of the lighthouses, and we were out in the open sea with no light in sight save the still bright stars in the clear sky, and the swaying stars in the mirroring water. There is an indefinable charm in being at sea on a fine night, intensified when the craft which bears one is a small one, which we now felt to the utmost, and disposing ourselves into the most comfortable attitudes, we prepared to enjoy it. The engineer in his hot den, and the man at the wheel, glancing from the bright circle of the binnacle to the circling darkness, were the only two workers. On either side of us our side lights threw faint red and green reflections on the water, and around us we could see at intervals red and green lights of some passing vessel, for we were now crossing the track of the coasting traders. Then as we got further out into the clearer and bluer water, it became strikingly phosphorescent. As the bows met and parted the swell, they seemed to be diving into a living translucent green, fairy like and unsupporting: then the surge on either side hurled over a mass of white shining crystals and brightly incandescent fountains, which melted together and joined the foaming, molten silver of the screw commotion, and subsided into a creamy glistening wake astern. Then, as the breeze sprung up a little, and wavelets formed on the swell, they flung their sparkling crests into the night, so that the sea was tremulous with light. Truly it was a lovely sight. Often as we have seen it, it is ever new and magical.

But I had not slept well the previous night, so I soon turned in and lay down in the little after cabin. But what horror was this? That demon of a screw was whirring and thumping around, shaking the floor under your feet, and making the bed vibrate in a most uncomfortable fashion. Oh, confound that screw! It is driving round in my own interior now, particularly when the yacht lifts her stern to the wave. Surely I am proof against sea-sickness. Neither a lively tossing nor a rolling calm has ever made me feel qualmish in a sailing yacht, but this screw! Will it or will it not make me feel queer? Is that a premonitory symptom, or is it not? Is sea sickness really as bad as people say it is? Shall I go on deck—shall I?—but fortunately I fell asleep before my doubts were solved.

But ere long I was rudely awakened by a violent jerk, and found that the yacht was heeling over like a sailing boat in a breeze, and on putting my head above the companion, I found that the foresail and staysail were set to a smart breeze, which had sprung up, bringing a little sea with it, enough to make the yacht lively, and dance up and down a bit. There was also a driving rain, which, however, only made matters more exhilarating; so, putting on my oilies, I went on deck, where all the others were assembled, similarly clad, and holding on as best they might. It was then between one and two o'clock, and having got beyond the coasting vessels, and not yet reached the North Sea fishing fleet, there was no light of any vessel in sight, and we were alone on the sea. After a time this grew monotonous and sleepy, so I went below again; but hardly was I asleep when I heard a shrill long-sounding whistle, and felt that we were only going half speed. What's up now? was the thought during the hurried scramble up the ladder. The answer was a disagreeable one. The wind was gone, the sea was calm, but there was a fog so dense that I could not see the funnel from the stern. Groping my way forward to the wheel, I met the forecabin lot, and learned from the crew that we had had rather a narrow shave. A large full-rigged ship had, without any warning or sound of fog horn, passed us so close that we could have flung a stone on to her stern. She had loomed up "like a town," her sails towering above us being the first sign of her presence. As our funnel barely came up to her stern, she would have been an awkward thing to have come in collision with, and as long as the fog lasted we all of us kept a sharp look out, and the whistle was sounded with great regularity and power every few minutes. Our own lights, though burning brightly, looked no better than two dim-coloured moons from the short distance of our bows, and would be quite invisible thirty yards away. The fog, too, played strange tricks with our eyes. We would see a shape loom up, and ere one could cry, "a ship is on the starboard bow," it had disappeared. The bright phosphorescence of the surge at our bow, and the boil of the screw astern were dazzling to eyes straining to pierce the misty circle, which hemmed us in so closely all around. At intervals, too, we heard the sound of a fog horn blown by some sailing ship, coming faintly from an uncertain quarter. It needed but an hour of this to make us under stand what a dangerous thing a fog at sea is. The wind was light and all round the compass, so that we could not guess from which direction the clearing would come.

With the first streak of dawn there was a sudden lifting, so that we might go full speed, and we passengers seized the opportunity to go below. The next interruption was a hail from Dendy—

"Come on deck, we are in the middle of the fishing fleet."

"Hang the fishing fleet; I am sleepy!"

"But we are now going to speak a smack, and ask where we are. Blake hasn't much faith in our compass, and we have just hauled the log and taken soundings, and they don't agree."

This news brought me out in a twinkling, but we were not quite so lost as the interpreter made out, although the first smack we spoke informed us that we were somewhere abreast of the Texel, which would be much to the northward of our course. This smack had probably lost her reckoning in the fog. The next one we spoke located us a little to the northward of the "new haven," Ymuiden, which was quite correct, and where we wished to be.

The mist had thinned so that we could see a mile on either hand, and in this silvery grey circle, luminous with the light of the morning, were a number of Yarmouth and Lowestoft smacks, with their nets down, and their tawny red sails flapping idly as they swung on the windless sea. The beautiful clear blue of the water beneath us attracted our attention and admiration, so ethereal was it, compared with the muddier hue of the coastal sea.

Five o'clock tea was very refreshing, although it was five o'clock in the morning when we had it. It was marked by our first and very nearly the only mishap and breakage of the whole cruise. I essayed to take two cups of tea from the cabin to the deck, one in either hand, and a sudden lurch of the ship sent me against the cabin table, which I assumed to be bolted to the floor, and so allowed it to take my weight in steadying myself. But over went the table, crockery, and all the hot contents of the teapot, finding a harbour on Blake's knees. In the midst of his expostulations I escaped to the deck with my two cups, leaving the captain to have a general mop round and gather up the fragments.

We had a natural reluctance to taking our meals in the cabin while at sea, because there was unfortunately no air space or non-conducting material between the boiler and the cabin bulkhead, and the cabin would grow insufferably hot after some hours of steaming.

As the day wore on we began to look out for land, but as the blue water, and the soundings of fifteen fathoms, showed we were yet some distance off, we had plenty of time to doze and eat, and do our best to kill time. With the exception of fishing smacks, English, French, and Dutch, we saw very few vessels. We found also that the "Atalanta" was not a very fast steamer, and with going slow during the fog, stopping now and then to oil bearings, and going out of our way to speak smacks, we were not, on the average, doing more than six knots an hour, as the log took care to inform us. So we went on over a fairly calm sea, but otherwise in all sorts and samples of weather, oilies off, oilies on, eating, drinking, sleeping, until the afternoon, when soundings of twelve and then of nine fathoms told us we must be nearing the land, for which we kept a keen look out, although the mist prevented anything like a far view.

"Yonder it is, on the port bow; I distinctly see the sandhills."

But in a few minutes the sandhills floated overhead.

"There it is to starboard. I can see a tower."

But the tower was the column of smoke from a steamer's funnel.

At last we began to feel a trifle uneasy. By the log we had run the distance, but if our compass was really out, as the captain asserted, we might be heading for the North Pole.

"Didn't somebody say that there were two towers at Egmont, where we laid our course for?"

"Yes," replied the skipper, "and one of them has a beacon top."

"Then I see them almost in a line," said the sharp-eyed one of the company.

The others could not distinguish them for full ten minutes, and then they loomed up largely enough. We had made a good "landfall," inasmuch as we had hit the very spot we steered for. The towers of Egmont rising out of the sand-dunes are well-known land-marks, and all we now had to do, was to steer to the southward for six or seven miles, and we should make Ymuiden.

The first appearance of a foreign coast was to me interesting, although it displayed nothing but dreary, barren sandhills, very irregular in outline, with here and there a church tower sticking up like a spike from behind them. But these sandhills were the fortifications of the country which lay in the hollow behind; its defence against the masterful power of the sea.

"We have made the land none too soon," quoth the skipper, pointing to the southward sky, where a dense black mass of clouds was rapidly sweeping towards us, below which the sails of the craft, near the mouth of the North Sea haven, were being blotted out by the rain storm. In a few minutes it was upon us, a deluge of rain and a squall of wind. The coast line disappeared, and the sea began to rise. The skipper steered us in as close as sounding would warrant us, for, as he said,

"We won't lose the land if we can help it, now that we have found it. It will be a dirty night."

So with an occasional glimpse of the sandhills through the blinding rain, we kept on until the lighthouses of Ymuiden came in sight, and our passage was safely made.

AS we steamed between the long and massive piers which project into the sea from Ymuiden, and form a long harbour leading to the sluices of the great canal which goes straight to Amsterdam, the sight which met our eyes was interesting in the extreme.

After clearing two or three tugs and smacks and a dredger, which left us little room at the entrance, we saw some fifty schuyts beating down the narrow channel, out to sea for the night's fishing. These curious craft had bluff bows, flaring high out of the water at an angle of forty-five degrees, long narrow leeboards, tall masts, with mainsails very narrow and pointed in the head, which were supported by short gaffs bent like a bow, giving the sails a sugarloaf sort of look. The jibs were fastened to the stem head, and there was no bowsprit, while at the mastheads they had long, coloured streamers. The boats seemed uncommonly handy, for they "came about" like tops, and seemed easily handled. It was ticklish work steering amongst them, as the space was so small, and they were so thickly crowded together. Two would be heading directly for us on the starboard side, and one on the port, and if we cleared these there would be a score crossing in front of us. As a steamer must make way for a sailing craft, we had to be very careful, but our good skipper was equal to the occasion.

"Starboard—ease her—stop her—port—steady—go astern—full speed ahead—shove that one's bows off with the quant—get a fender out amidships."

Such were the orders in rapid succession, and we escaped without a scratch, although the close shaves were numerous. The Dutch skippers knew that their solid oak sides would not suffer in a collision, but rather than spoil our paint, they came about good-naturedly in mid stream, or submitted to be fended off and put summarily about with a pole, and when two of them got aground with a falling tide in their anxiety not to go foul of us, their crews simply laughed as they got out their poles to shove. For ten minutes or so it was beautifully exciting.

"I never saw boats better sailed, considering that women were steering them all," remarked one of the men.

"They are not women," said another. "It is the wide trousers of the men which make them look like women."

And sure enough, it was at first sight difficult to say what the sex might be of the crews of these quaint, highly-varnished oaken vessels. Trousers so voluminous that petticoats are nowhere in comparison with them, gathered in with many creases and folds at the waist and knee, blouses ballooning out in the wind, broad belts with many silver buckles, gold buttons at the throat, and long lank hair streaming from beneath a close-fitting cap; such was the costume of these brown-faced, blue-eyed, hardy-looking fishermen, who looked with much amused curiosity at the little English yacht threading her way among them. If I could have photographed that first scene on Dutch waterways I should have valued the picture more than any other. But the wind and the rain forbade this being done.

We noticed many powerful little tugs, and some of them ran close under our stern, in order to read the name of the yacht. It was curious to see the way in which the steering wheel of these tugs was arranged. The wheel was horizontal instead of vertical, as in English boats, and the steersman hauled at the spokes as at the bars of a capstan. It looked extremely awkward to our notion, but we found it to be the universal method in Holland.

"Do you want a pilot to take you to Amsterdam?" sang out a young man in a small boat which came alongside.

"Jump aboard, and we will see. What is your charge?"

"One pound, sir. Dat is what all English yachts pay."

"Go to Jericho!" cried the captain, wrathfully; "it is only seventeen miles, and the canal is straight."

"Dat is the proper charge. I not go for less."

"Then go ashore at the sluice. We won't pay it."

We were now entering the great locks which connect the North Sea canal with the sea, and stupendous pieces of engineering they are. Three large basins side by side, of varying capacity, serve as locks. We went into the smallest one, and there was so much shouting of directions, on the part of the officials on the shore; so many things which it appeared we must not, or must do, that as we did not understand one of them, it was rather confusing. Here our would-be pilot, whose name was Peter, proved himself useful, as he was the only Dutchman of the lot who spoke English, and it was clear to us at the outset, that if we didn't have him as pilot, we must as interpreter, and we offered him ten shillings to take us to Amsterdam in the dual capacity, which he declined.

While the "Atalanta" was in the lock, we had to go ashore with the ship's register to the haven-master's kantoor, and pay the dues, which, owing to our calling the yacht twenty-three tons, came to ten shillings.

We were besieged by a crowd of people all offering assistance or seeking custom, thrusting their cards into our hands, from which documents, rather than from their lingo, we understood that they were severally prepared to sell us anything in the way of provisions, cigars, and tobacco.

"Have you telegraphed to the harbour-master at Amsterdam for a place?" said one.

"No, surely that is not necessary," replied we.

"Oh yes. All English yachts do so, and the harbour-master will keep you a place at the quay," said everybody.

We refused to believe that this was necessary, until the master of a schooner, which came through the lock at the same time as ourselves, and who spoke a little English, assured us that it was advisable to do so, and he accordingly wrote out and despatched a telegram for us. All this didn't happen so clearly as hereinbefore is stated. It took half an hour of broken English and very broken Dutch to get to this stage, and, as it afterwards appeared, we only made fools of ourselves by listening to such advice (the only time in the cruise, good reader). The harbour master at Amsterdam, expecting a large yacht something like the "Sunbeam," or the Royal yacht, "Osborne," which came to Ymuiden a few days afterwards, took the trouble to shift several ships, and prepare a swell berth for us, whereas we were small enough to slip in anywhere.

We were now summoned on board the "Atalanta," which was ready to move out of the lock. Master Peter was still at the wheel, and the captain instantly ordered him ashore.

"Will you give me fifteen shillings to pilot you to Amsterdam?"

"No!" roared the captain, who was getting savage at the fellow's pertinacity. "Go ashore at once, or we'll chuck you overboard."

"Is it ten shillings, then?" said Peter, quite quietly and respectfully.

"Yes, we will give you that, you paying your fare back again." And so it was agreed.

Going about three hundred yards along the canal, we moored to the side, the shallow, sandy bottom not allowing us to approach nearer than seven or eight yards at that spot. There was of course a good depth of water in the middle of this fine, broad canal, which has done so much to forward the trade of Amsterdam. The sea traffic used to be carried on through the North Holland Canal, running all the way up to Nieuwe Diep, and before the construction of that, through the fast shoaling Zuyder

Zee. Near us were moored several large vessels, in comparison with which we were a very pigmy. Fussy little steamers passed and repassed, growing fewer as the evening advanced, so that at last we were comparatively quiet. The rain had passed off, and after a good dinner, wash, and change of clothes, we felt refreshed, and stepped ashore to explore Ymuiden.

SLUICES AT YMUIDEN.

There was not very much to see, however. The great sluices, and the ships moored hard by, the schuyts already running back before the rising gale, the heaped-up sand-dunes showing yellow against the pale-green windy sunset, a few streets of clean and tidy houses did not promise much. But there were little details which interested us. On a highly varnished oak barge, which had come up with a cargo of bricks, was a woman, not only neatly dressed in dark brown and spotless white, but with a gold helmet covering nearly the whole of the head; this helmet would cost, as we afterwards learned, some twenty pounds at the least. It was a curious contrast to the dress and appearance of an English bargee's wife. The husband's dress, it may be remarked, though tidy, was not, I should say, so expensive, by a long way, as his English brother's would have been, and that is not saying much. There were plenty of bright, healthy children playing about, and every one with either pink or white stockings on, quite clean and fresh-looking at that time in the evening, although they had probably been played in all the day.

We took a stroll on the dunes, but had to abandon them in the vicinity of the village, on finding that the cleanliness and sweetness of the houses was decidedly obtained at the expense of the sandhills which were used as a common midden. There was an inn overlooking the sluices, where we sat for half an hour over our coffee, and then, as each of us was yawning dreadfully, and it was ten o'clock, we agreed to turn in at once.

About the middle of the night I was awoke by a heavy bang in our cabin.

"That's Blake, risen up suddenly and knocked his head," thought I, mindful of my own first experience, the berths being partly under the deck; and, without opening my sleepy eyes, I listened for the expostulation with fate which must surely follow. But no sound came; and looking in wonder, I perceived my companion sitting on the floor, smiling seraphically.

"What on earth is the matter?" I exclaimed, in alarm.

"Why, I dreamt that we were at the island of Urk, in the Zuyder Zee, and that I made a pun by saying that something was *irk*some, and I laughed so in my sleep that I rolled out of bed. You see I have blown my air bed out so much that it is too round. But listen to the wind outside. It is blowing a gale. We only just slipped across in time."

Between laughter at the captain's adventure, and the noise of the wind, I did not get to sleep again for some time.

CHAPTER IV.

YMUIDEN TO AMSTERDAM.

IN the morning it was still blowing hard from the south-west, and on the bar the sea was breaking heavily, the white spray being visible above the hollows of the sandhills.

After breakfast, Dendy and I went ashore with the camera, and set up the dainty and valuable instrument on the top of a sandcliff in order to take a view of the sluices. But a strong gust carried my precious apparatus over the cliff, and in an attempt to save it I went over also. It was soft falling, however, and anxiously extricating the camera from the avalanche of sand which accompanied us in our descent, I found it had received no damage except a few scratches on the varnish. After that, when it blew strongly, Dendy had to sit between the camera legs and hold on to them. This liability to be blown over is the one defect of a light apparatus.

We took a general view of the sluices, and one of the

crowd of schuyts which had run in for shelter, and which, with their trawl nets hoisted to the mast-head to dry, looked very picturesque. My struggles with the black focussing cloth in the high wind caused much amusement among the onlookers.

A sturdy fisherman coming up, they seized him, and pointing to his gold neck buttons and voluminous breeches, wished me to take his portrait, but the old boy was surly and shy, and so we let him alone, and went back to the Atalanta.

A large ship had just hoisted sail, and went driving along the canal at a good speed. It seemed so strange to see a sea-going vessel sailing along a straight artificial cut, which although broad to us, was narrow to her. We were soon under way, and the banks, which near Ymuiden are very high, became much lower, so that we could see over the surrounding country. The canal was also less artificial in appearance, and the margin was fringed with reeds, tall grasses, and bulrushes. There was a wide prospect on either hand, flat, indeed, but not monotonous, for the bright-green polders and meadows were diversified with groups of houses and clumps of trees. The houses had pointed gables, generally painted a brilliant green, great sloping roofs like four-sided pyramids, covered with tiles so highly-glazed that they shone like mirrors in the sun. Then there were quaint farms and taverns, quainter groups of peasants, barges sailing and barges towed; steam tugs, and passenger steamers, giving variety, life, and motion to the busy water highway and its peaceful banks.

We stood in a group round Peter, the pilot, who was at the wheel, and pumped him to the best of our ability, and to the extent of his broken English. The morning was cheery and pleasant, with a wind strong enough to take one's breath away when one faced it, and making it almost impossible to bring guide books and maps on deck, and difficult indeed to retain one's head gear. To right and left canals branched off, and red-sailed barges moved briskly over the meadows on unseen waterways. Peter was anxious to show us anything worth seeing, and told us names of places to the right and the left.

"Dat is de canal to Haarlem," and so on; and at length, as a heron rose from the bank,

"Dat is de bird dat pick de eel from de vater."

"Oh yes," said our skipper, "that is an old trick of theirs. We have plenty of them in our country."

We kept a look out for storks, which we supposed would be crowded about everywhere, but, to our disappointment, none were to be seen. A heron wasn't half foreign enough for us

"Look yonder," said the skipper; "is that where they store the surplus windmills of Holland?"

And truly there was some reason for this question. For, in the near distance were windmills in rows, in dozens, in twenties, and apparently in hundreds, stretching away to a vanishing point, and each one trying to twizzle round faster than its neighbour.

ZAANDAM.

"Dat is Zaandam. Dere is dree hondered and sixty five windmills, one for every day in de year," explained Peter.

"But why have they put all the windmills in one place?" asked Rowland, who was of a very inquiring turn of mind.

"Dey is not all in one place. Dere is nine tousand windmills in all Holland. Plenty more in oder places, as you see for yourselves when you go about."

"But what do they all do?" persisted Rowland. "They can't all be pumping water at Zaandam."

"Saw wood, grind corn, and many oder tings—like you use steam in your country," replied Peter.

"There seems something wrong about those mills, Rowland," said I. "What is it now?"

"They do seem wrong, sir. I see that every one has canvas sails, instead of the vanes, which we usually have in Norfolk, but there is something else too."

"I have it. They turn round the contrary way. Our millsails always turn with the sun, or over from right to left. These go backwards, every one of them from left to right."

"So they do. Well, one must expect things to go differently in a foreign country. I notice the handles of the doors of the houses and the carriages turn down instead of up, and all their door handles are egg-shaped or oval, instead of round, like ours."

Peter (whose broken English it is too troublesome to write) chimed in to inform us, that his grandfather told him, that the first windmills were made fixed, always facing the north-west, and not veering round to face the wind, from whatever direction it blows, as they do now. I believe that this was so, but it was long before Peter's grandfather's time; he, no doubt, repeated the tale which had been handed down to him.

We passed through two railway bridges; the first of which was opened to us without any delay, but the second remained obstinately shut, in spite of our continued whistling. The men on the bridge simply looked stolidly at us, while the strong wind blew us right into the opening, and we had to hold on to the dolphins with all our might. I know I got the first hold with a boathook, and held on so tightly, that for some few minutes afterwards I could not open my fingers. After keeping us waiting ten minutes, the bridge swung open, and we passed through. It appeared that steamers must not exceed a certain fixed rate of speed, and, by way of check upon them, the bridges are not opened if the space between them has been covered too quickly. The inducement to quick steaming is thus effectually removed.

The reed cutting and peat gathering, which we saw at intervals on the banks, was familiar enough to us from the Broad District, which is, indeed, but a smaller edition of the Hollow land, less artificial perhaps, and certainly prettier, in its conjunction of wood and water.

The idiosyncracies of our party speedily manifested

themselves, and happily fitted in very conveniently for the common good. Thus, the captain, in addition to his nautical knowledge, developed a keen regard for our creature comforts, especially eels, the abundance of which made Holland particularly interesting to him. Dendy was fond of diving into guide books, and ferreting out useful information, which he judiciously retailed to us. In all sight-seeing matters, we surrendered ourselves unresistingly to his guidance; while in all dealings with the natives, his guileless appearance and ready address (Blake and I called it cheek) were invaluable to us. As for me, I fear that I and my camera were the troubles of the trio. The appearance of the apparatus was the signal for Blake to go off hot foot in the opposite direction, trying to look as if he had no connection with the long-legged man under the black cloth, for Blake is a shy man, and hates nothing so much as being stared at. I must say that I don't like being the centre of a curious crowd, as was my fate whenever I wanted to take a picture, and I lost many opportunities through my bashfulness in this respect.

But this is a digression—not the first nor last, I fear. The canal grew wider, and the banks less formal, and we had entered the Y, as the long arm of the Zuyder Zee on which Amsterdam is built, is called. The strong wind raised a respectable sea, and out of the Zaandam canal, a red-sailed barge came hissing gallantly along, her sails close-reefed, and her bluff bows completely hidden in the cloud of foam and spray she drove up in front of her. These flat-bottomed Dutch craft are built to go over the water rather than through it, and this being so, flat sloping bows are apparently better than fine ones, while the vessel, for a given length, carries more cargo.

The barges or schuyts grew more numerous, large steamers and sailing vessels were visible in numbers, the Y broadened out to its full and goodly proportions, and there, on our right, was Amsterdam. The appearance of the city from the water is exceedingly fine. There are large and handsome buildings wedged in between crowded gables of every variety of height and form; spires, towers, and steeples, masts and sails, all mixed up together: and not only is there every variety of form, but every variety and tone of colour is there also. Houses and water and vessels are entangled together in an *olla podrida* of colour and form, which the delighted eye in vain attempts to separate.

It is easy to draw a map of Amsterdam. Draw a straight line which will represent the Y, with its crowded quays, plant one leg of a pair of compasses on this line, and draw some twenty half-circles, one outside the other, these are the canals. Then draw a number of straight lines radiating from the point like the spokes of a bicycle wheel. These are the streets, with a bridge at every intersection of the half-circles. Now you have as good a map of Amsterdam as you want, if you are a man of principles, and don't go in for details.

The Atalanta glided alongside one of the many little little piers which jut out from the quay, forming a number of nice little harbours, and was scarcely moored, ere our visits began. The first to come, and, alas! the last to go, was a voluble washerwoman, with a very white apron, and fat legs in very white stockings. As each one of the passengers and crew put his head out above deck, she would hand him a big business card, and repeat the same tale in a very shrill voice,

"You want me do your washing? I do it better and cheaper than any one else. A great big fat woman will come here by and bye, and ask for your washing, but I am here first, and do it best. Don't you give your washing to that fat woman. She not do it as well as I," and so on.

Then when we put on our shore-going toggery, she took us for fresh members of the ship's company, and gave us more cards and more talk. In vain we told her we hadn't any dirty things. She thought that was for the sake of bargaining, and that we were waiting for the big fat woman to come, and she offered a reduction in her prices. We got quite a collection of cards from the crowd of would-be vendors, and by studying these we made excellent progress with our Dutch vocabulary, as far as articles of food and drink were concerned. Most of the people were content with one refusal, but the sight of the white stockings feeling their way down the companion steps while we were at lunch, showed us that the washerwoman still believed in us. I had just cut my thumb with the carving knife, and thrusting an ensanguined handkerchief into her face, we said we would give it to her to wash and to keep for her very own for ever, if she would only go—and, thank goodness! she went.

Then a very polite man came into the cabin, and represented himself to be the agent of a certain yacht club, and did we know Lord This, and Sir Somebody That, and this yacht, and the other yacht?

"Will you kindly tell us what you want?"

"Nothing, nothing, but to be of assistance to you, if you require it."

"And what will your assistance cost us?"

"Nothing, nothing—no expense at all, I assure you."

We said this was very good of him, and to stick to him for a moment, he changed a little money for us, made us taste some excellent curacoa, was of more trouble than use to us, and finally considered us a fraud, I have no doubt, as he did not succeed in selling us anything except a ton or two of coals. We thought he worked very hard for his money.

CHAPTER V

AT AMSTERDAM.

OUR next visitor was the dock policeman, who politely shook hands all round, and asked to see the yacht's papers. He only knew a few words of English, but after some trouble, we understood that yachts were free from harbour dues, but it was necessary to produce papers from our club to prove that we were a yacht. The dues are really so small, that they were hardly worth troubling about except as a precedent, so we explained that the yacht was a hired one, and did not belong to any club, but that two of us were on the committee of the Norfolk and Suffolk Yacht Club, if that was of any use. We also produced the certificate of the vessel's registry, but what was wanted was evidently an Admiralty warrant, though, no doubt, any formal-looking document on a sheet of foolscap, signed by anybody, attested by a notarial seal, and setting forth that the yacht Atalanta *was* the yacht Atalanta, would have sufficed.

The dock inspector talked a great deal; so did another official, who carried off our certificate of registry, and who shook his head mysteriously, when we told him he might please himself whether he charged us or not: and finally the harbour-master himself came and looked at us, and returning our registry, politely told us that we were free of dues. We afterwards found that much of the preliminary palaver might have been saved by the judicious application of a quarter guelder. We frequently had the same trouble in proving that we were a yacht afterwards, until Blake hit upon the bright idea of responding to the question, whether we belonged to any royal yacht club, by saying, with a lordly air, "Oh, no! nothing so common. We belong to '*une société particulière*,'" at the same time pointing to the nautical buttons on his coat and mine. This gave ample satisfaction; but I should recommend any small yachtsmen—or crews of small yachts, rather—to provide themselves with something to prove that things are what they seem.

We now thought it time to go and see some of the sights of Amsterdam, but a fresh delay arose. One of the crew had foregathered with the captain of a tug which lay near us, who could speak English. This captain knew of a good pilot, and brought him to us. He was an old man, seventy-three years of age, and he had been pilot on the Zuyder Zee for forty-two years, and had now retired upon a pension. He was a little wiry man, with an honest countenance. He asked three guelders (5s.) a day, and his "grub," and we were so prepossessed with him, that we would have engaged him on the spot, but Rowland called out in a hoarse whisper down the skylight,

"Don't be in a hurry, gentlemen, there will be plenty more come, and we can take our pick."

This was very proper advice, and we followed it. But the next man who came was a bottle-nosed old boy, who said Peter had sent him, and who asked 10s. a day and his food. So we chose our first-comer, old Klaus de Jonge, and a rare old boy he was, as honest as possible. He did not cheat us himself, and he was particularly careful that no one else should cheat us.

He only professed to speak a little English, "Go-ahead," or "Astern," and so on, but this was only his modesty, for in a day or two he spoke with considerable ease and fluency, when the first strangeness had worn off.

On his arrival with his kit, he said to us, "Now sirs, you must not call me pilot, because I pensioned. I am de man at de veel, or de interpreter. But no new pilot as good as I, because dey not know de Zowder Zhay. De ships all go by de canals now, and de pilots not learn de Zhay. I learn it as a boy, and know every sandbank, because all de ships came dat way when I began piloting. Now, sirs, listen to me. Ven we go through de sluices give de man vid de ropes on the locks, a quarter-guelder (5d.), and dey make de ropes fast properly. We do noting for noting in dis country; and if you do not give de men something dey take no care, and you perhaps make de ship break someting."

We discovered that this was extremely sound advice, and that "tips" are as necessary in Holland as in England.

At last, and late in the afternoon, we got under way for a stroll round, making at first for the Post kantoor, the first object of interest to us in every town. A profane legend on every tram-car told us that the central part of Amsterdam is called the Dam, and we reached this place in a heavy downpour of rain. But the natives did not seem to mind the rain in the least. The men had no umbrellas, and we didn't see a waterproof coat in the whole of Holland, except the oilies worn by the pilots. The clean-looking women of the servant class, with their white frilled caps and white stockings, paddled about the sloppy streets with only slipshoes on their feet—the ordinary Dutch slippers with a thin leather sole, and vel veteen or carpet uppers—and an old lady from Friesland with a gold helmet and lace cap, seemed indifferent to the drops which rattled against the precious metal, and soaked her fine lace. The rain was clearly too akin to the constant washing of all things of the Hollanders to be minded.

It is not my intention to trouble the reader with any particulars of our sight-seeing. We did the usual things at Amsterdam as at every other town. One of us carried Baedecker, another Murray, and the third a dictionary, and between the three of us, we ferreted out all that was worth seeing. We would stop at a street corner, open our books, unfold our maps, fall into a heated argument as to the points of the compass, and cool ourselves with a glass of *bierisch* at one of the *eafés* which seemed to be at one's elbow wherever one stood.

I can't stand much museum and picture-gallery work myself, but I found abundant amusement in wandering up and down the narrow streets of the older part of the city, looking at the various types of people who were going in an orderly way about their business, only the smaller fry taking much notice of us. The groups of people from the provinces, which we constantly met, interested us most, because of the distinctive costumes which they wore and seemed proud of. It was also great fun poking about the quieter streets, and looking into the shop windows, and making a few purchases. Dendy was gone upon pipes, and could never pass a tobacco shop without stopping for a long look. Blake liked the jewellers' shops, and took a long time speculating what he would buy for his wife if he had one; but if I wished to stop and look at a scientific window, both declined, and would hurry on in the most unfeeling manner.

It struck us that the prevailing idea of every Dutch architect is to design a more striking gable and ornamentation than any of his professional brethren, and that he keeps experimenting. In no other way could we account for the diversity of pointed gables which topped the high and narrow houses, and made the streets look more like a stage background than real places existing in the nineteenth century. Then each gable had a crane projecting horizontally out of it at the apex, for the purpose, as we learnt, of hoisting furniture and other articles up to any storey of the lofty dwellings, without the risk of chafing paint and plaster on the staircase.

Of course there is never a straight vertical line anywhere; the crowded houses lean against each other with a gravity which does not look a sober gravity. If it were necessary to pull down or alter any of these mutually supporting tenements, the others would surely fall like houses of card. When I show any of my photographs of Amsterdam to candid friends, they remark, "I say, old man, either you or your camera must have been very unsteady when you took this." And when I reply, that it is Amsterdam which is unsteady, they smile incredulously.

It is, of course, well known that the foundations of Amsterdam are artificial, consisting of wooden piles driven into the soft mud, and every fellow quotes that other fellow, who said that he knew a city where the inhabitants dwelt on the tops of trees, but it takes a little thinking to realize that these piles are driven in so close together that nothing can be forced between them. In the foundation of one steeple 6,000 trees were rammed into the ground, and the wooden foundations of the Stadthuis cost £100,000 sterling.

It can easily be imagined that a large proportion of this wooden land must be rotten and yielding, and, indeed, some years ago, a large building did subside, through failure of its foundations.

The numerous canals, some broad, some narrow, but almost all with a busy street alongside, and shaded by rows of trees, were interesting to us, because of the abundance of barges, schuyts, tjalks, and snibs, which thronged their green surfaces. Loading and unloading, punting, towing, or sailing all day long, there was a constant movement of vessels; while in the evening, when work was done, the women and children made themselves very neat and clean and tidy, and sat on the tops of their little cabins and sewed and talked, while the shadows deepened on the canals, which were now so still, mirroring the tall, straight masts and tall, crooked houses on their smooth surface. The barges are all carefully washed and scrubbed when the day's work is done, until the varnished oak shines again; and the men aboard them spend their leisure time in giving a touch of varnish here and there, or polishing the brass work, which, in the shape of thin sheet brass, is nailed on to every spot where there is a decent excuse for putting it.

A favourite place is along the curved top of the long rudder and around the tiller, and when brightly polished, it gives the effect of massive brass castings. Even a coal barge is made spick and span, bright with brass and colour. As Jack, our deck hand, said, "They are hard on varnish and green paint here, sir." The very watertubs on deck are painted green, with polished brass bands around them, and sometimes with landscapes of gorgeous and rainbow magnificence painted on the ends. The barge is the only home of the bargee and his family, and hence partakes of the neatness of all Dutch homes. In the stern, on each side of the rudder, windows are cut through the solid oak planking, which is there quite eight inches thick; and these windows, which are barely a foot square, are gay with festooned curtains, and a pot of flowers or other ornament, and many have a toy *gate* fixed across the outer opening. We were much smitten with these dolls' house windows.

GROUP OF TJALKS, AMSTERDAM.

We noted a few of the best places to photograph—not the stock sights—visited the Krapolownski Café, a very large place, brilliantly lighted with electric light, and where we were amused at the funny little billiard tables, some curved like a half-moon, or right-angled like the letter L, which no doubt imparts an agreeable variation in the mode of play.

While returning to the boats, we smelt the canals rather strongly. At least the others did, for my sense of smell is so defective, that I cannot honestly say, that with my eyes shut I know the difference between a honeysuckle and an ancient boot. No doubt the heavy showers of the afternoon had stirred the water up; but at one bridge even I caught it, and was glad to reach the sweeter water of the Y. I believe that advantage is taken of the slight rise and fall of the tide in the Y to flush the canals, or rather, to cause a slight circulation, and consequent refreshing of the water in them. But I must say I should not care to live at Amsterdam in August.

The next morning, before breakfast, I hurried out alone with my apparatus, to try and get a few pictures. It was, however, extremely difficult, owing to the high wind which was blowing. The boats and trees in the foreground, which, from their colour, required a long exposure, were in a constant state of movement, and my Amsterdam photographs were not very successful. But I went dodging about into all sorts of queer places, and found the people, who crowded about me everywhere, very civil and polite. True, they always smiled audibly when I put my head under the black cloth, but then I laughed too, as if it were a good joke, and all was pleasant. Once, in a very low quarter, as I put my head under, I saw by the reflection in the focussing screen, that a big, rough-looking fellow made a motion as if he would bonnet me; but, without turning my head, I stretched my arm out behind, and shook my clenched fist at him, which turned the laugh in my favour. It was sufficient for me to say that I belonged to an English

AT AMSTERDAM.

yacht lying at the quay, to make everybody very civil and pleasant.

I must say I was very pleased with Amsterdam and the Dammers. The streets were clean, we saw no drunken or disorderly people, and there was no importuning by street vendors. I was extremely surprised to read the reports now appearing as I write, of riots and bloodshed at Amsterdam, caused by the suppression of some popular sport of torturing eels, strung across a canal, the details of which I cannot learn. Possibly there was a *kermis*, or fair, on. As the Dutch are so fond of eels, they may like to use them as playthings. By the way, we saw plenty of dried eels in the shops, straight and stiff, and strung together exactly like tallow candles.

After breakfast, Dendy and I went on the Y in my jolly, which I had brought in addition to the lifeboat jolly belonging to the Atalanta, so that I might prowl about without interfering with the others. Our object was to photograph some of the schuyts which were cruising past at a rare pace, so we fastened the camera to the stern of the jolly, by means of a brass clip with universal joints, and Dendy rowed me close to the vessels, and I fired at them with an instantaneous shutter as they passed. This was good exercise, but the artistic results were not very satisfactory. A little 12-foot boat, rocking on the swell, was not quite steady enough even for instantaneous exposures.

The view of Amsterdam from the Y is especially interesting, and we just drifted about here and there, admiring it, as it lay in a blaze of bright sunshine, which came for a short time out of the windy sky. Numbers of schuyts were sailing to and fro, at what seemed to us a great pace, considering their clumsy hulls, and the small amount of canvas they carried. Rowland asserted, and possibly he was right, that our Norfolk wherries would have beaten them hollow, and that it was simply the foam and splash made by their bluff bows that gave them the appearance of speed. But, at all events, they were wonderfully handy, and the huge leeboards, which take the place of our centre boards, seemed to cause but little trouble when they tacked. It was curious to see how these craft would sail away towards the city; a bridge would swing open, and the vessels would be swallowed up by the houses as they entered the canals. Again, these hidden canals would disgorge group after group of the schuyts, which would rapidly scud away eastward to the Zuyder Zee, or westward to the sea, or the many canals branching from the great one to Ymuiden.

When our plates were exhausted, we found our way to a little haven where the pleasure yachts of Amsterdam were kept. In a quiet basin, surrounded by trees, were a large number of quaint-looking craft. With the exception of a few American centre-boards, all the yachts were built upon the lines of trading craft, having an equal strength of plank and timber, but a brighter varnish, more polished oak, more dainty paint, and a greater abundance of resplendent brass. The cabin doors of these yachts were, in many cases, made of cast-iron gratings, of a decorative pattern, similar to the ornamental iron doors so common among the houses on land. The cabins were roomy, but, as far as we could see, lacking

YACHT HARBOUR, AMSTERDAM.

the internal comforts of English yachts. Not only was the brass work polished, but every bit of iron work, every shackle, every halyard eye and block and fitting, which with us would be galvanized iron, were plain iron, polished like steel. The white sails were hoisted upon the same short, crooked gaff as the country schuyts, and the great leeboards upon each side were hoisted up out of the water, looking, for all the world, like the wings of a great butterfly. We examined these curious craft long and minutely, but, as throughout the whole of our trip we only saw one yacht actually under way, and many a score at moorings, we came to the conclusion that Dutch yachtsmen spent more time in polishing up their yachts than in sailing them.

After rowing about, and visiting some of the bigger ships of various nations, which give portions of the Y a nineteenth-century appearance, strangely at variance with the old-world look of other parts of it, we went back to the Atalanta, and found Blake with a list of necessaries for our housekeeping, and Dendy departed, armed with his dictionary, in search of what was wanted, presently returning loaded with his spoils, and triumphantly declaring that he had not any fear of Dutch.

We visited the splendid new Rijks Museum, which is near completion, and has gathered within its walls the pictures and other objects of interest in Amsterdam, which were formerly scattered in various buildings. But of these pictures, much as they interested us, and much as we admired their bright colours and vivid realism, it is not now our province to speak, because our readers will do as we did, and look at Murray or Baedecker. Dendy and I had the museum all to ourselves, for Blake was indisposed, owing, as he said, to drinking Amsterdam water, but we are very sure that no Amsterdam water, unless boiled or safely diluted, had passed his lips. Talking about water, we had the tanks filled up this day from a barge that came alongside, by the order of our friend the Jew. For about a hundred gallons of the precious liquid we were charged six shillings, whereupon I said, "We might have filled up with Dutch gin at a cheaper rate." The man replied, "Yes, sir, it is easy to bring you Dutch gin in bottles, but it is hard to bring you good water in barges. We come from Haarlem, and we have to pay lock dues, and men to work the barge, and it costs us as much to bring you a little as to bring you a great deal." After some argument I paid him, although I believe it was a "do," but afterwards we made our bargain beforehand, and had no reason to complain of the price.

In the afternoon, Blake had recovered sufficiently to come with me to the tollhuis on the opposite side of the Y, where is the entrance to the North Holland Canal. Here there was a *eafé*, and a pleasant grove of trees with seats and swings and roundabouts scattered round for the amusement of the Amsterdammers, with whom the place is a favourite resort. In a branch of the canal hard by, we came upon a water-squatter, the first of the many fixed habitations of the kind which we afterwards came across in the quiet corners and rushy bye-ways of the waterways of Holland. A description of this one will serve without much alteration for that of all. In a little bay of the still, green canal, lay a boat, which might have been the original ark, or a less ancient Dutch barge cut down, securely moored against the bank. Upon this boat was built a house, with many attempts at ornament on a small scale, with little bridges to the land, and toy gates which a child might step over or around. A wooden platform accommodated a hen-house, and another wooden platform supported a shed, and a small garden of imported earth. Between and around the boat and the platforms the reeds and rushes grew thickly, and a fence of latticed woodwork shut off the floating house and its appurtenances from the rest of the canal. So far as we could learn, the tenants in these floating houses are simply squatters in unwanted corners, paying no rent or taxes, and living at least as free as the frogs which croak in the fast-growing marsh around them.

A fine, still evening succeeded a somewhat blustering day; and as we sat under the trees in the Zoological Gardens, sipping our coffee by the light of many lamps twinkling among the branches, cheered by the strains of a remarkably good band, amused by the crowds of people who were as interesting to us as we appeared to be to them, our feet protected from the damp by little wooden stools, and our souls soothed by English tobacco—not Dutch—we agreed that life in a foreign land had considerable charms. At twelve o'clock that night we turned in, the weather calm and fine, the glass high and steady. Two hours later, I woke to hear the howling of the wind and the beating of the rain over our heads. Amid the sound of the splashing of waves against the ship's sides, I heard the bumping of the unfortunate jolly-boats, which appeared to be beating themselves to matchwood. The glass had fallen four-tenths of an inch in the two hours, and there was a hard gale blowing from the north-east, which made us on a lee shore, with a good lop setting in from the Y. It was clearly necessary to get the smaller boat aboard; but as, on putting my head out of the companion, I got my hair immediately wet through, I hailed two of the crew, who cheerfully turned out, lifted the smaller boat out of harm's way, and secured the larger, after which I wiped my head and turned in for another sleep. But it was not for long, for a heavy thunderstorm sent the gale round to the south west, and it was morning ere I got to sleep.

CHAPTER VI.

THE ZUYDER ZEE AND HOORN.

ONCE again the black pennant was hoisted, and on Thursday morning the Atalanta steamed away from Amsterdam quay, bound for the Zuyder Zee. Old Klaus, who was at the wheel, began to talk at once, and all the time he was with us there were few moments in which he was not talking to somebody or other. Rowland was of an enquiring mind, and plied "Kloster," as he persisted in calling the pilot, with questions, which the latter answered very fully in his broken but improving English. He pointed out to us the prominent buildings of Amsterdam, as they were visible from the Y, the steamers and sailing ships of various nationalities, which we passed or met; and as a schuyt, laden with peat, passed across our bows, he called out, "Dere, dat is Dutch coals." We told him about our being stopped at one of the railway bridges over the North Sea canal, and he explained that the passage must occupy two hours, and that if a pilot takes his ship along faster, "dey would shoot him," by which we understood he would get into trouble.

The wide expanse of the Y, and its good and even depth, excited our admiration of it as a sailing ground, yet not a single pleasure boat or yacht did we see actually sailing upon it. This day there was quite a sea upon it, as the wind was still blowing half a gale from the south-west. We had heard so many tales of the dangers of the Zuyder Zee in a breeze, that we made special enquiries of the pilot, who assured us that these were much exaggerated, and that a run to Hoorn would not hurt us.

The only thing he was doubtful about was our draught of water, and whether we should be able to enter the harbour. Ordinarily there was but eight feet of water in many parts of the southern portion of the Zuyder Zee, but this was affected by the prevailing wind. A north-west wind filled the North Sea, raising the water at Ymuiden at high tide twelve feet above the Amsterdam level, and naturally raising the water in the Zee a foot or two. But the recent prevalence of easterly and southerly winds would have the contrary effect, and lower the level one or two feet or more, which would make a serious difference to us.

We now reached the massive sluices at Schellingwoude,

where the old arm of the Zee, known as the Y or I, was hedged across by great dykes, and the water controlled by locks. We passed through these locks in company with a large light-draught steamer, bound for Zutphen, up the Yssel (which was also our intended course), without difficulty, and without any charge being made, except the gratuity of a quarter guelder to the men, whose duty it is to make fast the ropes to the cleats on the lock walls. Then we steamed out of the lock, and got our first sight of the renowned Zuyder Zee.

It was in a somewhat alarming state of bubble. Lashed by the half gale into a foaming yeasty expanse, it was not at first attractive. As soon as we got beyond the lee of the land, we encountered peculiarly high and steep waves, caused, of course, by the shallowness of the water. The little jolly was on deck, but the larger one was towing behind, and speedily began to fill. So we had to stop while it was hoisted unto the davits, a heavy job, with a weight of water in it. As soon, however, as it was clear of the surface, the plug was knocked out, and the water ran out. The delay brought the engineer on deck. He was much impressed with the boil and bubble around us, and was of opinion that we were going to catch it. As the steamer proceeded, she seemed to create a hollow, into which she sank, drawing a curling wave astern of her, which threatened to break on board in a deluge. Sounding with our boathook, we found that there was hardly sufficient water to float her. However, there was nothing to hurt us, and, hoisting the sails, and getting the wind to help us as well as steam, we kept ahead of the waspish waves, which only occasionally tumbled overboard. Still the deck was kept wet enough with the water of the Zuyder Zee.

It was a curious scene; the seething sea, yellow with the mud stirred up by the waves, the low green shores, with here and there the sharp spire of a village church, and a cluster of red roofs of some larger town, groups of trees scarce rising above the universal level, and above all, the vast dome of the sky, where dark and ragged clouds hurried across the windy blue. There was no other vessel within sight on the sea, save the Zutphen steamer, which had got ahead during our delay with the boat.

As we went northward, the water became a trifle deeper, and we ceased to have any anxiety about running aground. The land was often hidden in thick blue rain clouds, but in the pale gleamy intervals we could see the island of Marken, and the "dead cities" of Monnickendam and Edam. We were most anxious to land at Marken, but our pilot assured us that we could not enter the harbour, and that it would be impossible to land in the boat with the sea that was running. So perforce we contented ourselves with running as close by it as we could, and getting a good view of its verdant shores and clusters of red roofs shining brightly in a sunny gleam against the blackness of a thunder cloud.

I am not an artist, but it struck me that it would be extremely easy to make a typical sketch of Marken, and other islands of the Zuyder Zee, from the sea, thus: draw a straight line for the sea, a curved line will make a flattish hump, like a stranded jelly-fish, which colour green. In the middle of this hump, draw a series of zigzags, which colour red, with a taller and thinner zigzag in the middle for the church. Then throw in the colours of sea and sky to taste, and there you are. Looked at frontways, it will be Marken; backways, through the paper, Urk; and upside down, Schockland.

Old Klaus presently gathered us round him to hear an awful story of the deep, *apropos* of the very spot where we now were. There was an Englishman who had a small sailing yacht, and who engaged Klaus as pilot. This yachtsman was a very strange man. After breakfast, he laid his vessel to in the Zuyder Zee, took off all his clothes (very impressively), and (solemnly) jumped overboard.

"Good Lord! and drowned himself!" exclaimed Rowland, horrified.

"Yah" (Dutch for yes, and spelt Ja), *"every morning."*

"Why you mean that he bathed," cried Rowland, much disgusted at his "sell." "We often do that in our country."

Presently, while some of us were studying the chart laid out on the top of the after cabin, there was a great clattering forward, and a warning cry, "Look out." Something hit the boat in the davits over our head a resounding thwack, and we threw ourselves flat to escape the mysterious danger, which disappeared with a final rattle astern.

"Who hove that brick?" queried Rowland, in wonderment, as he gathered himself up.

"It was an eel stick," answered the captain. "Klaus was talking so fast, he did not look where he was going."

And now we were in the midst of a curious evidence of the shallowness of this inland sea. All around were rows of large sticks on posts, fixed in the mud, and projecting eight or ten feet above the surface. To these were attached eel pots and eel lines belonging to the Zuyder Zee fishermen, among whom the eel is the staple object of pursuit. There were also numbers of anchored trimmers or "liggers" baited with worms.

THE PORT OF HOORN

Threading our way through lanes of these sticks, we came within sight of Hoorn, the port to which we were bound, and the dispersing clouds gave promise of a fine afternoon. The appearance of Hoorn from the sea is particularly fine, the imposing Tower or Watergate, dominating the harbour, being very picturesque, rising, as it does, in front of clusters of trees, masts of vessels, and houses.

The Atalanta felt her way carefully into the harbour, as at the best there was but seven feet of water on the bar, and a varying depth inside. There was an outer bay, partly protected by a breakwater, and an inner harbour, with just enough room in it for the Atalanta to swing; and after much dodging ahead and astern, and poling with quant and boathook, the Atalanta was moored alongside the jetty, just under the tower. A curious crowd had already assembled, and the harbour mistress, for the *haven meister* was on this occasion a woman, hardly gave us time to throw our ropes over the mooring posts, ere she was down upon us for the sum of 75 cents (15d.) for harbour dues. Uncertain how long the sunshine would continue, Dendy and I clambered up the high jetty, with the willing help of many assistants, and photographed the tower, with the Atalanta blowing off steam below it, a contrast of the old and the new. The stormy wind and threatening clouds prevented any further attempts at art that afternoon, for tossing branches of trees and swaying masts, and nets shaking in the wind, produced a sense of so much movement, that the very houses mixed up with them seemed to reel.

It will be sufficient simply to remind the reader that Hoorn was at one time a large, prosperous, and populous city; which, with the shoaling of the Zuyder Zee, has declined to a tithe of its former importance, and so become a dead city, within the purview of M. Havard's excellent book. He has therein gathered up and told the salient points of its history, which, need not therefore, be repeated here. The same remark will apply to Enkhuisen, Stavoren, and other places which we subsequently visited. Although the historical aspect of the places we visited does not come within the scope of our simple narrative, yet the reader must not suppose that we neglected a topic of such surpassing interest.

We, of course, had studied the history of the Netherlands; and Motley's "Rise of the Dutch Republic;" Havard's "Dead Cities of the Zuyder Zee," and "Picturesque Holland," and other books formed part of the library of the Atalanta, and were constantly referred to by us. It would be a great mistake on the part of any one following in our footsteps, not to do likewise; failing it, a large portion of the enjoyment of the cruise would be lost.

Dinner time claimed us ere we could examine the town, for the regularity of mealtimes is of the highest importance to the successful cruise. Then Blake, being a shy man, objected to the crowd, which, densely packed in three rows, sat, knelt, and stood, stolidly watching our movements, peering down the hatchways in the endeavour to see us eat. Blake hated being stared at, and this gathering of crowds was a constant trouble to him. Two or three small boys surrounding him, and fixing him with their glittering eyes, would put him to flight at once. But the crowd was so good-humoured that it was impossible to attempt to disperse them, and the infliction had to be patiently borne. After lunch we made a start, taking the old pilot with us as guide and interpreter. We found that beyond the harbour in which the Atalanta lay was a sluice or lock, leading to a very fine inner basin, margined on one side by a grassy bank and grove of trees, under the shade of which were broad and well-kept walks, and on the other side was a broad quay studded with limes. Beyond the quay lay the town, with its houses richly decorated, and having varied gables, with canals leading here and there with drawbridges over them, which were constantly opened for the passage of vessels. This inner basin, which looked like a lake in a park, and having on its banks Old London from the Healtheries, was crammed as full as it could hold of the fishing schuyts from the Zuyder Zee. These vessels, with their low sterns and high slanting prows, lay side by side with their stems projecting over the grassy bank

HOORN HARBOUR.

to which they were moored. Yet, though there were perhaps a couple of hundred of them so moored, such is the Dutch neatness of character, or respect for the law, that the grass was untrodden and unsoiled, and the shrubs unbroken.

After our experience of the short waves of the Zuyder Zee, we could well understand the value of these bold projecting stems and bluff flaring bows, which would enable these small craft to ride over the steep surges, where a sharp-bowed vessel of the English type would take them all aboard. The great oaken beams which formed the stems had a groove or hollow at the top, in which rested the anchor, and this anchor was invariably a grapnel, with four or six flukes, but no stock. These rusty anchors were now, in many cases, hidden in the green bushes, which came so close to the water's edge as to enwrap the stems of the vessels. The small trawlnets carried by each schuyt, were hoisted up by the small end to the mast-head to dry; and the whole basin, with its fleet, was apparently caught in the folds of one vast brown net. We saw no signs of any fish, except numbers of small, flat fish, the size of a child's palm, which in Norfolk are called butts. Long strings of these were suspended on twine across the rigging, and from end to end, of some of the barges to dry, particularly on the barges which had come from inland by canal, and whose crews had purchased them of the fishing boats. It would be difficult to get a single palatable mouthful from any one of these little dried fish, and that they could be caught and attempted to be used for human food, shows the minute and careful economy of the Dutch character.

A rumbling noise called our attention to the quay at the back of the tower, where there were barges laden with cheese, which were being unloaded into the warehouses across the street. A long wooden trough was supported on trestles from the barge to the door, the end next the barge being the highest. The yellow balls of cheese were thrown on to this trough and rolled into the warehouse, where they were stored on racks so arranged that no cheese touched another. These warehouses held a goodly store of the golden globes. But it was market day at Hoorn, and presently, following the drift of the people, we came to the weighing house, around which was a crowd of peasants, and in which the process of weighing was being actively carried on by means of several huge balances. These balances themselves were not painted, as we had been led to expect, with a distinctive colour for each province; but the men engaged about them wore huge shiny hats, with capacious brims, and painted bright green, yellow, red, or blue, evidently with the intention of ear-marking them in some way.

We were anxious to see the town hall, Blake and Dendy having developed a mania for exploring town halls; and we wandered hither and thither about the clean, neat streets, asking everybody for the Hotel de Ville or the Stadt-huis, but in vain, although the latter term is most excellent Dutch, and in common use everywhere but in Hoorn. Old Klaus, after talking volubly to a native, led us off on a hot scent a long way, and finally brought us into a private club-house, from which we had to retreat with many apologies. Klaus then gave it up, saying he was pilot for de Zuyder Zee, not for the land, and that his old legs would not stand much walking. Cast upon our own resources, we tackled every likely building, and at last hit upon the right one. We never experienced this difficulty in finding the town hall in any other place; in fact, the town halls were so obtrusively anxious to make our acquaintance, that it was difficult to keep out of their way.

There was nothing particularly interesting in the Stadthuis at Hoorn, except that in the council chamber every town councillor had a great big ash tray in front of him, containing an unreasonable quantity of tobacco ash. But outside of the Tribunal was a trophy captured from the English, being an English shield, taken in some naval engagement in which the Dutch got the best of it. Looking at the number of pictures and trophies and statues in every Dutch town, commemorating occasions on which they licked the Britishers, we concluded that much of English history has yet to be written. That evening, Rowland came into the cabin, and eagerly suggested that it would be a fine thing to rescue that British shield, and steam away with it; but we pointed out to him that Dutch laws were severe on larks of that nature, that there was a large prison within two hundred yards of us, and that three Dutch men-of-war had hove in sight, and he reluctantly abandoned the project.

It seems rather ridiculous to talk of men-of-war in this shallow part of the Zuyder Zee, but during the afternoon a large gun-boat, drawing, as we were informed, not more than nine feet of water, had steamed up to just outside the harbour, and there anchored, while boats from her kept passing and re-passing close to us. Another similar man-of-war was making for us, but got aground a mile off, while a third man-of-war was descried in the offing.

It seemed too absurd to suppose that we were the object of attraction. Still, it was conceivable that they had come out of curiosity to see us. At all events, it was clear that we were well blockaded, and must behave ourselves.

The clock in the tower, like most of the old Dutch clocks, had but one hand, and the time had to be guessed within a quarter of an hour, which was quite near enough for all practical purposes in this land of no haste. The clock here was also puzzling in another way, as it struck the full number of the hour at each half-hour as well.

We did not find this out at first; and that night, when lying awake and listening to the howling of the wind, it bothered me very much to hear two twelves, two ones, and two twos, and so on. Then, after each stroke, the watchman at the prison hard by called out the hour, with some addition of his own, and this was repeated from point to point all over the town, sounding musical enough in the distance.

How it did blow that night, and I am a wretchedly light sleeper. From the south-west it sent a sea into the harbour, which, catching us broadside on, made us roll more than we had done crossing the North Sea. We stood it until, as the tide rose, the yacht began to bump against the quay, and then, at three o'clock in the morning, we had to turn out in the wind and the rain, and shift the yacht alongside another pier, where she would be head to the sea, after which there was comparative quiet.

CHAPTER VII.

HOORN TO ENKHUISEN.

IN the morning the wind was blowing hard, with rain-squalls at intervals. The Zuyder Zee was a foaming yellow expanse, with not a vessel of any kind in sight.

"Well, pilot, shall we make Kampen, to-day?"

"No, master. I will not take you out on a day like this."

"Surely the Atalanta will stand any sea that this big pond can raise," said we, to chaff him.

"No, master, no. The sea it is short and steep, and come aboard over your fine bows, and we go down. The sea very bad to-day in the middle of the Zuyder Zeē. It is not fit to go. We stay in harbour to-day, and get fine day to-morrow."

"But if the Atalanta does go down, her deck won't be under water when her keel is on the bottom."

"I not go, and I pilot. You must do what I tell you as long as I be pilot. There is deep water between here and Kampen," said the old boy, in a sturdy and determined manner; so we pretended to be swayed by him, notwithstanding our valorous love of adventure. And, in truth, it was easy to see that one of the fishing schuyts, high prowed, bluff bowed, and strong as oak could make them, would be safer to be afloat in than the steamer.

Before breakfast, as the sun was shining brightly between the squalls, I had gone out with my camera, and secured as many plates as the wind rendered possible, and then we debated what we should do with ourselves for the rest of the day. Somebody suggested Enkhuisen which is another dead city, lying about ten miles to the north-east of Hoorn, on the extreme point of the promontory of North Holland, which projects in to the Zee. The guide-books told us there was a tram there along the road, passing through the interesting village of Blokker, but one of the crowd of curious natives who watched our every movement, and took the greatest interest in our deliberations, informed us in decent English, that there was a railway, and no tram, and that the tram started at twenty minutes to ten.

Our watches still had English time, so we asked him if he could tell us the time by the one-armed clock above us, to which, after some study (the difficulty in these clocks being that the hand is raised above the face, permitting you to see under it, the apparent position varying with the distance of the observer from the clock, and the height from the ground), that it was either a quarter or half-past nine, and that we had better make haste, and he would show us the way. So off we started, and as we neared the station, and saw the train already in, our kindly guide said that if we would give him the money, he would run in advance and get our tickets. This he did, and we were just in time to bundle into a carriage. It was a third-class one, which of course are the most interesting to travel in, in a foreign country. It had several compartments, with a passage down the middle. The end compartment was reserved for *dames*, and was full of peasant women, in the costume of the province. We got so that we could peep through the door, which was left open by mutual consent, and we scrutinized the ladies while they scrutinized us.

The elder ones had broad gold bands encircling the back of the head, and tipped with ornaments and bangles at the temples. The younger or poorer had silver crowns of a similar pattern, with a plain oblong projection on each temple. They wore clean lace caps and linen kerchiefs, and various things which I can't for the life of me recollect. If our wives had been with us, now, we should have been able to preserve every detail of these quaint costumes. One girl in particular was quite loaded with silver ornaments, on head, throat, waist (or where the English have their waists), and wrists. She had a nice fresh complexion, and was rather comely, and she sat so still and demure, that she appeared to take no notice of us, but I'll warrant she took more accurate stock of us than we did of her, down to the fact that Dendy and I hadn't shaved. I can describe a boat, but I'll be shot if I can a woman's dress.

We were rather amused at the qualified permission given to smokers on the railway in a land where the little baby boys just able to toddle, smoke cigars. The notice to "*rookers*" ran thus :—"*Smoking allowed here unless objected to by any passenger who has not been able to find a seat in any of the compartments in which smoking is prohibited.*"

The brilliant green of the rich flat pastures struck us as being brighter than any English meadows. The grass was luxuriant almost to rankness, and the blades, wet with the rain, gleamed in the flying bands of sunshine so that all the fields shone with a lustrous emerald hue, which had a richness and depth all the more effective because there was but little contrast of those yellow and white and blue flowers which make English pasture land and marsh so variegated in tone.

The Dutch meadows were bright, living green; and instead of our hedgerows, the fields were parcelled off by dykes, which either glistened like bars of silver in the sun, or were as green as the fields with the weedy scum upon them.

In these lush meadows there were numbers of cows, all black and white, and not a single red one among them. This is a distinct loss from an artistic point of view, for while we dearly love a group of red and white cows in a landscape with verdure clad, black and white is too hard, and when, as throughout the length and breadth of Holland, every cow is black and white, there is a monotony in it, which might be avoided if the Dutch would only paint their cows as they do their trees.

We were amused to notice that many of the cows were provided with complete, and very well-fitting *coats*, thus showing that extreme care is taken of these big, long-legged, and sleek animals, if they are delicate, or when first turned out to grass in the spring. These Dutch cows are valued more for the quantity of milk they give than the quality, and it was a constant complaint with us that we could never get really good milk. Probably the first cream had been skimmed off before it was sent out for sale. We also found that the butter was by no means as good as the pure country article in England.

From a "Description of Holland," printed by Knapton, in 1743, I find that these black cattle are, or were then, brought from Holstein and Denmark. They were bought by dealers at 50s. per head, sold to Dutch farmers at £4 per head, and after two months feed, sold to butchers at from £6 to £8 per head. This presumably refers to bullocks, but as there is not much attention paid to making prime meat for the market, an old cow past milking will, in Holland, make as good beef as anything else. We were rather out of the way of obtaining information on agricultural matters, and have not troubled ourselves to look it up since.

On our right we passed a long village of a single street, the houses in which looked more like the toy houses with trees which one buys for children at toy shops. The description of one house will serve for the whole lot. An accurate square of ground is surrounded by a dyke with a bridge across it to the road. In the middle of this square is a square house, with low walls, and a high pyramidal four-sided roof. The lower part of the house is painted a bright red, the upper part and the gables green. The great roof is partly thatched and partly tiled in regular ornamental patterns, the tiling generally being in the region of the windows. The front part of the house is for the accommodation of its human inhabitants, the back part contains the byres for the cattle. Man and beast are in the winter time stowed under the same roof and within the same four walls, which has the advantage of compactness and convenience.

Four rows of small formal trees encircle the square, and each tree is painted a light blue to the height of six feet or so. The surrounding dyke is covered with a light green scum, that looks as if it had been painted too, but is probably natural. This stagnant dyke receives the drainage of the house (as is evident by the neat wooden structures which project over it), and it also supplies the drinking and washing water, which is drawn by buckets from little wooden stages. True, we sometimes saw wells, but, from the nature of the soil, this extra filtration cannot be of much avail. All this does not sound healthy, but the general opinion is, that brandy, beer, wine, and gin are real safeguards against the dangers of the marsh and bad water, and that a full stomach is an excellent preventive against the ague.

CHAPTER VIII.

ENKHUISEN.

UPON alighting at Enkhuisen, which is emphatically a dead city, the first thing that struck us was that the city gate was a very long way from any houses. The gate had been preserved, for the Dutch are very fond of gates, big and little, but the city to which it gave entrance, and which formerly crowded up to it, had dwindled to comparatively small proportions, and large green fields, from which all traces of ruin had been carefully swept, now intervened between the still large town and the gate.

We walked through the painfully quiet streets, which were so clean, so quiet, and so still. The houses were, many of them, old and quaint, the best bearing date early in the 17th century, when, religious liberty assured, a wave of enterprise, and rich moneyed contentment swept over the land, so that people built themselves fine houses, and ornamented the fronts with pictures, carvings, and mottoes, expressing the intense satisfaction then established, and still a characteristic of Holland.

The houses did not appear to be actually empty, inasmuch as they were so clean, and the muslin curtains and flowers in the windows were bright and pleasant. But doors and windows were shut. There were no faces at the windows, no sound of children's voices, no gossiping of neighbours at doors. From end to end of the long winding streets no person appeared, save a few flat-breasted women, and a few old men and women kneeling on the stones, leisurely and patiently picking the grass from the streets. It appeared to us that they had much better let it grow into hay. There was no carriage or vehicle of any kind save a small cart or two, drawn by dogs, carrying peat. Upon one of these small carts, drawn by three dogs, was perched an immense big Dutchman, who might have put carriage and steeds in his breeches' pocket. We yearned to upset him, but we had heard dreadful things about Dutch law, and were satisfied with yearning.

Presently, seeing a barber's, I entered, and rubbed my chin with my forefinger, which is excellent Dutch for "I want a shave, please." Silently and solemnly the barber selected a short, broad razor from a large collection of short broad razors on the wall, held a soup plate under my chin, and slopped some soapy water over my face. But it was the best shave that ever I had, for the razor was perfection. Enkhuisen ought not to be a dead city with such razors and barbers as that. I held out a handful of small change, from which he selected a *dubbeltjee* or twopenny bit, and we parted: without a word being spoken on either side, or a smile showing that the transaction was anything out of the common. It was certainly the queerest shave I ever had but one, which was when I discovered that a dead man was lying on the bench behind me covered with a sheet, and awaiting an inquest.

The women we saw were very ugly. The city is dead in the matter of beauty. More than any other part of Holland, we noticed here the hideous custom of flattening in the breasts, by means of bands wound round (we were told about the bands), and as waists are unknown, and we suppose that stays are not worn, the effect may be imagined. We were informed by a resident, that this custom was adopted in order to check the admiration of the men. It certainly checked ours.

Quite depressed with the absolute torpor of the place (which has still 5,500 inhabitants, and formerly had 40,000), we found our way to the harbour, where there was some sign of life, inasmuch as there were some fishing boats in the harbour, and men baiting lines and mending nets. A tower or "port," somewhat like that at Hoorn, but plainer, guarded the entrance, and hanging from the outside of it were two anchors, which formerly belonged to Spanish vessels, and rusted away to mere skeletons of anchors. Outside the lock there was a goodly harbour, within a fine breakwater, with nothing but fishing vessels therein. Inside there was a broad still canal, with barges moored, and a shipwright's yard on one bank, with vessels hauled up on it, but no sign of work or workmen. At the corner of the canal next the sluice, where a smaller canal branched off, was a group of small dwellings, curiously old and small and quaint, with outside stairs, and tiny balconies, and boat landings with old boats moored to them; here a net, and there a bundle of dried fish. Every bit of woodwork was painted a bright colour, and in the absolutely still water below, the conglomeration of fantastic form and colour was faithfully mirrored. We greatly regretted that we had not brought the camera, but it was ever thus.

The street by the side of the main canal was bordered with fine trees, and a shower driving us in search of a restaurant, we here found one. By the aid of a dictionary we ordered dinner, and while it was preparing, we essayed a game of billiards on the funny little table, with jack-in-the-box pockets, which delivers the ball ready to your hand on the outside, and we drank the cool Bierisch beer, which is so wholesome and palatable.

Dinner was served in a clean room, the floor of which was still damp from washing, while the stiff uncomfortable wooden chairs of American make were as shiny as beeswax could make them. The beefsteaks, as usual in Holland, were simply chunks of beef the size of one's fist, but were here fairly well cooked, as was the rest of the dinner, and we had the felicity of using paper napkins

It was at the time of the Home Rule debate in the English parliament, and we tried to make out the items of English news in the Dutch papers, turning out the words in our dictionary. We noticed, by the way, that Sir Wilfred Lawson was termed the "Water drinker," the English words being used, and in italics, indicating to us that there was no Dutch word corresponding with the English "teetotaller."

As we walked back to the station, we noticed that there were shops, to be sure, but there were no customers in them, and we felt sure that the only business done that day in Enkhuisen was my shave and our dinner.

We got back to Hoorn in the afternoon, and found the pilot sanguine as to the weather, because the sky was "clear to leeward."

"Why, we look to windward for the weather in our country," said Rowland.

"Ja! but a Dutchman knows better. He always looks to leeward, because if the sky clears to leeward, the bad weather is not following up, and if there is room in the sky, the clouds will melt away, and the weather be fine."

Now the sky was blue to leeward, but uncommonly angry to windward, but the fishermen evidently thought well of it, for the fleet in the harbour were hurrying out to sea as fast as they could. The schuyts were poled and pushed and towed through the bridge, jostling each other as if time were of importance. It was astonishing to see how lightly they moved—I suppose because they were flat-bottomed, although above water they looked as if hewn from a solid block of oak. When clear of the bridge, the short-gaffed sails were hoisted, the boats made a series of short tacks to the harbour mouth, where, on the bar, each seemed to leap at the first wave, and sent a cloud of spray to the mast head. At each succeeding wave there was the same rise and leap, and the same fountain of foam; and later on, the red sunset light streamed from behind the old tower and the trees, upon the wet sails, turning them into cloth of gold, and transforming the low clouds of foam into fiery spray.

So the great basin was rapidly emptied of its vessels,

Engraved by Annan & Swan, London.

HOORN.

and as the dusk fell, a large steamer from Amsterdam came into the port, and passed into the inner basin.

We strolled round the town, finding fresh subjects for sketches and fresh objects of interest. The great gate or port at the opposite side of the town, with the wide moat, and the bridge, on which brown nets were hanging to dry, was a capital subject for a sketch, in which some plainer details might be left out, but it did not compose itself well enough for a photograph, which can leave nothing out.

Dendy, in search of pipes (of which he ultimately secured a large and quaint collection), went into a shop, where I followed him. There was no one in the front shop, but I noticed a woman in an inner room rise from a sofa, and wrap herself in a shawl, which she drew over her head and face, so that we did not notice what was the matter with her at first. But as she was about to hand Dendy a pipe, I saw, and called out, "Don't touch it, Dendy. She has got the small-pox." One look was enough for him, and we both rushed out of the shop, jamming each other in the doorway, in our haste.

Passing by a jeweller's shop, we saw some of the gold and silver head ornaments, and I went in, and for eight guelders, bought a silver band, about three inches wide, made to encircle the head, and with bosses at the temples. The cheapest gold one was one hundred guelders, which we couldn't stand. The jeweller's wife had a nice gold one on, and she had also a pretty lace cap, which we were curious to know the price of. I took hold of her cap, and, with my blandest smile, asked, "What cost—what price?" She shook her head to intimate that it was not for sale, but presently went in and produced another cap like it, for which she asked ten guelders. The lace looked good and fine, and the cap was probably cheap, but I doubted if any of my lady friends would wear it.

Coming across a very old house, of 1610 or thereabouts, with many verses written upon it, we copied them out, each taking a third to save time. It was fidgetty work copying old Dutch, and after all, we did not take the trouble to translate them as we intended. We gathered, however, that they were commemorative of some naval battle, which had been witnessed from the windows, and for particulars of which see the guidebooks.

In the 18th century, out of the seventy men-of-war constituting the Dutch navy, fifteen were stationed at Hoorn, showing the importance of the city, and the convenience of the harbour at that time. Now there was a man-of-war aground outside, and another with only a foot of water beneath her keel. So big and beamy were they, however, that the rough, choppy sea had no appreciable effect upon them.

We turned in early, glad to see from the soft, blue, misty twilight over the Zuyder Zee, and the cessation of the wind, that a fine morrow was certain.

CHAPTER IX.

THE ISLAND OF URK.

THE morning broke bright and beautiful, with a calm sea in front of us; no longer the turbulent yellow waters of the storm-tossed sea, but blue and opaline grey, with glancing green ripples. The schuyts were trooping in in threes and fours, with all the reefs with which they had started the night before shaken out. It was a brisk, healthy morning, and as soon as the men had done marketing, and laid in a store of vegetables and the best meat procurable, which was, however, not very nice, we started at nine o'clock for a run straight across the Zuyder Zee to Kampen, a little way up the river Yssel, intending also to stop at Urk, for we were anxious to see a Zuyder Zee island.

As we approached the first man-of-war, we suggested to the captain that we ought to dip our ensign, which was displayed on a six-foot staff astern.

"Why, it is such a little thing, they will never see it, and if they do they will only laugh at us."

But we persuaded him to try, and as we passed under her stern, our little flag was lowered a couple of feet and hoisted again by way of salute. Off went the officer's cap, off went ours in return; an order was rapidly given and executed, and the Dutch ensign was lowered some twenty feet and hoisted, and our salute acknowledged. We felt we had done quite the correct thing, and the performance was repeated with the second man-of-war, which lay aground, with equal satisfaction. We asked Klaus how long she would remain aground, and he replied, until the wind shifted to the north-west, and sent more water into the Zuyder Zee; the normal rise and fall at this spot being only one foot, while at the Texel, to the north of it, it is fifteen feet.

It was twenty-four miles to Urk, and our course lay almost due east, over a sea so quiet, and so blue and clear, that the day of storm might never have been known and never be again. We steamed steadily on, with a slight rise and fall on the slightest possible swell, with no lap of wave save in our own creaming wake astern, and we had nothing to do but bask in the sunshine, dip lazily into "Motley" for historical information, or into the cabin for a cooling drink.

When we were some twelve miles out, the low shores were invisible in the blue and quivering heat-haze of the distance, and we were again on a circle of sea without land. But it was not a lonely sea, for far and near we were surrounded by schuyts engaged in fishing. There could not have been less than four or five hundred of

SCHUYT ON ZUYDER ZEE.

them in sight at one time, for the number of schuyts engaged in fishing on the Zuyder Zee is estimated at one thousand.

Seeing one of them with its flag half-mast high, we

supposed it was in some distress, and called Klaus' attention to it, but he told us that it was a fish-buyer's boat flying a signal that he was ready to buy fish and eels in advance of the usual market.

"Are many of these schuyts lost in storms, Klaus, or wrecked on the sandbanks?"

"Lost! wrecked! no master, how should they be? There is a harbour to leeward within a few miles from whichever quarter the wind blows, and if they should get on to a sand, why they just bump until the storm is over, or until they bump across. They are so strongly built that no storm and no bumping on sand will hurt them. They cannot be beaten to pieces."

Such was the effect of Klaus' speech, expressed in broken English, and got out of him by leading questions, and the aid of the dictionary, which was our usual mode of conversation. We also learned that the cost of building the hull and spars of one of these boats without sails or nets was two thousand guelders, or about £160; the size of the vessel being, as far as the eye could judge, 40 feet long, by 10 feet wide and 5 feet deep.

The eel fishery of the Zuyder Zee brings in 45,000 florins annually, and in addition to the miserable little flat fish which we have already mentioned, a sort of freshwater herring, called the *pan haring*, "anchovies," or more probably, sprats, and a "small bright fish, that smells like cucumber," no doubt the smelt, are taken. Hoorn, which we had just left, has the credit of having made the first large herring net used for fishing in the North Sea by a Dutch boat.

In reply to our suggestion as to the hardships of a fisher's life, the old pilot did not see it as far as the men were concerned, and as for the women, why, if a husband had gone to sea and was missing for three years, his widow could legally marry again, so there was no great hardship there.

But between the blue and shadowless sea, and the blue and cloudless sky, rose a small green islet, presently showing sharp red roofs, and tall yellow masts, and brown swinging nets. This was the small island of Urk, said to be quainter even than Marken. It is just a low hump about a mile long and half a mile broad, with a lighthouse on the higher end of it, where there was almost a hill, a crowd of houses in the middle, and at the other end a stretch of low green marsh, where a number of cows and sheep were grazing. But the harbour, which was a spacious one inside, had such a crowd of schuyts in it as made us wonder, and more were coming in. It was Saturday, and the good folk were coming in for the Sunday, on which day there is no fishing. There was a long narrow entrance to the harbour, between two curving piers, and as we were not sure of the depth of water, we anchored outside, just off the piers, in seven feet of water, with a hard bottom.

Leaving the engineer and pilot in charge of the Atalanta, we rowed in the jolly up to the harbour.

"Now," said Rowland, "I know this is a wild spot. We shan't find any one here who can speak English, and not many will know there is such a place as England."

"How do you, sare? I hope you quite well. Me speak English," resounded a voice from the pier, proceeding from one of a group of men seated, dangling their legs over the water.

"Well, I'm blowed!" ejaculated our astonished skipper, "here is the very first man we see, talking English to us."

We landed on a *"hard,"* covered with boats and sheds and drying nets, and immediately a crowd of men and boys gathered shyly around us. We struck at once for the highest point, where the lighthouse stood by itself on a grassy corner, where a few sheep were tethered to graze. Several men and boys and girls had followed us, and Dendy at once began to form a group. The men submitted to be placed in position, with amused smiles, but were very self-contained and quiet, even dignified.

Fine-looking fellows they were too, tall and strong, and looking as hard as nails. Men and boys were dressed alike, with wooden shoes on the feet, thick knitted stockings, breeches reaching to just below the knees, and as

URK ISLANDERS.

voluminous at the top as any old dame's petticoat, gathered in with many a tuck round the waist, where there was a belt with clasps made of silver. A tight-fitting cloth jacket, sometimes single and sometimes double breasted, met the breeches, and was confined by the same belt. A cloth cap with a peak, and a coloured neckerchief fastened with gold buttons, completed the costume. The belt clasps were, in so many instances, made of English Hanoverian dollars, and other English coins of the 18th century, that we could not help wondering whether they had not been recovered from the vast amount of silver treasure sunk in the Zuyder Zee, when the "Lutine" was lost in the year 1799, and of which some £83,000 is known to have been recovered by the fishermen from the Zuyder Zee, and the islands to the north.

The girls of the island were the bonniest lasses imaginable, amazonish in their size and strength, kittenish in their laughing glee. We tried hard to induce them to be photographed, but as soon as my head was under the black cloth, off they ran laughing, with Dendy in hot pursuit. The men suggested that we should bribe them with "*kussen*," which would have been nice, but we thought of our wives, and didn't. Besides, the great strong girls might have boxed our ears, and their great big sweethearts punched our heads, neither of which would have been pleasant. But somehow or other Dendy coaxed one into standing, and I am looking at her comely face, and her—no, not sylph-like figure as I write. Her face is round and rosy, her arms are plump and red, her figure is decidedly sturdy, with a fine firm roundness and a healthy strength, which we noticed as characteristic of the Urk girls. Her waist—well, she hadn't one, no Dutch peasant girl has. They have backs like Hercules, and there is not only no narrowing between the shoulders and the hips, but there is a decided broadening all the way, and the ultimate breadth is wonderful. The dress is a green or red woollen outer petticoat, with a sort of all-round woollen pinafore, rather than dress, of a purple or dark green; a close-fitting body with tight sleeves nearly down to the elbow, and fitting close round the neck. On the head is a cap, black at the top, but with a broad white band round the lower part of it. I noticed that there were three kinds of caps, or rather arrangements of black and white, apparently varying with matron, maid, and child, but I forget the details. No doubt, if we had stayed on the Sunday, we should have seen gayer dresses, but on Monday we saw no ornaments of any kind on the women.

When the photos were taken, they of course wanted to look at them, which was impossible, and we were at our wits' end how to explain to the urgent, though good-humoured, people, that the plates could not be developed until we returned to England, when a man came up who spoke a little English, and he put things right for us.

Engraved by Annan & Swan, London.

They were much disappointed, and when we promised to send copies to the pastor of Urk, they said that was no good, as he would not show them.

I then turned round to take a view of the harbour, which was densely packed with the same oaken, high-prowed craft we had seen at Hoorn, and with the aid of our English-speaking friend, we got a row of sturdy urchins in the foreground. Amongst these we unwisely distributed some English pence, which had the effect of bringing every boy in the place around me, vociferously begging to be taken. Blake and Dendy sloped, and I did not see them again until we got on board.

I went out on the pier, and took more views of the harbour, and schuyts entering it. The fishermen submitted patiently to be grouped, and showed but little curiosity, although an English yachtsman armed with wonderful instruments of brass and glass, and polished mahogany, and a black cloth in which he hid his head, could not have been a common sight.

I learned that there were two thousand two hundred inhabitants in Urk, and that they were a race by themselves, intermarrying and keeping the stock pure, kind to strangers on a visit, but jealous of additions to their numbers from those not born on the island. Big, brawny, and strong as men and women alike were, their diet was not a generous one, consisting chiefly of salt pork, fresh meat being rarely obtainable, and only as a luxury. There were, however, plenty of fowls running about, which I suppose laid eggs, and could themselves be eaten.

There is no manufacture of any kind upon the island, and no trade but fish. In the winter time, when the Zuyder Zee is wholly or partly frozen, the fishermen break holes in the ice, to which the eels congregate for air, and are there speared in great numbers. I have known the same thing to be done upon the Norfolk Broads.

There is an utter absence of Dutch neatness and tidiness in the village. The houses are ranged anyhow, and are neither better nor worse than the old parts of a north country fishing village in England, or on the wilder coasts of Wales. Although it was Saturday, a day devoted in Holland to washing of everything on the face of the earth, there was no particular cleaning up going on at Urk.

We were particularly anxious to know how much of the great *beam* of the Urk lasses was due to nature or to woollen petticoats, but we had no means of ascertaining. The place was full of petticoats, red, green, and blue, hanging out to dry; and in one small front garden I counted ten, which might well, as far as the male eye could judge, have belonged to one person, but how they could be comfortably worn on so hot a day was a mystery, when we found a single thickness of blue serge enough.

Many of the stalwart women had handsome, well-cut features, black hair and eyes, and as I walked observantly about, the elder ones took not the slightest notice of me, although the younger ones were merry enough, and evidently cracked jokes about me and my following of boys. These latter were now getting very troublesome. They would plant themselves in front of me, shouting at the top of their voices as if I were deaf, "Mahn! mahn! takken me." I went in search of my friends, but they were in hiding in the cottage of some old fellow, who had politely asked them in, and gave them some coffee. So I returned to the boat, where I found Jack in charge. Here I shook off my following and we rowed back to the yacht, where I stayed, sending the engineer and Jack back to the island.

Quietly drifting before the lightest of winds, and helped occasionally by sweeps, came schuyt after schuyt, making for home thus early in the day, for it was yet afternoon. Home! this lonely, self-contained island on the Zuyder Zee, so isolated from the outer world, though so near, and, as it were, in the heart of it. Here it was clear that peace and contentment reigned supreme. Politics and newspapers were not, all pleasure was absent save the pleasure of living in the pure air and on the salt water, and the pleasure of the love of wife and of children— the simplest of pleasures truly, but then there are no anxieties and no pains, save physical ills, which must be few in such a sturdy and healthy race, where the weakest have died off, and only the fittest survive.

Here, on the hot deck, gazing at the island lying in the bright sunshine, watching the happy and contented fishermen going to home, sweet home, for the quiet Sabbath, one wonders in what lies the happiness of the eager struggle for existence, for fame, for riches going on in our thronged England.

But as time passes I get wearied of lying on my back, I get the fidgets in my knees and my elbows, I begin to want to do something, and there is nothing to do on board a steamer, not a rope to set up or a sheet to haul in; so I begin to think of what I shall do in this matter and that, how I will support this and oppose that, when I get home, busy home, and I feel that there is more to be done than to bask in the sunshine, and that it is better to strive and to work in England, than to live and eat and sleep on a quiet island, even though there is the happiness of toil on the sea as a foil.

At last, when I had taken to the "Rise of the Dutch Republic" for amusement, the crew came off, bringing with them a man who had begged a passage to Kampen. He was a trader, who had been to Urk on business. He could talk very little English, but, led by Dendy, we began to interview him. We began to talk about the Zuyder Zee freezing in the winter, and he told us about the skating. He had a daughter who was one of the best skaters in the country. She was, in fact, a champion, having won no less than seven races from the best men. She was so big and strong that she could—and he caught hold of me round the waist and shook me, from which we gathered that his "*dɔchter*" could make mince-meat of me if she chose.

Now Dendy had read somewhere, probably in "Havard," that the girls, when they skated races, threw off their garments as incumbrances, and he was anxious to find out whether our friend's strapping daughter did likewise, so asked as delicately as he could, and elicited the unexpected reply, "Oh yes, she has seven feet of water."

Explanations ensued, when it appeared he thought we were asking about the depth of water in the harbour of the town where he lived—I forget the name of the place —so we went at him again, getting his mind back to the skates, by touching one foot, and to his "dochter's" vestments by pulling his coat and his trousers, when it ultimately appeared that she shed a considerable quantity, and that what remained on her bust was red, and on her legs blue, possibly a red guernsey and blue knickerbockers

CHAPTER X.

SCHOKLAND AND KAMPEN.

WE were now in sight of Schokland, a long, narrow strip of low land with but two or three signs of habitation upon it. By the chart it appears to be three miles long, and narrow enough to clear with a hop, skip, and a jump. Its name indicates that it is or has been subject to shocks of earthquakes, as is currently reported, or more probably to subsidences due to its precarious position in the midst of the waters, and it was possibly built on a bad foundation.

Our passenger informed us that there were only "dree vaders and dree moders" upon the island, by which we understood that it was only inhabited by three families. We saw, however, two or three masts in the little harbour which it boasts: but as the afternoon was drawing on we did not stop to land.

We were questioning our passenger as to the depth of water in the Yssel, the mouth of which we were approaching, and took occasion to ask if he could procure us a pilot up to Arnheim, as old Klaus only knew the Zuyder Zee. Now Klaus looked upon us as his exclusive possession, and had been looking very grumpy for some time past at our prolonged conversation with the passenger. At the mention of pilots, his jealousy broke out into a storm of abuse directed against the passenger, accusing him, as the latter informed us, of endeavouring to supplant Klaus in our affections. Then ensued an altercation which was most amusing, although the words were unintelligible. Dutch appears to be an excellent language to quarrel in, owing to the length and solidity of the words. The dialogue was loud, and the expressions evidently strong, but it was slow, sonorous, and dignified, each man taking his turn, like divines arguing on a controversial platform. We moved to other parts of the yacht until the storm had subsided into a scornful calm.

A long curved line on the calm surface of the sea showed the sharp division between the flood of fresh water coming from the Yssel and the salt water of the sea. The difference in specific gravity was also noticeable by the waste pipe from the washing basin, which was set somewhat low, refusing to run, owing, of course, to the greater immersion of the yacht in the fresh water.

We were now entering the broad mouth of the river, between the stone piers projecting into the sea. We looked back with regret upon the Zuyder Zee, which we thought we were seeing the last of. Its surface was absolutely still, unruffled by any flaw of wind. There was a slight haze, which made the sky a greyish blue, full of diffused light; and the water was like frosted silver, with here and there large spaces of a pearly lustre. In the distance, the dense layers of mist near the water shone like the dew-wet gossamers on an autumn morning. The numerous schuyts which lay motionless, seemed lifted up by a mirage effect into the lower air, and in the extreme distance seemed far above the water level. To the westward there was in the sky a brighter glare from the declining sun, and in the mist a slightly rosy tint heralding the sunset. So fairy-like was this cloud-like translucent Zuyder Zee, that we were tempted to turn back and anchor upon it for at least one night more, but we expected letters at Kampen which we were anxious to receive.

There was a steady current flowing between far apart banks, and several barges had gone close in shore and were preparing to tow up the stream. Here we saw our first stork or, *ooyevaar*, which event we celebrated in the way that Yarmouth yachtsmen celebrate the passing of the half-way stake on Breydon Water, and as in former and more wicked days they used to mark the windmills (seven to the mile on the average), namely, by what Yankees dub "smiling."

We were disappointed at the scarcity of birds of any kind either upon the Zuyder Zee or in the country generally; and here it may be mentioned that we did not meet with a single person of natural history tastes. Of the many we questioned on the subject, none indulged, nor had they any friends who indulged, in such childish pursuits.

It is some three or four miles from the sea to Kampen. On the north bank of the wide river are numerous breakwaters jutting out thirty or forty yards, with beacon marks on the ends of them, from which it appeared that in flood time the strength of the stream played on that bank. Klaus told us that the reclaimed land on the bank belonged to the municipality of Kampen, and was a valuable possession.

With the faint gleam of sunset, a light air came from the west, and the barges spread every stitch of canvas in the shape of topsails, spinnakers, flying jibs, and watersails, to catch the favouring gale (gale poetically, not actually).

No persons are so ingenious as the Dutch in the variety

of sail, which they will set wherever they can get a spar to stick out, or a line to be suspended. Of every colour, red, brown, black, and yellow, and of every shape, bar an actual round, were the incongruous canvasses spread by the large barges which slowly stemmed the stream.

KAMPEN BRIDGE.

Illumined by the evening glow, these picturesque sails were sharply defined against the pale blue river, and the pale blue eastern sky, and then as we passed them they rose darkly in our crimson wake.

The spires of Kampen had long been visible, and now we saw the splendid bridge which spans the stream, its centre drawbridge being then open for the passage of a large barge or tjalk, whose lofty red topsail set above a yellow mainsail, white jib, and brown foresail, towered above the uplifted beams of the bridge. The quay at Kampen was a pleasant sight. There are fine houses all along, with the old Town-hall and the city gates, and on the broad street, beween the houses and the clear river, rows of fine trees are planted. So thickly were schuyts and tjalks moored against the quay, that we could not find a vacant place, and had to moor outside the Urk Post boat. On throwing a rope ashore, it was seized and made fast by a very ill-looking fellow, of whom more anon. We were soon properly moored, and the usual girl, carrying the usual milk-pails on a yoke across her shoulders, was alongside, crying, " Melk, melk." So was the usual man with a basket of loaves, and the usual man with a barrow of greens, and the usual men anxious to supply us with *vleesch* and other necessaries, and, much to Blake's disgust, the usual crowd of sightseers.

A very swaggering fellow came clattering down on the Urk boat, crossing her decks, which were being freshly varnished, with the greatest disregard for them, and boarded us.

"Do you want a pilot to Arnheim, gentlemen?"

"Yes, we do. Is there enough water for us?"

"Plenty. I will take you there safely."

"And what are your terms?"

"Ten shillings a day, and an engagement for a week certain, and my fare back."

"Oh, really you are too good for us," said Dendy and I politely, but Blake roared at him, "Go ashore, you lubber, no seaman ever boarded a boat in the awkward way you did. You don't know anything about it. Clear out!"

And the man cleared out with a flea in his ear.

While tea was getting ready, Blake and I made for the post-office, and were followed by the ill-looking chap who had made our ropes fast. He demanded a "tip" so insolently that we refused him, and as he kept mobbing us, we made him understand that we should resort to physical force, whereupon he went back to the quay, where he found Klaus, and began to mob him. He was getting very wild and had given old Klaus a push, whereupon Rowland climbed ashore, with the intention of giving the fellow a hiding, which he was well capable of doing. At this juncture a bobby arrived, who carted the fellow off to gaol, saying he was an evil-disposed man, and would be kept shut up until we had gone. This was the only disagreeable incident we had on our cruise, and the only time we met with anything but the very greatest attention, civility, and indeed friendliness.

Next Blake and I met an official who turned out to be a telegraph messenger, and who wanted to say something very particular to us. He didn't know any French. Dendy was not with us to guess at his meaning, and the more we didn't understand him the more excited he became, and the faster he talked, dancing about us the while in a most ridiculous way. We laughed at the absurd predicament we were in, but he thought we were laughing at him, and grew more wildly voluble. Suddenly a happy thought struck him. Holding out a leather portfolio which he carried, he wetted his forefinger, and traced some words upon the brown cover, which he held up to us with a triumphant air, which plainly said, "If you don't understand that, you must be fools." But Dutch written in spittle was no easier than when spoken, and a blank silence fell upon us. At last the man took us solemnly by the arms, and led us to a building, and upstairs therein to a telegraph-office, where he handed to us a telegram from a friend at Zwolle who wished to have the earliest news of our arrival, and to which we at once replied. This man was the only excitable man we saw in Holland, for the people were always most good-humoured and patient when we could not understand them.

We then all went for a stroll in the dusk, through the

quaint clean streets and along the old fortifications, which were now turned into a park, with pleasant groves, shady avenues, and placid lakes. We rested on a little bridge, to watch two men babbing for eels in our well-known Norfolk way, but instead of lifting the eels into a boat or on to the ground, they had common washing-tubs, with a pole pushed through the handles. The poles were stuck in the bank, so that they held the tubs floating in the water just above the bab. The eels could thus be lifted easily out of the water and shaken into the tubs. We afterwards noticed this dodge to be universal where the babbing was done from a bank. On my return to the Broads I mentioned it to a professional eel fisher, who told me that he had used an *umbrella* for the same purpose, with the advantage of portability. A horizontal stick held the umbrella in position, just floating on the surface, and he had cut several slits in the apex of the covering, and sewn a bag at the bottom. The eels soon found their way through the slits into the bag, where they were kept alive and cool. One night he had been very successful, and dropped a great many eels into the umbrella, but in the morning when he came to look, he found that he had forgotten to tie the string of the bag, and that the eels had returned one by one as he caught them back to their native water. He was so wild that he smashed his umbrella by way of revenge.

GATE AT KAMPEN.

The old gates of the city have been preserved as ornaments, and are massive and striking. With one exception, they are so overgrown with trees that I could not photograph them.

When we got back to the yacht, we heard that "a very nice young gentleman, as smart as any Englishman," had been to see us, and had gone in search of us. This was our friend from Zwolle, who had started immediately on receipt of our telegram, and he presently found us. We went with him across the long bridge, to a fine *eafé* at the other side, and sat long in the warm soft night, talking, watching the lights of Kampen, and the ghostly forms of the barges dropping down with the tide, and drinking the cool biersch out of tall glasses.

Our friend stayed with us on board that night, having arranged to carry us off to Zwolle on the morrow.

A CHANGE OF ROUTE—ZWOLLE.

BLAKE woke me in the morning by saying, "I say, old man, here's bad news, our cruise has come to an end."

"Good gracious! What's the matter?" my mind going to telegrams from home.

"We can't get any further up the river, owing to the water being low."

Joining him on deck in my pyjamas—Blake's costume also, and fairly presentable even before a crowd—I found that Klaus had brought a pilot, who was prepared to go with us upon the same reasonable terms as Klaus, but he feared that we drew too much water. The river was unusually low above Zwolle, and it would not be safe to count on there being five feet. We might get stuck for a considerable time, and he could not advise our running the risk. This was annoying, especially as we hourly saw large steamers passing up and down. But they only drew four feet of water, and we drew five.

Herr Kalff, our Dutch friend, suggested that we should leave the decision until the afternoon, when we could drive to Katerveer, about ten miles up the river, which was said to be as far as we could go with the steamer, and make enquiries on the spot.

It was a fine hot morning, and the river looked cool and limpid, so we rowed to the opposite side, which was quite far enough from the houses, and had a delicious bathe off one of the breakwaters. The bottom was hard and sandy, and I should imagine that it would be a good place for angling, more especially as we saw many very large carp floundering about amid the weeds, in the shallow bays between the breakwaters. We waded after them, armed with the oars, and on murderous thoughts intent, but they were too wary for us. Unfortunately we had not brought any suitable tackle with us, and we rarely saw anyone fishing for anything but the universal eel. We were anxious to discover if there was any good pike fishing to be had in the numberless canals, meres, and rivers. Many a likely spot we saw, but never was there the slightest rush of fry, or other indications of a pike. We constantly enquired if there were *snoekje* about, but we might as well have enquired for the *snark*. If there were any, no one fished for them. It is possible that the peaty water of Dutch meres is not favourable to them.

After breakfast, I pulled in my smart little dinghy up the river, in search of pictures. I took a Gate or two, and the long fine bridge, but it was too hot for much exertion, and I just floated lazily about on the broad, blue stream, watching the barges drifting by, for even on a Sunday there were some moving, though not many. There was not another pleasure craft of any description on the river, and my little boat, with the club burgee on the bows, attracted considerable attention.

The bells of Kampen rang out musically over the water, with that peculiar but pleasant metallic tone or jangle, so unlike the deep and sonorous tone of our English bells, but which is characteristic of the bells in Holland and Belgium.

In the clear air, I could see from the river the rows of bells suspended *outside* the tower, and played upon by little hammers, which we afterwards noticed was the usual arrangement.

We left by train for Zwolle, nine miles distant, about the middle of the morning. This we found to be a large town, very quiet, very clean, and with many handsome modern houses. We lunched with Kalff, who is a bachelor, and a very good English scholar. His sitting-room was full of English books, and adorned with curios and pictures just like the rooms of his English contemporaries.

"How is it, Kalff, that so many Dutchmen speak English and French, and so very, very few English speak Dutch?"

"We are a small nation, and as we must do business with foreigners, and they will not learn our language, we are forced to learn theirs."

We asked him about the skating, which had not been very good last winter, and he showed us a pair of Friesland skates, which have the blades long and very low, so that the foot is close to the ice. The skates are not strapped tightly to the foot as ours must be, and instead of laced-up boots, many people prefer to skate in the slippers commonly worn by the poorer people. Dutch roads are so even and so well-paved, that shoe-leather lasts long, and a sort of carpet slipshoe, with leather soles, is the ordinary wear by the class above those who wear wooden shoes.

After lunch, we found a carriage and pair awaiting us, and we drove about the environs of Zwolle, which were very charming, the road being paved with clinkers or thin bricks set on edge, and well planted on both sides with trees, so that for miles we drove along shady avenues.

Arriving at Katerveer, on the banks of the Yssel, we rested for some time at an out door *café*, and on making enquiries, found that there would not be sufficient water for us. Blake expressed a strong hope that he would meet the swagger pilot, who was so ready to land us in a mess, but I fear Blake's Dutch would not have been equal to the occasion.

The river, as it curved away between grassy banks, looked so pretty and pleasant in the sunshine, the steamers went so gaily up stream, and the red-sailed tjalks glided so easily down stream, that it was somewhat regretfully that we abandoned the route by Zutphen and Arnheim, which we had taken such trouble to plan out, more particularly as Dendy had letters of introduction to people at Arnheim, and was anxious to get there. Yet we were not sorry to return to the Zuyder Zee, to which we had taken a great fancy; and our first plan being broken, we left our future route to circumstances, and the fancy of the day, so that there was a general forwarding of letters from "Poste restante," in consequence of frequent changes, but all were ultimately received in safety.

We asked Kalff about the projected draining of the southern portion of the Zuyder Zee, which was mooted many years ago. It is intended to run a dyke across from Enkhuisen to the mouth of the Yssel, and drain the portion thus enclosed, which would add a good sized province to Holland. Lack of funds at present stops the way, but the project is still alive and will probably be carried out in a generation or two. A writer in the "Edinburgh Review," of 1847, mentions the matter, and states that the expense of maintaining the dyke when made, would be considerable. But he makes a suggestion, which in his opinion is valuable. It is that the dyke should be *faced with indiarubber*, which he supposes would better resist the action of the water.

The rest of the proceedings of that day at Zwolle were convivial; inasmuch as we found our friend, and our friend's friends very hospitable. We attended an open-air concert, which was very nice. We were taken to friends' houses, and were given of the good wine, and finally we went home—how naturally the word fits one's yacht—feeling that nice Dutch people were very nice indeed.

When we got on board, Rowland remarked, "You have been enjoying of yourselves, sirs."

"Yes, Rowland, and what have you been doing?"

"I've been for a walk in the park, under the beautiful trees, and by the water, and I must say I think Kampen is a fine place indeed. There's a nice place all free to any man to go in and take his pleasure. Why, I sat on a seat in the shade, and folded my arms, and felt like a lord. I don't ask for anything better."

This was good all round, and Klaus was overjoyed at the change of route, as it kept him with us for some time longer. He said to me,

"Master Davies, I been seventy-three years old, and forty-two years pilot on the Zuyder Zee, and I never liked any vessel so much as dis. I have all I want to eat and

OUR PILOT.

drink. I sleep all night, widout any work to do, and" [very emphatically] "*de peoples is very well.*"

It was a great story on his part to say that he slept all night, for at three o'clock every morning he used to turn out on deck, and not go to bed again. He would pace up and down above our heads, and as soon as any loungers appeared on the quay, he would narrate to them all our adventures, in which the old boy's imagination made himself play a principal part. We had to tell him at last that he disturbed us, whereupon he went ashore for his morning walk instead.

Kalff had come back with us, as he was so taken with our account of the Urk amazons, that we had promised to revisit the island, and take him with us.

CHAPTER XII.

URK AGAIN—STAVOREN.

ANOTHER brilliant morning! A delicious swim, a hearty breakfast, and we were again under way, and ere long upon the Zuyder Zee, which was now blue and sparkling, and dotted all over with schuyts.

Our steam to Urk was without incident. We were all very lazy and very quiet and very happy, and there was no occasion to make talk. Each took up the most comfortable seat he could find, and with hat tilted over his nose to keep off the sun, gazed idly and complacently at so much of the universe as was visible from under its brim.

Of course, steaming is pleasant when you go fast and far, but on such a day as this, with a steady topsail breeze and a fairly smooth sea, I did long for my own good little yacht, the "Swan," and as we went along on a disgustingly even keel, I pictured to myself how the little four tonner would go dancing along, leaning over till her lee plankways were awash, and now and then taking a refreshing dash of silver spray over her bows.

Then also would there be some skill on my part in the steering, and some strain of muscle with the sheets. But steam!—well, it is a shame to grumble at what is serving us well—and here is Urk!

We anchored in the same place as before, and rowed ashore. The harbour was quite deserted, all the schuyts being out fishing. Consequently there were not many men to be seen about, while the women were all abroad gossiping, and we could take stock of them to our heart's content.

We were anxious to procure something made at Urk, as a memento of the place, and went into a sort of general dealer's shop, where with Kalff's aid we made enquiries. Nothing, however, was made upon the island save nets, and we had to content ourselves with buying some basins from Maestricht, which my children now use for their bread and milk.

There were several women and children in the shop, who talked a good deal to us, and satisfied their curiosity as well as ours.

We presently found our way into a ship-builder's shed, where we saw the process of bending the great thick oak planking of the oak schuyts. It is not made soft by steaming as with us; but the plank is bent by heat. It is propped up, with a heavy weight, such as a basket of stones at one end, while a crate containing burning peat is held under it, so that the flames play on the wood, which is often charred to the depth of a quarter of an inch before the desired curve is attained.

Then we bade farewell to the little island to which we had taken so great a fancy, and set our course northward for Stavoren in Friesland, eighteen miles distant, where we arrived in the afternoon without incident. Here we found a spacious and deep new harbour, constructed in connection with a railway from the north, the terminus of which is at Stavoren. We proceeded to the inner and older harbour, and made fast to a high stone quay, up and down which it was no easy matter to climb.

In the matter of houses and people, Stavoren looked uncommonly bare, and it was as quiet as the grave. The harbour dues, in the collecting of which all the male inhabitants of the place took a friendly interest, amounted to threepence. The people here were better looking than in other parts of Holland (save Urk and Wemeldinge), and were very like English peasantry in dress and appearance. Not only so, but the Friesland language is more like English than in the other provinces. They could understand us very well if we spoke English slowly, and, in cases of doubt we gave all the English synonyms of the salient words, one of which would almost sure to be like Fries.

Stavoren, two centuries ago, was a large and flourishing city, doing great trade, and having a busy port, and inhabitants who were so rich, that they used the precious

STAVOREN.

metals for articles of domestic use. Now it is but a single broad street, with a narrow canal running down the centre, with broad grassy banks, on which sheep were tethered.

This curious custom of tethering sheep is common in Holland, and it has the effect of making each sheep take a close crop of the grass within the radius of his rope, which is good for the turf, if not for the sheep.

A man was shearing his sheep on his front doorstep, and sheep which had been shorn were clad in canvas coats, looking most comically miserable. Another man was seated in the street, milking his sheep. A small pleasure barge was moored in the canal, the only craft there. It had an elaborately carved otter for its rudder head, and was otherwise ornamented, but was clearly out of use, and "laid up in lavender long ago," like the rest of the city.

In the street, on either side, there were gaps in the rows of houses, where ruined or unoccupied houses had been cleaned away with Dutch neatness, and the spaces left, reminding one forcibly of a human jaw, where several of the upper and lower teeth had been removed down to the stumps, and the dentist had not put in new ones. In the case of Stavoren, I suppose, he never will.

The legend of how Stavoren lost its greatness has been told in every book upon Holland, but on the spot we heard it with greater detail, and with certain corroborative testimony, which may make the tale worth repeating here, although, as a rule, it is my intention to refrain from relating anything that we did not ourselves experience.

A certain rich widow of Stavoren, very puffed up with

her own conceit, and wanting a new sensation, ordered one of her captains, who was bound on a voyage to Dantsic, to bring her the most precious thing the country contained. The unwise captain, instead of golden ornaments or jewels, or such like feminine fancies, brought a cargo of wheat, which from a stupid man's point of view he considered most precious. When he got back to Stavoren; "Well," said the lady, "what have you brought me?"

"A cargo of wheat," replied the captain proudly, conscious of having done a clever thing.

"And nothing else?"

"Nothing else! What so good?" said the captain.

"You great stupid dog!" exclaimed the lady, in a rage, "Is wheat what a woman wants? Go and throw it overboard? What you took in at the starboard, cast out at the larboard."

So the captain went sorrowfully, and emptied his cargo of wheat in the sea, outside the harbour.

Now the wiser people of Stavoren were shocked at this wastefulness, and predicted that the evil so done would come back to the wilful widow.

"Come back to me, indeed!" cried the woman scornfully. "Yes, it will, when this ring comes back to me." And taking a ring off her finger she pitched it into the sea.

But a week later, a fisherman of Marken was cleaning a cod which he had caught, and in its interior he found the ring. Recognizing the crest, he took the first opportunity of taking it to Stavoren, expecting a reward. He didn't get it, but the widow took the dumps, being superstitious, and died.

The shipload of wheat formed the nucleus of a sandbank, which quickly increased, until it stopped the navigation to the port, and the inhabitants having made their pile, were too lazy to remove it, and in consequence Stavoren died like its widow.

Now comes a curious corroboration. Our men, in prowling about, saw here and there in the houses, bunches of dried stunted wheat, and learned that at intervals, when the water in the Zuyder Zee is low for a length of time, the sandbank, which is called the *vrowenzind*, becomes dry, and a grass, which is clearly a degenerate wheat and grows there, can be gathered. The Stavorenites seize these opportunities, and gather bunches of the grass. After much enquiry and trouble, and the expenditure of a few cents, we succeeded in getting two or three bunches of the grass, which we have brought home in memory of Stavoren.

We visited the town-hall, and found that the burgomaster or the town clerk—we didn't quite understand which, probably the latter—lived in the main rooms, being permitted to do so by the town council. But there wasn't very much to see, except some pictures of Scripture subjects, very badly executed.

STAVOREN LOCK.

A stroll round the dyke which keeps out the Zuyder Zee, and behind which the remains of the town nestled, and a vain endeavour to find out the species of the first shore bird we had seen, brought us back to the harbour.

Here the passengers of the Atalanta insisted upon being photographed, although the blazing sun made them screw up their faces into unrecognisable contortions. But it is one of the trials of amateur photography, that our friends insist upon our taking them, and then never forgive us because we haven't made them much better looking than they really are.

A barge, laden with brown peat from the interior of Friesland, passed through the lock, which gave communication to the canals entering to the heart of the province; and afforded an instantaneous shot with the camera.

The interior of the country, for the dozen miles or so of which we explored it, seemed less interesting to us than other parts of Holland. It was, of course, as flat as flat could be, and as wet in parts, as Holland is after all but a raft awash with water. The meadows were not so green as in North Holland, but were more like the dull marshes near Yarmouth. They were intersected by narrow canals, the water of which at a little distance was invisible, their course being marked by the red-sailed barges and the steamers gliding along them. Then there were wide-stretching, coffee-coloured meres, of which it was not our good fortune to see the larger ones, and everywhere were square pools occupying the spaces from which peat had been cut.

It is rather a curious thing that in a country where land is so precious, so much of it should be dug up and consumed by fire, and that the space occupied by this burnt land should be given up to Holland's greatest enemy, water, but so it is. The use of peat is still increasing, and, heat for heat, it is still cheaper in Holland than coal, although weight for weight the latter gives twice the heat.

The Friesland peat is brown and spongy, while that of North Holland is blacker, more solid, and earthy. In Friesland, while some of the peat is dug out of the moor or less solid bog, a large proportion of it is scooped or raked from the bottom of the pools, dried, and compressed into shapes. Of course, it has been found necessary to control the digging and manufacture of peat, by law, to prevent irreparable injury being done to the land. Sometimes a peat bog catches fire and is burnt out, a lake taking its place. Such is said to have been the origin at Jonker Meer in Friesland, of a lake at Brabant in 1541, and one at Utrecht in 1567.

Seeing a large tree being unearthed from a bog, I made enquiries, and found that this often happened, and that such trees generally lay in one direction, as if overthrown by a north-west wind. The men working in this mixture of mud and water looked strong, healthy, and contented. They worked by piece-work, and one man said that he was a very good workman, as he could earn 2s. 6d. a day, and once, when wages were higher, 3s. a day.

A good deal of Friesland seems already to have been consumed by the digging of peat. It is an old joke that the Dutch, having with difficulty saved their land from the water, are now burning it as fast as they can.

It was our intention to take the Atalanta to Sneek, where there was to be a great fair on the morrow, and we set about finding a pilot. There was no difficulty about this; but everyone doubted whether there was sufficient water in the great meres, over which the route passed. The canals were just deep enough, but the channels over the lakes were doubtful. The whole male population of the village took a profound interest in the matter, and made enquiries of the tjalks coming down the canal, and of the many steamers which were bound to Sneek. The upshot of it was, that owing to the unusual lowness of the water, the channels were not deep enough for us. If we struck just in the middle of a great mere, it would be a difficult matter to get off, as no anchor would hold in the soft bottom. With six inches less draught, they would have advised us to try it, but not with five feet.

Very reluctantly, therefore, we gave up the idea, but it

was a great disappointment not to sail over the great expanses of water, which these peaty-coloured Friesland meres present. We had rather set our minds upon doing it in our own boat, and as we could not do that, we did not care about going to Sneek by rail or native boat.

In any future steam excursion, we shall take care not to hire a steamer with a greater draught than four feet. For the second time we had to change our course.

Looking at the map of Friesland, there seems almost as much water as land, meres and connecting canals are so thickly distributed.

The provinces of Friesland and Groningen suffer most from inundations; a severe one being expected every seven years. One of the worst was in 1825, when, not only Friesland, but Over, Yssell, North Brabant, and Gelderland were inundated. Of the horrors of these inundations, the anxious watching of the levels, the breaking of the dykes, and the consequent death and destruction, it is not in the province of a holiday book to treat, but the subject is a deeply interesting one, nevertheless. It may be remarked that the level of the land is still sinking, as the spongy soil consolidates through drainage, and the beds of the rivers are rising, as their currents deposit mud.

After all, Holland is but the muddy delta of the three

great rivers, the Rhine, the Meuse, and the Scheldt, as a glance at the map will show. To protect this delta against the waters of these rivers on the one hand, and the sea on the other, necessitates the severest attention to the solidity of the dykes, and the efficacy of the drainage arrangements.

In the province of Yssel Monde alone, there are 200 miles of dykes, although the province is but fifteen miles long by seven wide, and eight of the provinces of Holland have eighty-five per cent. of their surfaces under the sea level.

Dendy said the country wore a bridal veil of water. Blake said it was more like a funeral shroud, so much depends on the point of view, and the sunshine or gloom of the day.

CHAPTER XIII.

HINDELOOPEN.

HAVING exhausted Stavoren while it was yet early in the afternoon, on looking at the map, and seeing Hindeloopen was but nine miles distant, and accessible by rail, we determined to visit it. Kalff returned by the same train to Zwolle, having to go a long way round by Leeuwarden.

Upon alighting at Hindeloopen station, we started to walk to the village, which was half a mile away. We ranged up alongside an intelligent-looking man, who saluted us, and Dendy immediately asked him if he spoke French. He did a little, and Dendy began the exhaustive process of pumping, which he applied to every intelligent foreigner whom we came across, much to our benefit. This man immediately constituted himself our guide about Hindeloopen. Upon learning that we had come from a yacht at Stavoren, he asked how we were going back again that evening, upon which we replied that the time table showed a train back at nine o'clock.

"But you have the time table for June, and it is not the first of June until to-morrow. There is no train to-night."

Blake was awfully disgusted at this, and utterly refused to walk back, declaring that he would stay the night at Hindeloopen, unless we could find a vehicle, and drive.

"I will take you to a man who speaks English very well, and keeps an inn, and he can let you have a conveyance," said our guide.

So before doing anything else, we went to secure the conveyance. In a roomy old inn we found Mr. Oran van Elseno, who, by the way, was a roomy old man. In addition to being an innkeeper, he was also the baker of the place. His English we found extremely rusty, but as he lost his nervousness at speaking with strangers, it improved wonderfully, and from hardly a word being understood on either side, we got to conversing comfortably. We could have either a closed or open conveyance, and as it was then fine and warm, we chose the latter, and ordered it to be ready at eight o'clock.

Our host had been a steward on an English vessel for some years, which was where he had picked up his English. He had saved his money, and so was able to set up a "*logement*" house in his native town. As he said to us during the drive home, "the other men they spent their money in fun and drink, but I saved all mine, and lived hard. Now they are dead or in poverty, and I am *so*" (with a smile of great contentment).

He was having his tea when we went in, and it simply consisted of a cup of coffee and a big, unhealthy-looking bun. But from Elseno's appearance it pays to live on buns.

In a corner of the room was a very quaint old clock, which had all sorts of fakements about it. I went up to examine it closely, and Elseno asked me if I was fond of "antikishis?" I replied that I was, whereupon he intimated that as soon as he had got on the outside of his bun, he would show us a lot of antikishis. Presently he conducted us to an upper room, and then began a show, which it was worth going to Holland specially to see.

His wife had inherited from her father a rich store of old dresses, ornaments, and antiquities, peculiar to Hindeloopen. From a large glass-domed cabinet, he brought out in rare abundance, dresses for maid, wife, and widow, bridals and mournings, church-goings and festivities. Also men's apparel, only a little less quaint. As Blake says in his circular post-cards to his friends, " words cannot describe" the things we saw. At least, masculine words cannot. I did so wish my wife had been there.

She would have carried a minute description of the whole lot in her head. With me, there remains but a vague impression of wonderful garments, minutely finished, and ornamented with fine needlework, the intricacies of the various stitches being pointed out to us by Elseno. The general colours of these garments were rich and striking, rather than artistic.

I will try and describe the church-going costume of a Hindeloopen lady. On the head was a coal-scuttle straw bonnet, with the back of it turned to the front, and the base of it covered with a chess-patterned handkerchief. Under this was the golden helmet, covering nearly the whole of the head, but hidden by the bonnet when on. Across the forehead was a broad gold band, with corkscrews at the temples, and in the ears were large coral pendants. A violet neckerchief was tied round the neck. The substratum of the dress was a dark-coloured woollen gown from head to foot, but this was almost completely covered as follows: all down the back with a gaily-flowered dressing-gown kind of thing, with sleeves—the material linen, with a great deal of needlework and em broidery, particularly round the edges. The sleeves came down to the wrists, where they were confined by tight velvet bands. This garment reached to the ground, and indeed trailed upon it, but otherwise it only covered the back and arms. In front, up aloft, was a pink linen thing, covering the whole of the breast, and confined at the waist by a red sash. From amidships to the ground was a voluminous pinafore of pinkish check-patterned linen. On the feet were velvet slippers as prettily worked as any curate's. In one hand a Bible, and in the other a fire-box. Such is a Frisian lady going to church as the Vrouw Elseno displayed to us, and such is the costume still to be seen in use.

The fire-box is a portable stove, which a Frisian lady takes with her to church, or other cold public places, to serve as a foot-warmer. Externally it is a little wooden chest, like a large tea-caddy, ornamentally designed, with open fretwork sides. This contains a metal case, in which is set a piece of lighted turf. If this is carefully selected, it will keep aglow for two or three hours. The old boxes which Elseno showed us, were painted with a varnish or enamel paint, the secret of which appears to have been lost. In appearance it looks like the best Japanese work. The present ones, in imitation of it, are not so choice.

Elseno was thoroughly smitten with the idea that all old things were best. Only he called them "antique," which synonym was odd in some of its applications, as when he spoke of a friend as an antique man, and of his religion as antique Protestant.

The gold ornaments of various kinds for the head were of course very interesting. The Frisian girl makes her ornaments express the language of love. Thus, if a young man comes a-wooing, and the maiden dons her Sunday best gold things, he knows that he is the winning horse. If, on the contrary, she receives his visits minus the ornaments, he takes the hint, and goes elsewhere.

Elseno showed us also many silver ornaments, delicately fashioned, and quaint and odd in design, clasps for reticules or ladies' bags, buckles, brooches, spoons, and all sorts of things, china and pictures, finishing up with a large and very antique doll, beautifully dressed in the aforesaid church-going costume. It was a delightful doll, and I greatly coveted it for my little daughter. But none of the things were purchasable.

Afterwards, he and several others accompanied us for a stroll through the town. The harbour was very small and shoal, so that only a small boat could enter. In a bay just outside the little pier, the mud was covered with shore fowl of many different kinds, running briskly about, and filling the air with their cries. As this was almost the first indication of bird life in any quantity we had seen, I wanted a good long stare at them, but the evening was drawing on, and there was much to be seen.

The town had many little streets, crowded with many

little houses, all neat, compact, clean, and many-coloured. The very fowl-houses were like miniature villas, or large dolls' houses, ornamented to excess.

The emblem of the town, a couple of hinds leaping, was carved, and painted on every available place; but the chief curiosity in this way, is a large painted carving on a house at one end of the town. It represents the miraculous draught of fishes, but the boat is a pronounced Dutch schuyt, and the fishermen are in Dutch costume, while we were told that the flag, which had now disappeared, was the Dutch flag.

Asking us to wait a little, Elseno went into a modest looking house, no larger than, and in no way distinguishable from its neighbours, and presently emerged, stating that we were permitted to look inside it. We crossed a tiny little bridge, over a tiny moat, passed through a tiny and spotlessly clean yard, to the back door. The front door of a Dutch house in the country is for ornament only, and not for use, and is rarely opened save to be cleaned and painted afresh. This house was the most minutely clean and unique any of us had ever seen, and was a perfect and rich museum of the wealthier side of Frisian life. In the passage by the house door, was a well, and the polish on its mahogany cover was only exceeded by the glisten on the copper bucket, with brass bands, and the shining brass chain, which took the place of the ordinary rope. The floor of the hall, as well as the doors leading from it, looked as if they had only been painted yesterday.

The kitchen, the living room on the ground floor, the hall, a passage, and the staircase were lined with Dutch tiles, those in the passage and dark staircase and corridors being white, or with a pattern or figure of an animal painted on them. At the foot of the stairs were hung several wooden bowls, painted with cupids and flowers in many colours. Climbing up the narrow staircase, we were ushered into the sacred front room, which would rarely be used for any purpose but show. It was the museum of the house, where a collection of antique treasures were preserved in a place which was worthy of them.

The room was so jealously guarded from daylight by drawn inner and outer blinds, that we could see nothing distinctly until one shutter was opened, and as we crept about cautiously over the highly-polished oaken floor, we had an uneasy feeling that we ought to have taken our shoes off, and, in fact, did debate in whispers whether we should do so or not.

Three sides of the room were completely lined with tiles. Up to the height of six feet or so, the tiles were adorned with various Biblical subjects, the Dutch conception of which was, in many instances, extremely comical. Above this dado the tiles were plain white, except that a blue bordering went round the oaken beams which supported the roof. On the fourth side was a range of magnificent oak cabinets, with lattice or fretwork doors, through the interstices of which the contents were visible. These consisted of rare old china and antique silver articles of every kind, spoons, teapots, pins, brooches, and even a silver birdcage.

Many of the things were so curious that we could assign neither use nor ornament to them, and much of the interest of the collection was lost to us for want of some one to explain the uses of what we saw. Probably the following paragraph, which I have just seen in a weekly newspaper, may give the true explanation of the small size of some of the objects:—"The rich Dutch burghers of old believed very much in teaching children by means of their playthings, and used to give them elaborate dolls' houses, furnished with utensils in solid silver, that worked perfectly, and were exact models of those in daily use in the family. There were silver lamps and coffee-pots, dishes, spice boxes, and everything in miniature. Thus the little Dutch girls were housewives from their babyhood.

Along the top of this rare old piece of furniture was

suspended a row of porcelain plates. About the room were curiously carved and designed chairs and tables, some of the latter finely inlaid; and on the wall I particularly noticed mirrors with tortoiseshell frames. The waning light left us too little time to examine the contents of the room in detail, but we all thought it the choicest thing of the kind we had ever seen in public or private.

The lady of the house (who was pleased at our admiration, yet fearful that we should scratch or displace anything) wore the large gold helmet of the country, and her son, who could talk a little English, told us that his aunt possessed one so jewelled that it cost two thousand florins

As we went downstairs, the door of the living room was open, and we caught a glimpse of a trim and polished interior, and a glimpse also of a real Frisian beauty. Trimming the evening lamp, was the daughter of the house, a tall, stately, yellow-haired, and clear-complexioned girl. I could not get the other fellows away. They simply stood and stared, until the girl came out into the passage, and passed us on her way to the kitchen. She carried a large basin of water in her hands, but with her golden crown, and her apparent supreme indifference to our presence, she looked a princess at the least.

The brother walked with us back to the inn. On the way he pointed out a large chateau, which belonged to the squire of the place.

"Large chateau. Nothing there. My house small, but plenty there." To which we nodded an approving assent.

Our carriage was ready. It was a four-wheeled thing, without any springs, and our seats were loose boards put across. We jogged along the clinkered road in a very lively manner, which made conversation difficult and spasmodic. Elseno and his two boys accompanied us, and the former tried to find out our motive for coming to Hindeloopen. When he understood that we had come in a steam yacht, not for trade, but for pleasure, he cried, "Fine, fine."

The day had been broiling hot, but the evening turned so bitterly cold that, unprovided as we were with overcoats, our teeth chattered again. We noticed as a peculiarity of Holland, that in a moment heat would give place to cold. When a cloud obscured the sun, we had to run for a pea jacket, and the evenings were almost always chilly. Warm, woollen clothing is clearly advisable, even in hot weather.

We drove along under the shelter of a continuous mighty mound, whose steep slope rose far above our heads, and whose top was a firm straight outline against the darkening sky. It suddenly occurred to us that this was the dyke keeping out the Zuyder Zee, the level of which would be above our heads, and, jumping out, we climbed to the top, and, as we expected, saw in front of us the grey sea, which by this massive embankment was held up above the land. It was an impressive sight; the restrained strength of the water, which looked so vast under the gathering night; the solitary defiant dyke, standing guard over the sleeping land, and the only moving object the little pony and cart on the narrow track far beneath us, and beneath the soft ripple whispering away the precious stones casing the sea front of the dyke.

Here and there was the twinkling light from the window of some little house low down by a canal, and we pictured to ourselves the quiet contentment which might be found within that obscure home, while in England at that moment there was the fever of hot debate.

Dendy was so cold that he took to running along the top of the dyke to warm himself, and so ran the last three miles home, to the great amazement of Elseno, who kept staring at the ghostly figure up there as if it was somewhat uncanny.

Every now and then he would point with his whip, and,

imitating the action of running by moving his knees up and down, say, "Very good."

He and one of his sons came on board the Atalanta with us, leaving the other boy to mind the trap. We gave them their choice of eatables and drinkables, and they chose Bass's ale, and some fine white biscuits. The boy shyly asked if he might take one of the latter for his brother, and Elseno asked for one for his *vrouw*.

We turned in, feeling that we had experienced a very jolly day indeed, and remembering our then enjoyment, I now feel that I am giving but a very bald account of it.

ANOTHER fine morning made us congratulate ourselves upon our good fortune. Our steam to-day was simply to be across the Zuyder Zee to Medemblik in North Holland, a distance of thirteen miles. It was a brisk, exhilarating passage. There was a pleasant breeze, which tipped with white crests the waves, that otherwise were as blue as the interspaces of the dappled sky. Under a dazzling blue and white sky, over a dazzling blue and white sea, we sped swiftly without incident until Medemblik came in sight.

We steamed very slowly between the piers, sounding with poles as we proceeded. There was, however, about seven feet of water in the middle. There were two or three schuyts moored to the quay, and we presently moored outside one of these. The harbour is a large one, but shallow; and men were engaged in dredging up the mud in bags fixed at the end of long poles, and depositing it in lighters.   This operation we in Norfolk call "dydling."

The town lies on the north side of the harbour, and a high grassy bank, shaded by a row of trees, divides the basin from its bordering street of small quaint houses. A large inner basin was quite untenanted, although it

MEDEMBLIK.

was spacious enough for a fleet to be moored there. On the banks of this inner basin, is a large building, which in palmier days was a naval training college, and is now a lunatic asylum.

"Dendy has got hold of somebody already," said Blake

to me before we had been moored five minutes; and sure enough, the interpreter, spying two smart young fellows on the quay, had spoken to them in French, which one of them understood very well, and had invited them on board. One proved to be the son of the burgomaster, and the other the son of the pastor, and we quickly, through Dendy's help, made friends with them, to our own subsequent advantage.

The morning was still young, and our new friends were kind enough to take us round the town, which was gay with flags, on account of the celebration that day of two silver weddings. The town-hall was of course the first place, for Dutch cities are particularly fond of their town-halls, and collect in them, as in a museum, whatever is of interest, and belongs to the municipal body. One room was lined with embossed and painted leather, very old, beautiful, and effective as ornament.

The most interesting thing to us was a copper-plate, dated 1599, very clearly engraved with a plan of Medemblik at that date, showing the fortifications which then existed, and a large portion of the town to the eastward of the church, which has since been swallowed up by the remorseless Zuyder Zee. Fully one-fourth of the town appears to have thus disappeared, and the church now stands on the outskirts, and close to the massive

Engraved by Arnar Ashcar, London.

MEDEMBLICK

dyke, which, it is to be hoped, will prevent any further depredations. A print of the plate was presently discovered, which gave us a clearer idea of the contrast between then and now.

There was also a mighty two-handed sword, which formerly belonged to a chieftain, whose ruined castle or fortified chateau formed a prominent object on the other side of the harbour. The owner may have been a smart man, but before he could get that sword over his head and in a position for striking, his adversary would have time to take a pinch of snuff and run him through.

We next went to the church, which had a very lofty tower. The interior of the church was very charming, and so cool, compared with the sultry heat, gathering to a tempest, outside, that we lingered there a long time, and I took a photograph of it, to the scandal of the sexton. There was a large sounding board over the pulpit. The latter was of finely-carved oak, as was also the screen, or enclosure for the choir. There was a very fine organ with a number of symbolical figures at the top, and backed by a well-designed curtain, painted on the white wall. Large and handsome brass candelabra were suspended from the ceiling. The body of the church was seated with chairs, but round the sides were the old-fashioned pews, so excessively narrow and uncomfortable that they would effectually prevent any attempt at lounging. There was no room for my knees, and I had to sit sideways. To me they were reminders of the chambers of torture of my boyhood, with seats barely eight inches wide, and wooden footstools which

MEDEMBLIK CHURCH.

tilted up, and made an awful clatter, when the agonies of pins and needles compelled a move.

The general appearance of the church was that of quaint solidity, but the pavement was decidedly comical. It was covered with memorial slabs or gravestones, but then the designs and inscriptions on these were grimly humorous. Thus, on the grave of a man named Groenbroeck (green breeches) was carved a voluminous pair of knickerbockers, with the inscription across the seat. There were other punning designs, and many emblems of the trades formerly carried on by the deceased, such as a pair of scissors, or a drawing of a brass plate, with a mouthful bitten out of one side, which are hung up in the barbers' windows. (The cut-out place is intended to fit against the neck, while the dish full of lather is held under the chin.)

Then we climbed the tall church tower; up ladder after ladder, from floor to floor, up among the ropes and bells, and at last we arrived in a breathless condition on the gallery around the lantern at the top. The view from this height was magnificent, and well repaid us for the exertion. The air was beautifully clear, although in the distance the thunder clouds were gathering. But their gloom only emphasized the objects which were outlined against them by the brilliant sunlight. Beneath us were the red roofs of the town, the harbours and barges, and the great embankment against the Zuyder Zee. In the flat, and far-reaching distance to the westward, were a score of villages set in the verdant plain, each with its grove of trees, which sometimes so concealed the houses that only the tall church spire was visible. The land was patterned out with a lacework of gleaming dykes, canals, and pools, with here and there a red-sailed barge. To the eastward was the sea, looking silver-grey in the shadow of the rising cloud.

From the height we were, the extreme hollowness of the land was very apparent. It might be compared to a soup-plate floating on a pond, the level of the water being nearly up to the brim, which was represented by the curving embankment keeping out the sea. Dwarfed by the distance, the dyke looked but a poor protection to the country behind it, and as if a kick would shatter it and let in the waters.

Descending to the great clock, we waited for the bell to strike the hour, which it presently did, with a mighty and startling clang. It was the hour of one, and it awoke answering echoes in the places to which dinner was ready to go.

The afternoon was partly occupied by a thunderstorm, which cleared the air and brought on a fine evening, and partly by a stroll through the streets and to the old chateau. A sale of marine stores was going on in this, and the crowd of buyers was chiefly composed of country people, who stared at us as curiously as we stared at them. We know what we said about them, but we should much like to know what they said about us.

There was one wide street with a still canal down the middle and thick rows of trees on each side, which I wished to photograph. There was not a soul in it when I commenced to erect my apparatus, but in a few minutes a large crowd of children had assembled and hastened to plant themselves on a foot bridge over the canal, in order to come in the view, thereby spoiling my picture.

The little mirrors which we in East Anglia are not unused to see projecting from the sides of windows, in order that the inmates of a house may see who is coming along the street without the trouble of rising from their seats, are common enough in all Dutch towns, but we particularly noticed them at Medemblik. Of course they reflect what is inside as well as what is outside; and as we walked along close to the houses, we could see the faces of the women framed in them, and as it were projecting over the street, heads without bodies.

There was a small open sailing-boat, or yacht in the harbour, lying under our stern, which belonged to a gentleman from Leyden. He was cruising about in her, and came on board us for a chat. He was the only Dutch yachtsman we saw in actual movement, and looked a regular sailorman. His craft looked like a big beetle, with her leeboards triced up like huge wings. She was about seventeen feet long and six feet wide; flat-bottomed of course, and with timbers and planking strong enough for a twenty-tonner.

CHAPTER XV.

TWISK.

OUR friends, whose names, by the way, had so many syllables as to cause Rowland to remark, "it was a long way round to them," suggested that we should visit the village of Twisk, which was about an hour distant, and was a model pastoral village. The hour meant an hour's walk at a moderate pace, and this mode of measuring distances by the time occupied, seemed to be the one in universal use in Holland. There seemed to be no measure, corresponding to our miles, known to the public, and the replies to our inquiries invariably were, " It is half-an-hour, or an hour, or two hours' distance."

With this uncertainty of distance we declined to walk, so hired a conveyance of the universal type, that is, an oblong box on four wheels, with the back curving up like a chariot, and supporting a roof. So we started in the cool of the evening along a road, which for a considerable distance skirted the land side of the sea dyke. This road was paved with brick clinkers the whole distance, giving it a neat clean appearance, and drying rapidly after rain. Of course all the heavy traffic of the country goes by water, and only the light traffic passes over the roads, which thus have a better chance of being kept in good repair than an English road.

On arriving at Twisk, we put up the horse at a *logement* house, where there was good *uitspanning*, and proceeded to walk up the long single street which comprised the village. On one side ran a narrow canal, green with scum, which was brushed aside by the passage now and then of a boat carrying goods to and fro. On the green banks of the canal a few boys sat solemnly fishing for roach. Smaller canals branched off at right angles from this, and enclosed square plots of ground, on which rose square houses, with lofty pyramidal roofs. Each house had a bridge leading to it, which was mostly in a high state of ornamentation, and an imposing gate, which was there purely for ornament, as it was customary to walk round rather than through it. The pathways were painted in coloured patterns, the trees were in many instances painted up to the branches, a light blue or pink, the gables and sides of the houses were green and red, the steep thatched roofs were variegated with patches of tiling in regular patterns, and house and garden alike were as neat and as trim, and as brightly-coloured as a toy house in a nursery. Here and there was a house of greater pretensions, with more windows, slated roof, and ornate eaves, with a larger garden, polished metal sun-

FARM AT TWISK.

dials or shining balls on stands, like a school globe without maps on it.

Numbers of people came out to look at us, but in no instance was a front door opened. The front door was for ornament, not use, and many of them were decidedly works of art in the way of carving, gilding, and painting.

Each house had within it the whole of the farm establishment, the cattle being housed in the back portion during the winter time. There were no separate farm buildings. The cattle were now of course upon the meadows, and the men went to tend them in little flat boats along narrow little canals. It was a village of small farmers, no one being very poor, and no one very rich. As a rule, each man owns his own land, and works uncommonly hard, practising the utmost thrift.

Here was what some would call the happy mean; to me it looked the deadest of dead levels. No precautions seemed neglected whereby a little money could be saved, the very sheep were being milked, to say nothing of the goats, and many of the cows were encased in coats to protect them from the cold.

There were several gaps in the village, where houses had lately been burnt down. A strong wind had blown the sparks far and wide, setting fire to houses at long distances apart. In two hours about a dozen houses were demolished; one unfortunate man, in addition to his house, had twelve hundred guelders in paper money burnt. We understood that none of the houses were insured, as the Dutchman's thrift makes him object to pay premiums in the shape of money down against an unlikely risk. We walked on and on, and at last asked

Engraved by Annan & Swan, London.

how much further it was to the end of the village, and the reply was, it was like this to eternity, whereupon we thought it prudent to turn back.

And now Blake and I noticed that the people were regarding us not only curiously but pityingly, and we could not make out the reason why until we got back to the inn. There we learned that our Dutch friend, who was dressed all in white, and Dendy, who had been talking very enthusiastically with explanatory gestures, were taken for two of the lunatics from the Medemblik asylum, and that Blake and I, who were dressed in blue with peaked caps, were taken to be their keepers. At first we understood it the other way, and Dendy was exultant over us, but when the true state of affairs was discovered, we had the laugh on our side.

The village of Twisk is said to be one of the most characteristic in Holland; it is not mentioned in any guide-book, and we can strongly recommend the tourist to pay it a visit. The rebuilding of the houses burnt down, gave us an opportunity of inspecting the somewhat peculiar mode of construction. First a square framework of massive oaken beams, and of a considerable height, is built. This is the support of the whole house. The roof projects over this framework, and slopes half way down to the ground, where it is supported by exterior walls, only half the height of the inner frame.

It was dusk when we returned to our cosy little home, and there was a constant play of summer lightning on the horizon, sharply outlining at intervals the gables, trees, and masts. The town was early asleep, and it was very still except for the noise of the frogs, which were unusually lively. We noticed that they had a distinctly shriller note than English frogs, being more of a chirrup than a croak. The night watchmen patrolling the town awoke the echoes with their cries, and the springing of their rattles at regular intervals.

I had arranged to revisit Twisk in the morning with my camera, and as the other fellows wished to make an early start for Nieuwe Diep, I ordered the conveyance for six o'clock in the morning. Shortly before that hour, Rowland made his appearance at the top of the companion, with a bowl of hot bread and milk, the best possible material for an early breakfast. It is easily and quickly enclosed, and is satisfying. The wagon was punctual, and, taking Jack, the deck hand, with me, we started, on as merry a morning as well could be. We rattled our bones over the stones, through the quiet streets, and when free from the houses, past a picturesque windmill on the dyke, and through a feeble pretence at a gate, we enjoyed to the full the glorious beauty of the early summer morning.

In the brilliant sunshine, the grasses of the meadow

were in the stems a lustrous green, and in their ripening seed plumes a warm brown. Red flower spikes and masses of blue and yellow, of Dutch brightness, carpeted the plain. Over the vivid and gay meadow many a lark sang blithely, and bees hummed about the flowers, and blue and brown butterflies fluttered across the road. A cool and pleasant breeze tempered the heat, and the air was exquisitely fresh and light to breathe. Could this be the land of frogs and inundations, "*canaux, canard, canailles,*" the land so fishy, that its inhabitants were said to address their sweethearts as "my dear codfish," by way of the best term of endearment? Why, it is a sunny, cheerful, land, smiling with peace and plenty.

But we could picture this same drive on a winter's day, with a strong wind blowing the snow or sleet in one's face, and the verdant plain a howling desolate waste; the sea thundering against the dyke, and the land sodden with rain and melted snow. We imagine that summer and sunshine are necessary for the enjoyment of rural Holland, save when the frost is keen and the skating good.

On our arrival at Twisk we had to give orders to our driver, who knew no tongue but Dutch, but by this time we were clever at gesticulating, and by shifting the hands of my watch to half-past eight o'clock, we made him understand that he was to be ready for us at that hour. We had become so used to pantomimic speech that we found ourselves gesticulating to each other. Blake, in particular, was fond of addressing us in broken English, with appropriate gesticulations.

Twisk was extremely quiet until I had my camera fixed; then from every house there came the "clang of the wooden shoon," as inmates, young and old, came hurrying out to see what was up. They crowded round us in an embarrassing manner, trying to peep in at the lens, while my head was under the focussing cloth. Then when I was about to uncap the lens, they would rush into the foreground to appear in the picture.

I talked to them in vigorous English, which some man, who had a glimmering of what I required, paraphrased in Dutch, and between us we managed to get a few pictures. But my heart failed me when I saw the impossibility of giving any idea, in the final prints, of the bright contrast of colours which looked so well on the focussing screen. Holland is a country for the colourist, rather than for the photographer.

When the good-humoured but excited crowd became too troublesome, and got in the way of a special bit I wished to take, I duped them with a dodge which I have often employed in England with success. Placing them

A PIOUS FRAUD.   181

all in a position just out of the picture, but near enough to it for them to imagine the lens was pointed towards them, I pretended to focus them, while in reality drawing a bead on a moated grange. Then cautioning them to keep still and smile their Sunday best, I exposed, but not

DOGS AND CART.

on them. This is a pious fraud, which, as it satisfies both parties, will not, I hope, lower me in the opinion of my parish.

A group of three dogs drawing a cart, strongly objected to be photographed, and growled and barked at me for some time before I got them.

By the time I had taken six views the curiosity of the crowd was getting too pressing. I should like to have understood all their comments upon us and our proceedings, which were freely expressed, and appeared amusing. When I had packed my things up; the crowd and I took off our caps to each other with the utmost politeness, and we bade adieu to Twisk.

The drive back was hotter than the outward journey, but the mowers were busy cutting the hay on the great slopes of the dyke, and the warm air was filled with its delightful fragrance, and we loitered a little on the top of the dyke to enjoy it. We judged that the dyke was thirty feet above the meadow, and a hundred and fifty feet across the base. The stones, with which the sea face was lined, had been brought at great expense from other countries, chiefly Norway, for practically there are no stones in Holland.

We overtook a peasant woman trudging along with a big basket on her arm, and she evidently asked our driver for a lift, and in reply he shook his head. But we managed to make him understand that we should be delighted to give the lady a lift, and she climbed up to the front seat alongside of the driver. He told her that we were

English, whereupon she faced round and talked to and at us nineteen to the dozen, with variations of nods and becks, and wreathed smiles. She pointed to various parts of our dress during the criticism, and she appeared especially pleased with Jack, who is a good-looking, fresh-coloured fellow. She pointed to his white teeth, and black eyes, with evident approval, and the more Jack blushed and laughed in confusion, the greater was her delight. Then, as if she wished to make amends to me, she suddenly kissed her hand to me with great violence; as only a yard separated us, I began to be apprehensive that she might want to give me a proper kiss, and I am sure Jack was equally alarmed. We could only smile inanely at her, feeling that she had much the best of it, and were very much relieved when she got down.

We got back to the Atalanta in good time for a second breakfast, and made the others jealous by recounting our adventures at Twisk.

CHAPTER XVI.

TEXEL STREAM AND NIEUWE DIEP.

AGAIN under weigh, we steamed out of Medemblik harbour, our friends waving a farewell to us from the top of the dyke, which at the end of the harbour rose to quite a respectable hill. It was another perfect morning, sunny and hot; and as soon as we had got well out into the open, and the water was blue and deep, we gave the order to stop. As the sound of the engines ceased, the pilot looked round to see what was up, and appeared highly delighted as we rapidly shed our garments. It would give him something to talk about afterwards, and as a matter of fact he made a pretty tale out of the Englishmen stopping the steamer to bathe in the Zuyder Zee. As I think I have said before, it was his favourite diversion to recite to the sightseers on the quays our adventures, and we found that this bathing was never omitted.

It was delicious to quit the hot deck, which was quite

A DELICIOUS SWIM.

too warm for naked feet and plunge into the cool blue water, which was salter and more buoyant as we went northward. There was that nice lift in the sea, which makes swimming so much pleasanter than in either a flat calm or rougher waves.

We swam around the Atalanta as she slowly forged ahead, and enjoyed to the full the coolness of the water, the pleasant embrace round one's neck, and soft caressing of one's shoulders by the sparkling wavelets. We agreed that it was the most delicious swim we had ever had. Dendy made a diversion by attempting to get into a life-buoy feet first, which resulted in his head going down and his feet going up. The crew rushed to his rescue with boathooks and other sharp weapons, which, fortunately for his skin, were not needed. The skipper informed us that the proper way to get inside a life-buoy is to tilt it over one's head, which advice we perpetuate for the benefit of those about to drown.

The pilot looked on admiringly over the bulwarks, and we invited him to join, but he said his legs were too stiff, adding that he had bathed in his youth and could swim.

Resuming our course we left the island of Wieringen on our left, and entered the Texel stream, skirting the great sand known as the Lutjeswaard. Here the water was much deeper, and there was a stronger race of tide, which meeting the wind, now grown somewhat fresh, raised a highly respectable sea. The Atalanta danced from wave to wave, and bowed and curtseyed in a very lively manner. The curling green and white crests which tipped the blue waves—the transition from deep blue to translucent green being delicately beautiful—leaped on board with great activity and regularity, and kept the deck in a perpetual swish of purling water, which ran in little streams round hatchways and other impediments. It was most lively and exhilarating, and brought forth the frequent remark that "this was the best sail yet," a remark which was not novel, as we usually made it each day until we got into Belgium.

I was greatly struck with the manner in which my little twelve-foot yacht's dinghy towed behind. With a short scope of painter she came perfectly dry, skimming from wave to wave like a captive seagull, while it was advisable to have the lifeboat slung up in the davits. Often in towing her behind my own small sailing yacht, I have been struck with the same thing. She is a beautiful model, built by Mollett, of Brundall, Norwich, and will carry six people with ease, while you may stand upon her gunwale without upsetting her. Jolly boats are often such crank affairs that her good qualities are worth noting.

Presently, old Klaus de Jonge called us around him to hear a story.

"I am seventy-three years old," quoth he, "and I have been pilot for forty-two years on the Zuyder Zee, and I only lost one ship. This was the spot. She was a large barque, and it was in the winter time, with a strong gale blowing, and a very dark night. The channel was not so well buoyed as it is now, and even if it were, I could not see the buoys. The compass, too, was not a good one. The vessel would not answer her helm well. It was not my fault, but she struck the sand here. Well, the crew were very frightened, but I was not. By and bye a steam tug came up with a lifeboat, and offered to take the crew off, but I said to the captain, 'Captain, is there any water in the hold?' And he said,

"'No, pilot, there is no water.'

"'Then captain,' said I, 'I will not leave the ship.

"'Then if you stay, pilot, I will stay,' said the captain.

"Some of the crew went off in the lifeboat, but some stayed with the captain and me. When the gale was over we had the cargo carried on lighters to Nieuwe Diep, and so saved that, but we could not get the ship off, and afterwards she went to pieces."

This tale, told in broken English, with many dramatic

gestures, occupied some time, and the old boy sounded his trumpet very freely. But he was a sterling old boy, a regular honest sea dog, and, looking upon us as his peculiar property, did his best for our interests.

It is said that "in matters of commerce, the fault of the Dutch is giving too little and asking too much." Klaus cautioned us so often against this fault of his countrymen, that it would have been very much our own fault if we had been much taken in afterwards. But our experience of the Dutch decidedly is, that after making allowance for a little pardonable shrewdness, they are a very pleasant and reliable sort of people, obliging, courteous, and easy to get on with, being in all these respects a long way more uniform than the same class of people in England.

On every opportunity, Klaus would express his satisfaction with us. "I am seventy-three years of age, and I have been pilot, &c., &c., and I never as long as I live forget dis boat and dis voyage." This was extremely satisfactory, as we were not particularly indulgent to him. He did a fair day's work for a reasonable wage, and his food was the same as the men's. But the truth is the Dutch live much harder and on meagre fare, while the savoury meat meals which to the English waterman are a necessity are to the Dutch seaman a luxury.

Rowland used to look at the old man quite affectionately, and we suggested that he should adopt him as his father, and carry him off to Yarmouth.

Texel Island, which we passed close by on our right, had the usual crowd of sharp-peaked houses, with red gables, and we decided not to stop there, as we were all rather anxious to begin the canal work, which we deemed to be more peculiarly Dutch than the sea. So we went on to Nieuwe Diep, meeting at the entrance of the harbour two torpedo launches coming at a terrific speed, throwing a cloud of rainbow spray high into the air on either side of their sharp bows. At first it seemed as if they meant to run us down, so close did they come, but as Klaus kept his course manfully they sheered off sufficiently.

"They don't expect an Englishman to make way for a Dutchman!" growled Rowland, who found great fault with the Dutch for their arrogance. They *have* a rather pert way with them, particularly the younger men. They *strut* about as if they were monarchs of all they survey, but they don't really mean it. I think the fault lies in their legs, which we found were longer from the knee to the heel than is usual with Englishmen, and possibly their military training when young, and the officialism which prevails everywhere have something to do with it. A man would prance up to the quay and look at the Atalanta with the greatest superciliousness, but when spoken to he would be as amiable and desirous of obliging as anyone possibly could be. With Rowland, however, this putting on of "side" was always a sore point, and he delighted in taking the starch out of the poor fellows by some dry bit of witty chaff in the pure East Anglian style.

Rowland had been singing the praises of Nieuwe Diep, and raised our expectations to a high pitch. But since the opening of the shorter ship canal from Amsterdam to Ymuiden, the heavy traffic has deserted the North Holland canal, which formerly carried it from Nieuwe Diep to Amsterdam, and the Helder from being a busy seaport, is now little better than a fishing port.

As soon as we had moored to the quay, an official from the harbour master's office came up and demanded to know if we had a pilot on board, to which Blake, forgetting that our pilot was only to be publicly called the interpreter, answered, "Yes."

"Then why did he not signal as he came in?" a query to which we could make no reply, Klaus having gone ashore. The official demanded the yacht's papers, whereupon Blake growled at him that we would rather pay harbour dues as a trader than have any more trouble about the papers. But when we went up to the *kantoor* of the harbour master, we found him to be a very polite person, who took us upon trust, and informed us that there would be no dues to pay.

A very short stroll was sufficient to exhaust the interest of Nieuwe Diep and the Helder. We saw nothing that the guide-books will not tell you of better, but at every turn there was a statue or other piece of brag about the naval supremacy of the Dutch over the English. One statue of an admiral was the most ferocious thing in face and attitude that we had ever seen. There was a training ship moored to the quay, and Blake pointed out that her yards were not trimmed with the neatness and precision of an English man-of-war.

A long breakwater parallel with the quay forms the harbour, and an uncommonly hot tide runs along it, the rise and fall being about fifteen feet. Beyond the breakwater lay the Zuyder Zee, which we had at last left, but mean to revisit.

Schuyt after schuyt was running in with the tide, and mooring against the quay. It was easy to see the necessity of their being built strongly, for their method of stopping was to bump up alongside another schuyt with a resounding thump—and this, coming at the rate of six or eight miles an hour, was no joke.

During the evening, I was down below writing letters, and Dendy was on deck smoking, when I heard a conversation, which I give in detail, as an illustration of Dendy's manner of eliciting information wherever he goes. Two persons appeared to have arrived at the quay, to whom Dendy said, "Good evening."

"Good evening, sir," replied they in English.

"So you speak English, do you?"

"Yes, sir, a little."

"And where did you learn it? Have you been in England?"

"No, but I was nine years at sea, and part of the time in an English ship."

"Which do you like best, an English or Dutch merchant ship?"

"I like the English ship best, as it is not so strict with the men as the Dutch. On a Dutch ship the pay is much less, only one-half of the English; the food is worse and the work harder. On an English ship there is much more liberty. The men do not need to ask leave to go ashore after six o'clock if the ship is in harbour, but on a Dutch ship the men cannot go ashore at any time without leave."

"Why did you give up the sea?"

"I found that going about the world makes men older

but not richer. I would rather have ten shillings a week at Urk, than double that amount at sea."

"I see that you wear the Urk dress. I suppose you are an Urk man?"

"I am a Kampen man, but I married an Urk girl and settled at Urk, so I have to wear the Urk dress. I can live at Urk, board, lodging, and washing, for six shillings and sixpence a week."

"We went to Urk and saw some good-looking girls there," said Dendy.

"Yes, they are very nice-looking, but they are very shy with strangers. The Urk people keep to themselves very much. Many live and die without even leaving the island."

"Have they any amusements or games?"

"No, they go to the fishing, and then rest and go to bed. The young people sometimes meet at the public-house, but the married people don't go there."

"And do you go out fishing in a schuyt?"

"Yes, but in five years' time I hope to be able to buy a schuyt for myself."

"What will that cost?"

"Three hundred pounds of English money."

"Do several people go shares in one schuyt?"

"No sir, they generally belong to one man."

"What are tjalks?"

"The big round-bowed vessels with one mast. The two-masted ones are called snibs."

"Why are so many schuyts coming in here to-night?"

"Because to-morrow is Ascension Day. The fishermen are very religious, especially the Urk people, and these are mostly Urk boats. They always get home if the wind is favourable, but if not, then into the nearest harbour where they can go to chapel, on Saturday night or the eve of a saint's day. I think it is a good thing to be so religious."

"I see you have the gold neck buttons. Do they cost much?"

"About two pounds ten shillings, sir."

"And the silver buckles?"

"The men's buckles made in patterns, cost about the same, but the younger people cannot afford that, and have to put up with dollar pieces."

Dendy had no more questions to ask, and the men were bidding good-night, when I called up the companion, "Don't let them go away without a drink, after all that pumping." So he brought them into the cabin for a refresher, and I had a look at the Urk-Kampen convert. In spite of his accomplishments, he was not half the man to look at that the genuine Urk islander is, and we thought the Urk girl had bad taste to pass over her brawny cousins for him.

A pleasant stroll by moonlight along the quay brought us up to bed-time. During the night I was awakened several times by the thumping of schuyts arriving, and mooring outside of us.

CHAPTER XVII.

NORTH HOLLAND CANAL, ALKMAAR.

IN the morning we found ourselves hemmed in by a great number of schuyts. There were nine in tier immediately outside the Atalanta, and with a torrent of tide they were pressing her hard against the quay. Fore and aft of us, the schuyts were fourteen or fifteen in tier, and there was just a possible passage between the bows of our tier and the sterns of the next, which was, however, laced across by mooring ropes in every direction. We had let the time of slack water slip by, and at first it seemed as if we must wait for the next slack to get out. We shoved, and hauled upon ropes for a long time without moving her. At last the screw was set going, and the order given to stop talking and all shove together. This moved her, and as she slowly squeezed out, the schuyts filled up the vacated place, menacing my jolly, which would have been in another minute smashed to matchwood. I made a rush aft, seized the painter, and hoisted the boat unaided on to the gunwale of the Atalanta, a height of about five feet. I saved the jolly, and was uncommonly proud of the feat of strength involved in the operation. The Atalanta was now held across the bows of seven or eight schuyts, and under the sterns of an equal number; with less than three feet clear on either side, and a three-knot tide on her broadside.

"Let go all ropes, and full speed ahead;" and she swung out into the stream, with hardly a scratch on her paint.

"Well out of it," cried the captain, as he gave up the helm to the pilot. And in truth it was a nasty jam.

We soon reached the sluices at the mouth of the North Holland canal, and prepared to enter the lock. But the rush of tide, as the gates were opened, swept us across the entrance broadside on, and it was only after a good deal of "easy ahead, easy astern," pushing, and hauling on ropes, one of which broke, that we mastered the current, and got straight again. I did what I could to help, by pushing with a quant—a long pole with an iron spike at the end—and could not make out why all the officials on the lock were shouting at me. Not knowing what they meant, I went on using the quant as we should in Norfolk, sticking it into the wooden piles for a good hold. Presently the lock master brought me a copy in English of the regulations for the navigation of the canal, and informed us that it was contrary to law to place any iron-pointed pole against the lock, save in the sockets and against the cleats provided in the stonework for the purpose. He made us buy a copy of these regulations, costing, I think, eightpence, and in the appendix I give extracts from them for the use of yachtsmen. They are very carefully framed.

The regulation as to iron spikes is clearly a necessary one. On our Norfolk rivers every bit of timber about the bridges and locks is honeycombed with the marks of the quants.

When the Atalanta was safely moored in the lock, we were taken to the dues office, where we had to pay four guelders forty cents, which would free us to Amsterdam, except the usual tip of twenty-five cents to the rope men at each lock. At the office we found an elderly official who was in a great hurry to get to chapel because it was Ascension Day. He was in a fidget at having to attend to us then, but his wife, who was ready dressed and waiting, assisted him in making out the several tickets and counterfoils which appeared necessary. Both of them found plenty of time to talk, however, he in broken English, and she in French. He pointed out to us a large engraving which might have been cut out of the

British Workman, representing Queen Victoria reading the Bible, and entitled "The Secret of England's Greatness." The nice old boy said he pointed that out to every one who entered his *kantoor*, and that it ought to be put up in every house.

Seeing that he wore a blue ribbon, we remarked upon the rarity of such a decoration in Holland, to which he replied,

"We have not blue ribbonites in dere tousants as you have in England. We are too near Dutch gin for dat. Gin is the devil's drink. Still, there are some in Amsterdam. Have you any in your crew?"

"Yes, we have one;" for Jack is a total abstainer.

"Ah! God bless him! If I were not in a hurry to go to chapel, I would come and see him."

We now steamed steadily along a broad and deep canal, which was, however, quite deserted, save by small sailing craft and local passenger steamers. Still, although the paying traffic had left it, it was well kept, banks, bridges, and locks being in perfect order. It was somewhat uneventful, this gliding between high green banks, but not dull, because the day was fine, the breeze refreshing, and the wide, flat, green, cattle-dotted country rolling away to right and left, was at least strange, if not very beautiful.

Our general position on deck was in a group round the wheel, which was forward of the engine room. From this spot we could look over the dyke on either hand, and listen to the pilot, whom the skipper kept in a constant

TJALK ON CANAL.

talk, varied at times by an argument as to the naval supremacy of their respective countries at sea.

"Ah! we burnt your ships in the Thames," old Klaus would remark.

"Never mind. We swept your fleet from the sea."

"Yes, but we burnt your ships in the Thames," Klaus would constantly retort, and no amount of chaff on Rowland's part could check his satisfaction at this feat. If we tired of this post, we would sit on the top of the after cabin, where, inside the life-belt, our library was kept in the day time, and would dip lazily into Motley or Baedecker.

Many barges were sailing one way with a fair wind, or being towed the other way by horses. There were several horses patrolling the banks, each with a boy and a coil of line on its back, ready to render assistance in the way of towing when necessary.

We passed a great many villages, one in particular, called, I think, Koedy, stretched for a long distance along the western bank. It was close behind the dyke, so that only the gables appeared above it. These gables were all of them lofty and high-apexed, and were highly painted, with the roof partly thatched and partly tiled with the bright, glistening, highly-glazed tiles which appeared to be so popular, the junction of the thatch and tiles being scalloped and cut into fantastic patterns. If we stood on the cabin top we could see the doors, which were frequently bordered on either side by rows of milk pails hung on the wall. These pails were sometimes of wood, painted green, with polished brass bands, and sometimes all polished brass, but in every case were painted inside, generally red. This custom of painting the milk pails inside is universal in Holland, and seems rather foreign to our idea of cleanliness, when we think of the well-scoured milk cans of our English dairies.

Every village had its drawbridge, made in the form of a floating raft, which was drawn back into a recess in the bank at our approach. At the sound of our whistle the bridge would begin to move, and we would go easy through it to avoid making much swell.

It was comical to see the sheep tethered to the bank, each long and lank and brown after being shorn, and each wearing a canvas overcoat instead of its own wool.

After twenty-four miles of this mildly interesting work, we reached Alkmaar early in the afternoon, and moored under the shade of a pleasant grove of trees. We found Alkmaar to be a clean and pleasant town, with a fine new town-hall, and many quaint canals, along which the country boats were coming laden with round yellow cheeses, for a cheese fair on the morrow. The cheeses were being piled up in the market place in pyramids, as cannon balls are piled. We were tempted to delay and stay the morrow, but then we were so tempted at almost every place, and the majority of us had made up our minds to go on to Purmerend.

We strolled along the streets, and particularly examined the jewellers' shops, which were full of gold and silver curios, which we looked at longingly but dared not buy. We had a nice little dinner at a nice little inn, and left at four o'clock, one of us doing so with great reluctance.

We were passing through the country of *polders*. A polder is the bed of a lake which has been drained, and to look at on the map is like a chess-board, marked out with thin blue lines representing dykes (ditches and canals of water are dykes, as well as the great embankments), and surrounded by thick blue lines representing canals. North Holland was a land of lakes, or rather a leaky raft of land floating on the water. It had also such curiosities as floating fields, which might be anchored here and there on the lakes, and on which cattle pastured. We have these in miniature on the Broads, where many a bit of "rand" floats up and down the rivers. Many of the polders are twelve to fifteen feet below the natural surface of the land. During the first half of the 17th century, twenty-six lakes were transformed into polders in this province. In the Beemster polder, which is the largest, and stretched green and fertile to our left, on our way to Purmerend, there are no less than four different levels of canals, and the water has to be pumped from one to the other, and at last into the ring canal round the polder. The water is thus raised step by step, chiefly by windmills. If, in a wet season, there is a continuous wind from the north-west, the sea sluices have to be kept closed, and as the water cannot get away from the polder, the latter is more or less flooded until the wind changes. During a continuance of this wind, the tide on the coast rises as much as eleven feet above the Amsterdam level.

The drainage of a lake and formation of a polder, is sometimes undertaken by the State, and sometimes by private adventurers, and the reclaimed land is generally exempt from taxes for the first twenty years.

Old Klaus gave us a lot of information about polders, of which I regret to say I cannot remember very much, as I was too lazy at the time to note it down.

The level of the land is still sinking as the drainage is improved, just as a dried sponge shrinks up, and the beds of the rivers are rising from the accumulation of silth, so that the system of drainage becomes more and more artificial.

The moist atmosphere of the Low Countries is said to be very prejudicial to wood and metals, which perhaps partly accounts for the extreme care which the Dutch take of all constructions, in the way of constant washing and scrubbing, polishing, and renewal of paint. It is not only the inside of their houses that the Dutch keep so spotless,

They are always washing away at the outside; skeeting water on to the wooden walls and windows, and scrubbing with brushes at the end of long poles. The men scrub the outside, the women scrub the inside, and scrubbing and washing their belongings (not by any means themselves) must occupy a large proportion of the life of the Dutch.

One day I saw Blake gazing contemplatively at a small girl, who was regarding him with equal contemplativeness.

"What are you thinking of, Blake?"

"I am thinking what a great deal of scrubbing that little girl has to get through with before she dies."

We passed one very large mere and several smaller ones. There seemed to be navigable openings into them, and although on land there were frequent notice against trespassers, "*Verboden te gang,*" there were none of the notice boards on the waterways which, in the corresponding district of England, meet one at every spot where there is a chance of enclosure from the navigable channel.

From Alkmaar to Purmerend is fifteen miles, which were accomplished in a little over two hours, and, passing through a lock, we moored by a tree-shaded bank hard by the town.

Dendy got a line out to fish, and asked some boys near

to procure some worms, which they brought in the wooden shoe of one of them. The wooden shoe of the Dutch boy answers the same manifold purposes as the cap of the English boy, and makes the best of toy boats. During tea, the men called out, "There is a fish on the line," and we rushed up to pull out a miserable little eel, the sole result of the only attempt we made at the gentle art in Holland. The boys ashore caught up the English phrase, "a fish is on the line," and kept repeating it with great glee.

It was a very quiet anchorage. One or two passenger steamers came from Amsterdam. The turning round of these long "streets" was a matter of nicety, inasmuch as they are within a yard as long as the canal is wide. Not a single other craft passed during the evening, which was one of the quietest we had.

Engraved by Annan & Swan, London.

CHAPTER XVIII.

PURMEREND TO HAARLEM.

IN the morning we had a pleasant stroll around the clean quiet town of Purmerend, and found some interesting canal scenes, which were duly photographed.

Dendy and I created some amusement by purchasing a quantity of the common brown pottery of the country. The shapes of the various vessels, pots, and pans were very quaint and old-world-looking, and their roughness and imperfect glaze only improved their value as "art ornaments." The natives, seeing us struggling along with armfuls of these things, to them worth only a few cents, evidently thought us somewhat mad.

After breakfast we told the pilot that we wished to take his picture. He was highly delighted and said,

"Master Davies, you will do me great pleasure. I am seventy-three years old, and have been pilot on the Zuyder Zee, &c. [as before], but wait till I put on a clean shirt, master!"

"No no, the picture won't show whether the shirt is clean or not. Take your place by the wheel!"

"Oughtn't he to have a cigar in his mouth?" suggested Rowland. "He is always smoking."

The old fellow toddled gleefully forward; went, in his hurry, down the saloon companion, whence he re-appeared

PURMEREND.

most comically apologetic, dropped down the forecastle, and came out with one of the skipper's best cigars between his lips. Notwithstanding the wicked attempts of the crew and the interested bystanders to make him laugh, he grasped the wheel, with an expression of defying the storm, and never moved a muscle during the operation.

Klaus informed us sorrowfully that south of Amsterdam he would be of no use to us, and that he had spoken to the captain of a steamer which had started in advance of us bespeaking a pilot to be in readiness for us at Amsterdam.

It was a lovely lazy morning, and we congratulated ourselves on our good fortune with respect to weather. We passed between the Wormer and Purmer Polders, passing on the right many large sheets of water. The canal was broad, and had a somewhat winding course, being not unlike our Norfolk rivers, save that the banks were much trimmer and neater. It was curious to see pigs being carried to market in a small boat towed by their owner. The method of towing a small boat is ingenious. The line is fastened amidships and meets a small spar projecting sideways from the bows, thus forming a span like that on a kite, and when properly adjusted the boat keeps an even course without anyone steering.

We reached the Tollhuis sluices on the north bank of the Y, opposite Amsterdam. Here the new pilot was waiting for us, and came aboard. It turned out that he could not speak a word of English, so, rather than be delayed, we decided to take Klaus with us as far as Rotterdam, in the capacity of an interpreter.

The new pilot was a big fat man, whose rapacious appetite smote the crew with dismay, as they had to find him in food for eighteenpence a day. They called him the pelican, because they averred that he had a pouch somewhere in his inside where he could store superfluous food until he required it. The first day, they told him to go below and help himself to some cold meat, but were disgusted to find that he had polished off the whole of a piece of beef intended for the general dinner, which had weighed four and a half pounds before cooking; even the bone had disappeared. After that they did not leave him alone with their stock of provisions. They declared that he would swallow an egg without stopping to peel it.

"Why, he would take a windmill, sails and all, at a gape," said Jack, who was the messman. His thirst was commensurate with his appetite, and he kept Rowland in a constant state of growl, and Jack in constant laughter all the time he was with us. But he was a very good steersman; he could swing the steamer in and out, threading his way between other craft, and through locks and bridges, with a certainty and boldness which compelled our admiration. He surpassed Klaus in this respect.

Engraved by Annan & Swan, London.

PAARNDAM

He would not or could not learn a single word of English, and we had to get Klaus to coach us up in technical terms so that we might understand his orders,

We steamed rapidly along the Y and the North Sea canal half-way to Ymuiden, and then turned to the southward along the Haarlem canal or canalised river Spaarne. Spaarndam Lock was a very picturesque structure, with a village built round it. There were sluices for large steamers and smaller ones for small craft, under which latter category we came. The main pool of the lock was surrounded by quaint old houses and trees. Eel nets were hung up to dry, and eel trunks floated in the water. As we passed out of the lock through the drawbridge, a barge following us, I took an instantaneous shot from the stern of the steamer, which is here reproduced.

We were now crossing a reed-surrounded mere, the course of the deeper channel being very plainly marked by a double row of buoys. A smart breeze ruffled the brown peaty-coloured water and swayed the rushes and reeds, and, but for the colour of the water, we might have fancied ourselves at home, for the characteristics of Broad life were here present on a larger scale. But whereas in Norfolk the water is clear and reflects the colour of the sky, in Dutch meres it is coffee-coloured, and, to small-boat pleasuring, somewhat repellant.

This mere was perhaps as large as Hickling Broad, and had the same low shores, the same reedy horizon, with an occasional windmill, but, unlike Hickling, there was not a single white sail upon it, and not a token of any pleasure craft. A brown-sailed barge was bruising along behind us, and the foam at her bows was tinged like the foam of a Highland river in spate.

Entering the river again, we soon reached Haarlem. We had to hold on to the piles of the railway bridge for a quarter of an hour before it could be opened for us. A very fine windmill rises high above this entrance to the town, and numerous barges and steamers told of a busy traffic. The river winds through the town, its broad stream being bordered by quays thickly grown with trees, under the cool shade of which much busy trafficking in garden produce was in many places being carried on. Little country carts drawn by dogs, or, if pushed by men, having a dog harnessed underneath as an auxiliary power, brought piles of cabbages, &c., which were being rapidly sold by auction all along the quays. Houses and warehouses were quaint of gable, and full of ornament and colour, and there was always a crowd of barges of many types; very many loaded high with brown peat, and all shining with varnish and brass. We had to proceed slowly, threading our way between the vessels,

MILL AT HAARLEM.

constantly shaving stem or stern within six inches, but never actually touching.

We passed through many bridges, one of which was in course of construction, and where there was very little room to pass. Several small tolls were charged, not amounting to a guelder in all. It was only now noon

HAARLEM.

but we intended to stop to coal, and, presently seeing a coal lighter, we stopped alongside her, Dendy and I going ashore while the dirty operation of coaling was gone through.

It may here be mentioned that the Belgian coal sold in Holland is as good for steaming purposes, and as cheap as

Engraved by Annan & Swan, London.

THE GATE OF HAARLEM.

English coal, and we had no trouble in obtaining a proper supply whenever it was necessary, which was about four times during the cruise.

When we got back, we found the Atalanta moored by the quay in not at all a nice place, as the neighbourhood was a low one, and the canal was decidedly sewery, green, and unwholesome, with plenty of rubbish floating about. We ought to have pushed half a mile further, when we should have been in the suburb, by pleasant gardens and on a purer stream.

I rowed about in the jolly, taking photographs, and exciting much interest among the crews of the various vessels.

I found my way up one very narrow and dirty canal on my way to a fine gate, which I think is the "Amsterdam Gate," and picked my way among eel boats and eel trunks, regretting that I had not a third hand to hold my nose. Crowds of dirty little urchins followed me along the bank, and presently began to pelt me with mud and small stones. This was highly inconvenient, as if I had landed to punish them, I might rouse the neighbourhood against me. However, an eel catcher came to my aid, and soundly cuffing some of the boys, relieved me of my foes.

We did the usual sights of Haarlem, and, strange to

say, it is the only place which does not dwell in my memory. I forget the places we went to, and have the dimmest recollection of any part of it, save the river and the quays, which formed a picture I could not easily forget. I remember the church with its big organ, and the small houses clustering around and built against the sacred building. We had a shave in a cigar-maker's shop, and I saw the whole process of making a cheap and vile cigar.

Then in the evening we strolled in a wonderfully fine park, through glades of beech trees, and refreshed ourselves at a shady *café* under the trees, where we learned that our progress was duly chronicled in the papers.

We were too late to see the show of tulips and other flowers for which Haarlem is noted in the spring. As is well known, it is the head-quarters of a certain branch of floriculture, and I had, in fact, introductions to some of the prominent tulip growers of Haarlem, but forgot all about them until afterwards.

Haarlem was once famous for the bleaching carried on there. In my old book of 1743, I find it stated that the reason of linen washing so white in Holland, is that "the water of their canals is of a due thickness, and, perhaps their air is so too. Both these elements may be too rare and fine for that purpose." Further that the slimy water of Haarlem lake [since drained] was the best in the country for the whitening of cloth, and great quantities of fine linen used to be sent from all parts of Europe to be bleached at Haarlem. Either the drainage of the mere, or the discovery of chemical methods of bleaching linen [or both] has caused the bleaching industry to depart from Haarlem.

On going on board, we found a visitor—a nephew or cousin of our pilot—a young man who was an engineer at the railway works. He spoke English, and told us several interesting things, which I was too sleepy to take notes of.

It was a close hot night, and the smell of the canal was rather oppressive, so that we were glad when the morning came, and the black pennant was again hoisted.

CHAPTER XIX.

HAARLEM TO GOUWSLUIS.

ANOTHER sunny morning, and the outskirts of Haarlem looked rich and pleasant. The river was fairly wide, and on the banks were elegant villas, with gay gardens running down to the water's edge, where a gaudy summer-house would be placed.

Klaus told us that "They (meaning the Amsterdammers) shut up their house, and come to Haarlem for the summer,' and I suppose sit in their summer-houses in the evenings, complacently smoking, and watching the passing craft.

One often reads of the damp mists rising from the dank waters, and presumably interfering with the enjoyment of the occupants of these summer houses. But curiously enough, during the month we were in the Low Countries, we did not see a single evening mist of the white damp character which one might expect to see, and which, in the same period, one would see several times on Norfolk marshes; a low dense sheet making the land look like a vast lake with islands of trees.

The banks of the river grew—I was going to say *wilder*, but that is an adjective out of place on a Dutch canal or canalized river—at all events they grew more rural, being fringed with tall and flowering grasses, rushes and reeds, with quiet bays here and there, with occasional water lilies. There were rustics babbing for eels; funny little boats laden with country produce; and actually one pleasure skiff (save the mark) with red cushions, a little white sail, and brightly painted oars, and three or four people on board who were positively on pleasure bent. It was a comical rendering of youth at the prow and pleasure at the helm, in a sixteen feet massively-built model of a hundred ton tjalk.

Many little sailing boats with huge leeboards were sailing about on business, and appeared to move through the water fairly fast. In one place we saw a small sailing canoe, clearly home-built by the adventurous youth who was sailing in it, and who had possibly read one of Macgregor's books.

The clearer water, the prettier banks, and frequent groves of trees, and country residences, made this portion of the river very charming.

Presently we struck the canal skirting the great polder

which occupies the site of the late Haarlem mere; and one of the steam pumping stations is a prominent object in the foreground, with its great beams or arms slowly moving up and down. The drainage of this was only begun in 1840, so that Klaus remembered it well, and spoke of it as a splendid sheet of water. Well it might be, seeing that it occupied seventy square miles. It was in times past four distinct lakes, which became merged into one great one, many villages being destroyed in the course of nature's operation. It was fourteen miles long, and nearly as many broad. During the famous siege of Haarlem, the Dutch had one hundred and fifty small ships upon it, and the Spaniards not many less.

My 1743 writer says, that it was the only water which then gained upon the land. Although only six or seven feet deep, it was subject to violent storms, and its waves washed away and engulphed the low soft shores, seriously menacing Leyden, Haarlem, and Amsterdam. Its drainage was first suggested by a water engineer, named Leighwater, who lived in the early part of the 17th century, and who possessed the useful accomplishment of being able to remain under water for a very long time, and there eat and drink and play musical instruments. The jealousy of the said three towns, and their non-agreement as to their respective shares of the land to be reclaimed, was, in 1743, the obstacle to the drainage of it. When at last it was drained, it is curious to note that no vestige or relic of any of the villages or vessels lost upon it was discovered. They must have sunk in the ooze far out of sight.

By the way, my said old book gravely relates, that a mermaid was washed ashore here in 1403, and lived for many years at Haarlem. She learned to spin, but had an awkward habit at times of throwing off her clothes and running (had she legs or a tail?) towards the water. That is a fine old book of mine. It is so reliable.

It was most interesting to see the vast expanse of green meadow, so level, and lying so far below the canal on which we were steaming.

Two passenger steamers had started ahead of us, and we had been trying to get ahead of them, so as to have first turn at the locks, and we here managed to pass one, but it is not easy to pass such large vessels as they are, in the comparatively narrow water of a canal, where there is a decided back-wash to meet. We met and passed scores of barges, and dozens of steamers and steam-tugs towing barges. One small tug was towing eleven laden barges, each carrying not less than sixty tons.

The length of canal from Haarlem to Gouda, is, perhaps, the most interesting in Holland. We were told that we ought not to miss it, and therefore took the route by the Oude Wetering instead of going straight on to Leyden, the spires of which we saw in the distance. Every mile brought fresh objects of interest, and we stood in a group by the wheel, pointing out to this and that, and taxing our interpreter's powers to the utmost.

The barges (it is easier to call them by this familiar term than by the Dutch ones) seemed to glide along with great ease and the minimum of trouble, and when they came to a bend where the wind would be against them, they would avail themselves of the services of one of the horses and tow ropes which would be in readiness at such places. We were struck with the extreme politeness of the bargees. They invariably saluted us by raising their caps or waving their hands, and we all, passengers and crew, returned the salutes with equal politeness. When we got to meeting or passing a barge every minute, it became rather fatiguing, so we took "spells" at salute returning.

During the whole of our cruise in Holland, we did not meet with a bargee or waterman who was otherwise than well-behaved, civil, and indeed courteous. The civility was not by any means servility, for they are perfectly independent, and they were fairly free from that "*tip expectant"* attention so often characteristic of many English watermen.

Oudeshorm village, where the canal is very wide, would have been worth stopping at, if only to watch the passing craft, but Alphen was most charming. Here the canal was very narrow, forming, in fact, one very long water-street, on both sides of which the houses were built; so close indeed to the water that you might have fished it from the bedroom windows.

Here we saw our first and only stork's nest, built on the top of a chimney, which looked too weak to support the great platform of brushwood, forming the nest. The stork stood on one leg, and looked calmly at the busy scene just below him, where steamers and barges were passing through the bridge, and country folks and their carts were waiting to cross.

The bird and nest were so strikingly outlined against the sky, that I took an instantaneous shot at them, but it was unfortunately on a bad plate.

Both banks of the canal formed a moving panorama of exceeding interest. Blake hadn't time to light his pipe, and Rowland wished he could look on both sides at once. We all forgot our dinner until long past the usual time. The houses were all of the usual fantastic kind, and the poorer class allotted on the water's edge, while the smarter class of villas had gay gardens in front, ornamented with sundials on small pedestals, and having pretty summer-houses by the water. These summer-houses were adorned with mottoes, such as "*Wel Gelegen*"—well situated.

We tried to note down some more of these memorials of the owners' self-content, but have somehow mixed them up one with another, as we cannot now translate them or find the words in the dictionary.

It was Saturday, and therefore the chief cleaning day of the week, and the inhabitants were all hard at work washing and scrubbing; throwing water over the outside paint and windows, and wielding mops and brooms with extraordinary vigour. Only the young ones paused to look at the English yacht, but some of the bare-armed and short-petticoated lasses were irreverent enough to kiss their hands to us, and call out some chaff which amused our pilots very much, but which they did not translate for our benefit.

The washing boxes at every house amused us. To save the unnecessary labour either of lifting out the water of the canal in buckets, or of kneeling down to wash in the canal, a sort of square water-tight tub is sunk in the canal, so that a person can stand in it and have the water all round of a convenient height.

Many of these tubs were occupied by buxom women,

who fitted them tightly, their waists appearing to overflow, and these women were scrubbing away at their linen on the little platforms edging the tubs.

Then we saw a most romantic flirtation, which touched our hearts. A young man strove to snatch a kiss from a strapping young Venus, who threw a bucket of water over him, whereupon he retorted by tousling her head with a wet mop, amid shouts of laughter from the neighbours. As we passed quickly "into the infinite," we caught a glimpse of the youth's flying form, with the maiden's wooden shoe assisting him over the palings, and we can only guess what "might have been." It was so idyllic.

We passed through bridges where the small toll of a dubbeltjee was collected by a wooden shoe at the end of a line and rod; past lovely gardens, with pigeon-houses like Chinese pagodas of exhibition form, brilliant flower-beds, and little lilied bays.

Wooden shoes seemed to be staple articles of manufacture here, if one might judge by the many wood yards, where piles and rows of the white wooden shoes in various stages of completeness were displayed. We also saw several small yachts moored in dykes, which yachts were of the beamy, shallow American type, no doubt, centre boards. One of them was gaily decorated with flags; possibly its owner was getting married.

The traffic passing here is immense. We heard that some sixty steamers and two hundred barges would pass in the course of the day. It certainly is a most unique waterway: an artery of the real Dutch rural life, which may here be seen to the greatest advantage.

At Gouwsluis we came to a sharp right-angled bend in the canal. The long steamer which had kept in front of us was slewed round it by means of a rope thrown from the shore. The Atalanta got round by degrees, going ahead and astern several times. The Pelican steered us through a crowd of other craft, and into the narrow lock with a hansom-cab-driver smartness which won our encomiums. He was good enough to say that the Atalanta was a very handy craft to steer.

"Now I can light my pipe and take a drink," said the captain.

CHAPTER XX.

BOSKOOP TO GOUDA.

OUR interpreter informed us that the water in the canal at this point was good enough to drink, but it looked dark and peaty, and we were not inclined to try it. We met some very large barges, and in particular noticed one which had gay landscapes painted on the ends of its water-butts.

There were plenty of trek horses plying along the banks, but Klaus told us it was cheaper and better for sailing yachts to employ one of the small steam tugs. They charge yachts a little more than other vessels, but for a sixteen-ton yacht, the usual charge for a tow from Gouda to Amsterdam is eight guelders, which is not out of the way.

"Give the captain a little 'drink money,' and he will tell you the names of the places. Must give drink money in this country," said Klaus.

At Boskoop we passed another collection of small

houses, all close to the water's edge, the canal being also very narrow, as at Alphen, and the same busy scene of scrubbing and washing was going on. The whole population seemed at it with a considerable amount of larking as they worked. The women were clearly the busiest in both respects, the men stopping to smoke, and regarding the volatile leviathanesses with an indulgent smile.

From the open windows of a school came the voices of children singing a psalm tune, reminding us of a rural English school.

We were following a steamer and barge through an open drawbridge, not two lengths behind the steamer Immediately the steamer got through, the bridge was lowered right in our faces, and the engines had to be reversed full speed in order to bring us up sharp, and prevent our fouling the bridge. The canal was so narrow at this point, that my jolly, drifting alongside, got a jam between the steamer and the bank. I distinctly heard it crack, but no actual damage was afterwards apparent.

We were inclined to talk to the bridge keepers, particularly as a large sailing barge, coming up at a rapid pace with a fair wind close behind us, had to brail up and let go halyards and throw out ropes in a great hurry, in order to prevent running into us. It appears, however, that if there are people waiting to cross a bridge, the men in charge are bound not to allow more than two vessels at a time to pass through; the bridge must then be closed to give the road passengers their turn. So after the crowd of waiting people had crossed over, the bridge was again opened, and we passed through.

The canal on leaving the village again became wide, and passed through extensive tracts of trim nursery gardens, divided into square sections by numbers of narrow, still, and gleaming dykes.

As we reached another village, strange sounds issued from the Pelican, and from a certain rhythm in them, we conjectured that he was spouting poetry. He pointed, smilingly, to a large windmill on the right bank, on which was a large tablet, setting out in verse and in letters so big that those who steam may read, how the mill had been thrice burned down and thrice re-builded, and how the owner, having repented him of his sins, hoped that he might be spared further punishment.

Apropos of this mill, which was an excellent sample of a Dutch windmill, it is noticeable that the mills in Holland are usually thatched all the way down. How the straw or reed is retained on the nearly perpendicular walls, I do not know, but the result is a smooth brown coating, having the appearance at a little distance of moles' fur.

Gliding along this smooth water highway, raised high above the fertile land, passing and meeting steamers, tugs, tjalks, schuyts, and snibs, quaint toy villages on the banks, an ever-changing scene below, and a changeful blue sky above, this part of the day's journey was a rich treat. One peculiarity was not so pleasant, namely, the constant change of temperature. While the sun was shining or the wind at one's back, one's ordinary jacket was a burden. Let a cloud come over the sun, or a turn in the canal bring us facing the wind, and pea-jackets had to be donned and coat-collars turned up. In Holland, one great essential is to avoid getting a chill, the other essential being to avoid drinking the water neat or unboiled.

As we neared Gouda, the canal had many sharp curves, and at the points on the tow path side there were guide posts for the tow-lines, with rollers worn into grooves by the friction of the ropes. Seeing a highly-varnished and gilded schuyt with a fine flag, we took her to be a yacht, but were told that she was a powder boat. The canal was here so serpentine, that within a hundred yards the Atalanta, the powder "busk," and a large steamer occupied the relative positions of the three lateral curves of the letter S.

We had to wait at Gouda railway bridge for some time before it opened, in company with several other steamers and sailing craft. The Atalanta was sandwiched between two steamers, big enough to take her aboard, and to save my little jolly from being injured by the vessels coming up astern, we hit upon the happy thought of putting her inside the larger one. When the bridge was opened, the vessels passed through in their turn with the greatest order and regularity. Indeed, the traffic is regulated in the most admirable way, otherwise there would be constant blocks. From the railway bridge to Gouda, the canal doubles back completely upon itself.

"Dinner is ready, gentlemen!"

"Hang dinner," said Blake, "I shall not go below until we have passed Gouda. Look, how pretty it is!"

And it was pretty, and quaint, and picturesque, and old-world and foreign, and all the other adjectives which really fail to convey a realistic impression at all like what I could wish. There was a large basin crowded with craft, waiting their turns to go through the lock. Around the basin was the usual grove of trees, and around the grove, the usual crush of pointed gables.

While we were waiting our turn, Blake and Klaus went ashore for a pass, and when our turn came, they had not reappeared, and we conjectured, as the fact was, that they had stopped at a "*slitterij*" (excellent name for a tavern) for a glass of beer. We lost our turn, and had to let other craft pass ahead of us. When they came back, looking happy and guilty, we loudly reproached them, but they heeded us not. While we were waiting, a constant succession of steamers from all parts of Holland passed by.

On the shore, we noticed a stream of factory girls, neatly and cleanly dressed, and comparing favourably with their English sisters.

Upon passing through the lock, we found ourselves in a tidal river, called the Yssel, the muddy banks of which, laid bare by the ebbing tide, were not pretty.

"Now," said Blake, "I feel hungry."

So did we all, and dinner had been waiting for a long time, and must have felt hungry too.

CHAPTER XXI.

AT ROTTERDAM.

FOR some miles below Gouda the river was not very interesting. Perhaps it suffered by comparison with the lively canal we had just quitted. There were many brick-works on the banks, the mud for the bricks being obtained from the river bed. It was not pleasant to see barefooted girls in scanty dress wheeling barrow-loads of mud, but I have seen the same thing in an English brickyard.

Breakwaters jutted out from both banks, and here and there were little bays, then half dry; on the banks of which were little villages. As we descended, however, the river widened considerably, and the banks were prettier, with forests of reeds in places, and huge stacks of dried reeds.

As we neared Rotterdam, and entered the wide Leck, it was a pretty sight to see the numerous red-sailed craft turning up with the young flood. All sorts of barges were there, from the large ones like Thames spritsail barges to the long wooden boxes, unpleasantly like coffins, which, with a scrap of sail, jogged along better than we could have thought possible.

We steered for the docks on the north shore, just above the bridge, and after waiting about some time, we were admitted to the Haaringvleet basin, and assigned a berth in convenient proximity to the English Church. We had steamed forty-eight miles through most varied and interesting scenery, and were rather glad to rest and prepare for a quiet Sunday. Hardly were we moored, when a yacht agent came on board, and it was easy to guess that he was a brother of the one at Amsterdam. He had heard from his brother, and had been on the look out for us. This edition was quite a curiosity. He was intensely excitable, and talked with great rapidity. He was not pleased at being told he was like his brother, whom he abused dreadfully, and accused of the very fault of excitability he himself had.

"You want a pilot for Antwerp. I get you one who take you there in two days for £2 10s., which is cheap."

"Thank you, very much, but we have one who will take us there for 10s."

This rather took the wind out of his sails, as he was clearly determined to make more profit out of us than his brother had done. Meanwhile Blake had been eyeing him closely, and said—

"Do you remember the ship so and so?"

"Yes."

"Do you remember selling us some bad condensed milk, and we paid you a visit, and made you eat some of it?"

"Oh, I have a very important engagement ashore. I wish you a good evening," stammered the poor man, as he made for the companion in a great hurry. Out of compunction, Blake and Dendy paid him a visit afterwards, and got let in for a dozen of villainous claret.

We had at last to part with Klaus. We bade each other an affectionate good bye, for we had all got to like him.

"Good bye, Captain; good bye, Master Dendy; good bye, Master Davies. I am seventy-three years old, and I have been pilot on the Zuyder Zee for forty-two years, and I never was so sorry to leave any ship as this. Give me a guelder for drink money, captain, and I drink your good healths."

We were now left alone with the Pelican, and began to feel that a man who would not learn a single word of English, and who ate and drank as he did, was an awful being to be weighted with.

Of Rotterdam, with its numerous and crowded havens and canals, its long and busy quay, called the Boompjees, its wide river thronged with steamers and sailing vessels from all parts of the world, immensely long Rhine lighters, and schuyts and barges from inland canals, I have little to say.

AT ROTTERDAM.

At Rotterdam we were simply British tourists, dependent upon a Baedecker and Murray. We did a certain amount of sight-seeing, but were not so interested as at Amsterdam. At least I wasn't. Blake seemed to enjoy it; no doubt because he found friends there, which makes a difference. We had perhaps grown accustomed to the peculiarities of Dutch towns, and had lost some of the first keenness of appreciation.

The next day, Sunday, it was very close and hot. The sun shone into the square, the centre of which was occupied by the placid heat, and light reflecting water, with power untempered by any wind.

I took the jolly, and pulled out into the river, where there was a slight breeze, and drifted down with the ebb tide under the huge and lofty bridge. But taking warning by the rate at which I was drifting, I seized the sculls and turned back. The tide was so strong, that with ordinary pulling I could not even stem it, and I had to pull my very hardest to make headway. It took me half an hour of the hardest pulling I ever had, under a blazing sun, to get back through the bridge and into the basin. This was hard, as I had gone out for coolness. If ever I take a sailing yacht to Rotterdam, I should give that bridge a wide berth in selecting an anchorage. It is one of my favourite nightmares to dream that my yacht is dragging her anchor on to a bridge.

After a necessary change and wash, I concluded to go with Dendy to the principal Church. As service had commenced we were actually refused admission, so we hauled our wind, and came back to the dilapidated looking English Church by the yacht. The British parliament in

1812 gave £2,500 to complete the English Church at Rotterdam, and it now needs another grant from somebody. Repairs were going on inside. The congregation was scanty, but the sermon was good, and the place was delightfully cool and restful.

We had noticed a small, clipper-stemmed yacht lying at anchor above the bridge, which was decidedly English, and looked like the "Keepsake." So after church we rowed out to her, and found that it was the "Keepsake."

"Is Mr. C—— aboard?" we asked of a gentleman on deck.

"Yes, but he is shut up in the dark, developing a photograph, and you can't see him yet."

Photographers everywhere! Nature will presently begin to complain.

When the plate was developed, the blankets were taken off the skylight, the hatches opened, and the extemporized dark room returned to a cosy cabin, where we sat and chatted awhile before lunch. The "Keepsake" had come from the Schelde, and was bound by the route we had come to the Zuyder Zee, but I fear her draught of water—seven feet—would be against her there.

Our basin was very full of barges, and Sunday being a day of rest, there was much polishing of brass-work going on. A Dutch bargee is never idle if there is anything left to polish. The vessels were clean and shiny, the people were clean and neat, the women with the whitest of caps over their silver ornaments; there were pots of flowers, and even miniature gardens in the tiny windows and on the decks, and there was a charming air of home comfort and independent contentment about the vessels.

Inside of us there was a barge with an aged couple, a married son and his wife, and grandchildren, and an unmarried daughter, all living on board; and, peeping curiously into their abode, we saw how beautifully clean and tidy it was kept, and how cleverly every corner was utilized. There was also no lack of little ornaments and knicknacks of an inexpensive kind. The hold being empty of cargo, the family availed themselves of the greater space by having their meals there.

For clothes washing, a strong wooden tray is suspended out-board from the bulwarks, so that the water falls overboard. The basin was very impure to look at, but the people drank the water, and we saw a bucket of slops being emptied over at one end of a barge, while at the other a girl was letting down a small copper bucket and drinking out of it. But impure as it seems, the river water is drunk by all Rotterdam. We had to fill up our

MILL AT ROTTERDAM.

tanks here, out of a water boat which came alongside. The water she brought was fairly clear, and had probably been partly purified. It is my habit to drink a tumbler of water night and morning, but I had to give it up in Holland. The first drink I treated myself to on my return to Norwich, was a glass full of the excellent water which is fortunately supplied to the city.

Many row boats passed out from an inner basin, but not a pleasure sailing craft of any description. We could not understand how a maritime people like the Dutch should make so little use of their waters for pleasure and exercise. Every *eafé* was thronged with young fellows, whose pasty faces ought to have been tanned by the sun and wind, and whose big, but flabby, forms ought to have been hardened into muscle on the water so close to them.

In the afternoon we strolled through the public gardens, and had a good dinner at an excellent *café*, in company with the "Keepsakes," finally ending an uneventful day by going early to bed.

CHAPTER XXII.

THE HAGUE AND SCHEVENINGEN.

HE Pelican was getting troublesome. He would follow each of us about whenever he had the chance, with a pocket almanac, in which he pointed to the figure of the moon, and told us much in Dutch, which no amount of consulting the dictionary enabled us to understand, with wonderful gestures, pointing this way and that, and to the hands of his watch. Seeing that he was troubled about something, we would calm him by nodding amiably, and saying, "Ja, Ja." But this, presently, lost its effect, and we fled the sight of the Pelican and his almanac.

It was amusing how each of us, when the others were not looking, undertook to sit down with the unfortunate pilot, and get at the bottom of his mystery. The result was that we had three several versions, equally improbable.

At last we found an interpreter, and learned that the

pilot desired to start at five o'clock in the morning in order to save the tide.

"You won't get me up at that hour," said Blake. " Tell him that we can steam against the tide, and we won't start until after breakfast; that we will go by Dordrecht, and stop at Wemeldinge for the night, going on to Antwerp next day. Then we shall not want to talk to him any more until we get to Antwerp."

With this answer the pilot had to be satisfied, although he evidently thought it a sad waste of power to steam against the tide, when we could get it with us by rising early.

As we were not to start until Tuesday, we took the opportunity of sending a quantity of linen to be washed. It came back to us beautifully white and clean, but they starched Blake's pyjamas all over. How he did rustle when he went to bed!

Having duly sampled Rotterdam, and having found out where the coolest *bierisch* was drawn, we turned our attention to the Hague.

Dendy was the great sight-seer, and used to drag us about everywhere with untiring energy, Blake generally lagging a yard or two behind, keeping up a running fire of grumbling at our indecent haste. But at the Hague we rebelled, and, finding a good restaurant, we concluded that the best scenery was to be found therein, in the shape of a good *déjeuner*. Very good it was too, and we consider the Hague an extremely interesting place.

Everybody knows that it is the aristocratic quarter of Holland. It was, therefore, lacking in the truly rural old-fashioned aspect, which had in other places so charmed us in Holland. Still it is a noticeable place, with its clean wide streets, handsome houses, gardens, public buildings, and fish-ponds. There were plenty of well-dressed people, apparently well to do, and looking just like English people. We purchased some photographs at Parsons, 19 Plaats, where a very excellent series of photographs of all parts of Holland, including the Dead Cities of the Zuyder Zee may be obtained.

But as far as sight-seeing went, the only thing which made much impression upon me was the chamber of horrors in the old prison, in a tower by a gateway. Here hideous scenes were enacted in the times of the Spaniards, and it makes one's blood run cold to see in these dreadful dungeons the instruments of torture which made poor human bodies suffer surpassing agonies. The racks, breaking wheels, brad-awls for thrusting under nails of hands and feet, thumb-screws, and many other fiendishly ingenious device of torture. As we passed from cell to cell, and realized the terror of them all, it made us wonder how men in the image of God, and, professedly acting in the interests of the worship of God, could act so inhumanly, yet, with human inconsistence, we at the same time felt that there would be a rare joy in compelling to the same torture the devils who inflicted it.

One refinement of devilry consisted of a starvation chamber, where, within full sight, and almost within arm's length, of the abundant cooking of things going on in the kitchen, a poor wretch might starve to death.

Seventeen forty-three does not see much horror in death by breaking on the wheel. He says: "This kind of death has more of terror than pain in it. The executioner first strangles the malefactor, so as to put him next to entirely out of pain, after which he breaks his arms and legs at four different blows with a long round bar of iron, the fifth blow is the finishing stroke on the breast. I saw a rich farmer executed in this manner at Delft."

Breaking on the wheel was at that time the punishment for premeditated murder, and this said rich farmer was a Roman Catholic, who had made his crime worse by offering the judge a bribe of £10,000.

From the Hague we journeyed by tramcar along a pleasant avenue, shaded by trees, to Scheveningen, a place always associated in my memory with the invention of sailing chariots. The tale is an oft-repeated one, but 1743 tells it so well, adding a comical experiment of his own, that I give my readers the benefit of it.

"This village is famous also for a sailing chariot belonging to Prince Maurice, and kept here. It was made by Stevinus, a great mathematician. The form of it was simple and plain. It resembled a boat, moved upon four wheels of an equal bigness, had two sails, was steered by a rudder placed between the two hindmost wheels, and was stopped either by letting down the sails or turning it from the wind.

"That it far exceeded any ship under sail with ever so fair a wind in swiftness. That in some few hours' space it would convey six or ten persons twenty or thirty German miles; and that with little labour to him who sits at the helm, who may easily guide the course of it as he pleases. That eminent person Peireskius travelled from Paris to Scheveling for the sight of this chariot, and frequently talked of the incredible swiftness of its motion with astonishment.

"Though the gale was ever so brisk, it could not be perceived by those in the chariot, because they went as swift as the wind itself. Men who ran before it seemed to go backwards as it passed them. Things seen at a great distance being presently overtaken and left behind.

In two hours it would go from Scheveling to Putten, which is fourteen horae milliariae, according to the same author, or forty-two miles with twenty-eight persons in it.

"I once made an experiment of this kind on a child's chair, by doing some things to it, and adding a sail, which succeeded beyond expectation, but with an unforeseen circumstance that was very near giving me great cause to regret my mechanism. For the wind being brisk, carried away the little machine and passenger in it with such rapidity, that myself as well as the nurse, who almost swooned away, was in no small terror. There was, indeed, a precipice before it, which I thought at too great a distance for any danger. The sailing chair had almost reached the brink of it before I could overtake to stop it, and my being able to do so, was more owing to some large pebbles that retarded the motion, than my own speed, though I ran as fast as I could."

Fancy the curtain lecture he would get from his wife for playing such an experiment with his child.

The fisher-folk of Scheveningen are a race by themselves, marrying and inter-marrying like the fisher families of our own north country fishing villages. Sturdy, independent people they looked, the men in baggy canvas trousers and blouses, and sabots made white with pipe-clay; the women with large bonnets, shaped like a three-quarter moon set athwart the head, with white caps and gold head ornaments.

But the great feature of Scheveningen is the beach, where there are hundreds of fishing craft, unique in design and appearance. Owing to the beach being very flat, and the water shallow for a long way out, it is necessary to beach the vessels. They sail bang ashore with the flowing tide, and are left dry when it ebbs. To get off again they wait for the tide, with an anchor down, until there is water enough for them to get under-weigh. If it is not intended to proceed to sea again soon, they are hauled up the beach by horses, planks being laid on the sand in advance, and rollers placed underneath the vessel, to make the operation possible.

The boats are of great size, many being larger than the largest East coast smack. They are so bluff at the bows and stern, as to look like an oblong box with the corners rounded off. The bottom of the hull is also rounded off, but the middle length of it, of a canoe shape, is flat, and it is on this flat wide sort of keel that the vessel rests on dry ground.

We watched the operation of hauling one of them up. There were two teams of six horses each, harnessed to ropes, passing through blocks fixed ashore at the top of the beach and to the vessel, forming a very powerful purchase tackle. There were also some twenty men helping, either by shoving or shouting. Planks were laid before the bows, and by all the men putting their shoulders under the hull and lifting in unison, the hull was lifted so that a roller could be slipped under. Then the horses were whipped up and hauled on the falls of tackle, and the vessel moved a yard or two, and another roller was inserted. By repetitions of this laborious process, the vessel was moved her own length in about an hour.

Far along the beach lay a serried rank of similar vessels, gay with bright paint, and red streamers at the mast heads, and, bumping in the surf, lay several others, waiting the incoming tide, their sails ready for a beat out to sea against the fresh easterly breeze, which was knocking up white horses on the yellow sandy water. As the surf struck their bluff bows and flat sides, it burst in clouds of spray clean over them, and the craft rolled and bumped in the most alarming manner. But it was only the normal state of things, and the crews sat quite unconcerned, waiting for the water to rise.

One by one the boats floated, hauled up to their anchors, and made a cast off. One of them missed stays, and drifted ashore again twice, but got off the third time.

They are built immensely strong to stand all this bumping.

I suppose it was too early for the season, as there were no visitors at Scheveningen, although there is plenty of

FISHING BOATS—SCHEVENINGEN.

accommodation for them, the place being a fashionable seaside resort.

Back again, thankfully, to the cosy cabins of the Atalanta, and orders were given for a start in the morning.

CHAPTER XXIII.

DORT AND WEMELDINGE.

SOON after nine o'clock on the Tuesday morning, the Atalanta picked her way out of the crowded dock, through the drawbridges, two of which were within two Atalanta lengths of each other, with a right-angle turn between, and out into the Maas.

It was again a sunny morning, and as we slowly forced our way up the Maas against the strong ebb, we had ample leisure to note the great number of barges dropping down the river—red, brown, and white sailed, in twos and threes, their varnished hulls reflecting the sunbeams—they came in great variety, their crews invariably giving us a cheery greeting.

On the banks of the broad river were many shipbuilding yards, where immensely long iron lighters of light draught were being built.

Leaving the Leck on the left, we turned off to the right, along a broad branch of the many-armed Maas, which on the map is labelled "Noord" only, and came in sight of Dordrecht, or, as it appears to be more generally called, Dort, leaving on the left another branch of the river, with a pretty village named Papendrecht on its banks.

The appearance of Dort from the river is singularly fine. On the broad and rapid stream, great numbers of barges and other vessels were anchored. By the long line of the busy quay, numerous craft were loading and unloading, under the shade of the fringing trees. Close upon the quay were the rows of quaint old houses and picturesque gables, which are quainter and more picturesque at Dort than at most other Dutch towns. Above the close clusters of the town, rises the grand tower of the Church or Cathedral, which seemed, however, mixed up with the tall masts of a brig in an inner dock.

Dort is one of the oldest towns in Holland, and certainly one of the most typical. Except Amsterdam, it had the finest appearance from the water of any town we saw in our cruise. It is said, by the way, to be a travelled town, inasmuch as it once changed its site. During an inundation early in the 15th century, the upper, and more solid stratum took a slide over the bog below, so that, to an appreciable extent, the whole town moved bodily.

Engraved by Annan & Swan, London.

We had not intended to stop at Dort, as it is only twelve miles from Rotterdam, and we had a long journey before us; but a great railway bridge spans the river, and, notwithstanding our whistling, it remained obstinately shut.

We steamed as close to it as we dared on account of

DORDRECHT.

the tide, and whistled loudly time after time. But not a soul appeared upon it. The pilot asked the men on board several of the barges anchored out in the stream, when it would open and they said in half-an-hour. So we circled about the river, dodging in and out among the barges, and whistling loud enough to wake the dead, while the bargees gazed at us with indolent curiosity. Then somebody shouted that the bridge would not open until one o clock. So we decided to make fast to the quay, and go for a stroll, which we did. Dendy went off for some fresh fruit, and Blake offered to accompany me and the camera.

A picture meets one at every turn at Dort. There are streets in which the street is a canal only, and the tall, many-windowed houses rise straight from the water, high above the masts of the barges in the narrow canal. Very many of the windows had projecting ledges, trays, or even little glass houses, all filled with gay flowers; and every house, old as it looked, and no doubt was, was as spruce and neat, externally, as possible.

We blocked the traffic on a little bridge for some time, while I took some photographs. Glancing just now at a print of one of these, I caught sight of something white at a window, which a magnifying glass resolved into a woman's head, with an immense cap on, with broad flaps extending over the shoulders, which cumbrous, but snowy-white headgear, is usually worn at Dort. Scanning the rest of the picture, I observe many curious heads at the windows, which we did not notice at the time.

In a large basin in the centre of the town were many ships and barges, and in one corner of it were two or three house-boats, veritable cottages, which appeared to be permanently moored there. I tried to photograph one, the housewife obligingly posing herself in the act of peeling potatoes, but unfortunately I exposed the same plate on another subject, and so spoilt two views.

While we were perched on the crown of another little bridge, photographing the Cathedral, with a group of people waiting good-humouredly at each end, Dendy came running up, to say that the pilot had found out that the bridge only opened for seven minutes at one o'clock, and the hour was just striking. So gathering up the apparatus anyhow, off we rushed, and jumped breathlessly on board. We shot out into the stream, and approached the bridge whistling loudly. A man crossed it, but made no sign to us, so we turned back again, and did this three or four times. The Pelican was evidently getting into a stew, as we pestered him with questions which he could not understand. After more hailing to bargees, he made straight up the river as far as Papendrecht, and by the aid of a dictionary, we thought we made out that the bridge was broken, and that he would try another way round. But just as we were consulting the chart to see how this could be done, back he turned, and we gave it up as a bad job.

Again and again we steamed up to the bridge, and

whistled, without avail. By this time we were getting rather short-tempered all round, and the Pelican was reduced to helplessly shaking his head, to intimate that it wasn't his fault.

At last we went alongside the quay, and Dendy and the pilot started off to the bridge, which was a long way by land, to make enquiries. A small boy about ten years old came up, and spoke English to us. Rowland at once seized the chance of securing an interpreter, and started off with the boy in pursuit of the others. This boy and his companion, who stayed behind, had never spoken to an Englishman before, but they had learned English in school, and had the wit to make use of the present opportunity to utilize their knowledge. Fancy an English schoolboy of tender years doing the same with French.

"Look, sirs, the bridge is opening," cried the other nice little boy. So it was, and the barges at anchor were hoisting their sails and getting up their anchors.

With the seven minutes limit in our minds, Blake and I determined not to wait for the rest of the crew, but to drop through at once, and pick them up afterwards. And we had cast off the ropes, when they hove in sight at top speed, Dendy first, and the poor pilot, who was a big, fat man, panting and puffing along a very bad third. They tumbled aboard, and the pilot held on somehow to the wheel.

"Beer, beer," he gasped.

"No. No beer until you get us through that bridge," cried unfeeling Rowland.

We were soon through, and then the skipper consoled the Pelican with his beer; but the latter was much exhausted, and I really feared he was going to have a fit. Why the bridge did not open before, and what the regulations really are, we did not find out. We guessed that it might be in the discretion of the bridgeman to open when he thought there were a sufficient number of barges waiting to make it worth while. At all events, there is no certain time for opening.

We had waited over two hours at the bridge, with a full pressure of steam on all the time, and it was afternoon, while we had still forty-five miles to go to Wemeldinge, where we proposed to stop the night.

Our course lay along De Kil into the Hollandsch Diep, where the estuary is very wide indeed. On our left, as we entered the Diep, was a branch leading from that desolate tract of water and reed beds, known as the Biesbosch, which was laid waste by an inundation, and never reclaimed.

At Willemstad, a fortified town, where we saw large numbers of horses being shipped, we entered a channel to the south-east of the island of Overflakke, thence into another channel between Duiveland and Tholen, called Keaten Mastgat, and so through into the East Schelde.

It was somwhat monotonous steaming along these wide sea channels, the shores, in some places, being barely visible, so distant were they, and so low. A dark group of trees, with a tall church spire in the horizon, would mark a town or village, and on learning its name from the pilot, we would mark off our position on the chart.

By half-past seven we were nearing the opposite bank of the Schelde, which looked black and forbidding under a threatening storm cloud. Soon we could distinguish the houses of Wemeldinge, and the entrance to the sluices. Here our attention was attracted by the clearness of the water, and the extraordinary number of jelly-fish floating about in it. The water looked so tempting for a bathe, but we stood in wholesome awe of the jelly-fish, and we certainly could not have taken a dive without coming into contact with a score at least.

We entered the sluice in company with several fishing craft, the bows of which were more praam-shaped than any we had seen. Their crews, too, had more colour about their costumes, and with their brown faces and gold neck buttons, were sufficiently picturesque.

Looking back as we were entering the gates we were impressed by the gorgeous sunset. The smooth, undulating water stretched away like an ocean of blood, and the huge red disc of the sun had a church spire sharply defined across it. The thick cloud which we had noticed over Beveland, was passing away to the south-east, pursued by the sunset fire, which consumed the ragged fringe of its rearguard.

"Look at those jolly little girls," cried Dendy, "we must photograph them, although the light is going. Be quick, there's a good fellow."

"And look at those jolly young women," echoed Blake. "We must have them in the background. Be quicker, old man, or it will be dark."

I hastily put my apparatus together on the lock wall, while Dendy arranged several bright-eyed little girls, with big white caps, and silver head ornaments, and two really pretty girls in the same costume, with the addition of broad coral necklaces, in a group. I rapidly exposed three plates, and, much to my surprise, considering it was dusk, and the red glow of the sunset (very *non-actinic* in colour) shone on the clear brown faces of the girls, all three negatives were successful. A reduced reproduction of the group is here given as an illustration, but in the process of reproduction, the broad flaps of the caps of the elder girls, which rested on their shoulders, have become invisible It is difficult to photograph a white thing against the sky, and they were only faintly outlined in the original print, from which the smaller block is produced.

We were immensely pleased with these nice little girls, and with two of their elder companions. Strongly built, yet well-shaped, with the first *waists* we had seen among

GROUP AT WEMELDINGE.

the Dutch peasantry, firm red arms (we all think red arms are as nice as white if they are plump), regular features, and serious, kindly grey eyes.

The Atalanta was now ready to go out of the lock into the canal, and we descended to her with some difficulty. At half-tide there was a fall of ten feet from the sea or estuary to the canal level, and the latter was higher than the land. More than ever, Holland seemed to us to be afloat, and that if we could cut her moorings, she might drift away.

As it was getting dusk, we moored in a basin by the lock, and spent a very pleasant evening. The somewhat stormy sunset was followed by a clear starlit evening, which made the deck a pleasant lounge until late.

TO ANTWERP.

WE were now in the province of Zeeland, which, as a glance at the map will shew, is cut up into several islands by wide sea channels, or estuaries of the Schelde and their branches. A deep canal, about six miles long across the eastern part of the island of South Beveland, connects the East and West Schelde, and our route lay along this.

It was a dull and drizzly morning as we left Wemeldinge, but it speedily turned into a sunny and broiling hot day. The water of the canal was so clear and deep that we longed for a swim, but the great abundance of jelly-fish floating about again deterred us, as we knew they often cause irritation of the skin if they come in contact with it.

A fleet of schuyts came sailing after us with a very light wind, and they closed upon us when we were delayed at a bridge, but we soon left them far behind, and in about an hour emerged into the Lower Schelde, and headed for Antwerp.

The canal had not been interesting, because the banks were so high that we could not see over them. We were not charged any fees for passing through, and had no trouble.

It is said that the people of Zeeland are weak and unhealthy, owing to the excessive dampness of the soil. So far as we saw them, however, this was incorrect, and our impressions were decidedly the other way. The rich dank pastures are said to be suitable for fattening cattle, but sheep rot upon them.

The pilot had been eating and drinking too voraciously, having had a run among unaccustomed good things, and he was very much upset in consequence. Rowland had clapped a wet handkerchief on the poor man's head to cool it, and with the corners of this peeping from under his cap, and the drops of water running down his puffy cheeks, the Pelican looked distressingly comical. Whenever any of us looked at him, he would place his hand on his waistcoat, and shake his head solemnly, to intimate that he was very bad. But he stuck to his work gallantly. We had the tide against us the whole of the day, meeting the fresh ebb as we ascended the river.

After a few slight showers, the day turned very sultry

and oppressive. The water was a glassy grey, with a misty calm, which caused vessels to seem to float above the actual water, and be suspended in the air. It was quite a mirage effect, disturbed now and then by the commotion caused by some large screw steamer coming down. What air there was blew right aft, at about the same speed the Atalanta was going, so that the blacks from her funnel fell upon the deck, and speedily made everything filthy. The barges and vessels coming down with the tide, drifted listlessly past us. Ours was the only craft going up, and we went boring on against the heavy current, making at best not more than three knots over the ground.

We counted the buoys as we slowly crept up to and passed them, and we nearly fouled one of them. The pilot kept as close to the edge of the channel as he dared, in order to cheat the tide, and the engineer, without warning, stopped his engines to oil the bearings. The consequence was that the Atalanta began to drift back upon a buoy, over which the rush of tide was regularly foaming. The pilot yelled out in alarm, and the engines were set going again, only just in time to escape the buoy.

There was thunder in the air, and what with the heat reflected from the wide glassy water, the glare of the misty blue sky, and the general breathlessness of the day, I shall not forget that long steam up the Schelde. We did not know where to go for shade or coolness. No sort of drink gave us any relief or comfort. If we tried to read, the glare from the paper made us giddy, and we could only puff and pant, and wish the storm would come and clear the air. I felt quite sorry for the pilot, who was obliged to stick to his post of duty at the wheel, particularly as his back was against the steam-pipe, and his only seat the casing over the dome of the boiler.

When we went into the cabin to dinner, we stripped to our shirts, and gazed ruefully at the steaming dish of stew on the table. Now Atalanta stew was our staple dish. We had it most days when we did not dine ashore. To make it, get some chunks of meat, as many varieties of vegetables as can be had, with plenty of potatoes, and stew in the ordinary way, but add to it a tin of soup. This gives it a body, which it otherwise lacks, and we can heartily recommend the stew with this addition, duly christened Atalanta stew. The dish it was served up in was big enough for a foot-bath, but so great a reservoir of heat in our small cabin was too much on this hot close day, and our appetites were not worthy of the crew of the Atalanta

It was twenty-five long miles from the mouth of the

South Beveland Canal at Handsweert to Antwerp, and it was mid-afternoon (we had left Wemeldinge at nine) when we sighted Antwerp.

The thunder-clouds were gathering above the Cathedral spire, and the tempest was close upon us. The new quay which is being built, has spoiled the appearance of Antwerp from the river, inasmuch as the old houses which fringed the bank have been pulled down to make room for it, and the work is still unfinished. We met two or three smart little yachts turning down with the tide. They had very much the look of our Norfolk river yachts.

On going up to the dock entrance, we found it was not yet open, and there were numbers of barges waiting to go in. We moored by the quay wall for a quarter of an hour or so, and then the lock-gates were opened. The Atalanta steamed in athwart a tremendous rush of tide, which made it very ticklish work, and in the midst of such a crowd of barges, that when the lock-gate was at last closed, there was not room even for another jolly boat, so closely were we all crammed together. It says much for the skill of the pilot that we did not get a scratch.

What made us most nervous was the way in which the big tjalks carried their anchors suspended over their bows, and just below the surface of the water. A prod from the flukes of one of these anchors would go through our quarter-inch iron skin, where it would only dent the six-inch thick oak planks of the local vessels. So we were particularly careful in all jams in locks to look out for the anchors, and have our poles ready to fend off.

It is surprising how easily these great barges can be fended off. They come shooting into a lock as if they meant to smash into you, but a man puts out his pole, and the way is stopped directly. They float so lightly on the water that they are easily moved or stopped, even when laden.

While all the shoving and shouting attendant to entering the lock was going on, the storm burst. It was sharp while it lasted, but short, and cleared up as we were leaving the dock for the inner basins.

The harbour official directed us to proceed to the *Bassin aux Briques*, and politely informed us that there were no dues to be paid. We moored in a quiet corner, outside a Dutch yacht and a Belgian steam yacht, about three times the size of the Atalanta.

The Dutch yacht, which was nothing more than a pleasure schuyt, had lately been bought by a new owner, who was having her polished up. He was having the solid oaken bitts coated with thin sheet brass; also every possible place where there was a decent excuse for metal. When the brass was polished, it gave a sham appearance of brazen solidity, which must have been very gratifying.

We were near the spot where the exhibition had been, and now that it has disappeared, the streets look very strange. They are properly laid out, but the only houses are the *cafés* at the corners of the streets, and of these there are a great number. We found a really splendid swimming-bath, unnecessarily deep even for diving, but with shallow portions for non-swimmers, and every precaution to prevent accident. I never saw such extensive baths and so well arranged, and we had a glorious swim there, which I shall not soon forget. Indeed, with the exception of the cathedral, where I spent some thoughtful and happy hours, the swimming-bath is my pleasantest recollection of Antwerp.

I don't like towns, and I hate sight-seeing. I go through the mill as a duty to one's friends at home, and am glad when it is over.

Following out my plan of avoiding any descriptive writing about the towns, I will simply say that we stayed at Antwerp on the Thursday, and let Blake be our guide to various places of amusement and instruction, which, as an old *habitué* of the place, he was anxious to show us.

Here we got rid of the Pelican, and secured a most

excellent pilot, named Storm, who spoke fair English, and quite equalled the other pilots in his skill in steering.

From a man on the Belgian steam yacht we learned that the bridge at Termonde on the Schelde, which we should have to pass through on our way to Ghent was broken, owing to a ship having run against it; also that the canal from Bruges to Ostend was under repair, and that it was closed to traffic. This was unwelcome news, but Storm said that if we lowered our masts we could pass under Termonde bridge at low water, and that we could return from Ghent by the canal to Terneuzen, on the south bank of the Schelde. So we determined to proceed by that route.

"Let us go for a ride in the tramcar as far as it will take us," said Dendy, that evening.

"Agreed," said I.

"Where to, messieurs?" asked the conductor.

"*Au diable*," replied Dendy, gaily.

"Ten cents, messieurs," replied the conductor, gravely.

CHAPTER XXV

ANTWERP AND TERMONDE.

ANTWERP docks proper are at the other end of the town, but the basins at the Exhibition end are very large; yet they were well filled, chiefly with country trading craft, and there was always a rush to gain a front place on the opening of the lock at a certain state of the tide.

Between nine and ten on Friday morning, the Atalanta forced her way in between the contending craft, and there was a repetition of the Wednesday's jam. When the lock seemed quite full, a barge would come charging against the rearmost row, and wedge her bows in, and then there would be any amount of squeezing to find her a place. At last the lock was really full, and the gates closed.

Next to us on one side, was a low, narrow, wall-sided canal barge, with a whole family on board. The man and his wife looked respectable, but careworn and workworn to the highest degree. Even the little children had a grave expression, far removed from the gladness of youth. They were pleased, however, when we allowed them to peep into our engine room.

When the river gates were opened, there was a general scramble out, and we had the same anxiety as before, in respect of the big anchors of the larger craft. We were towing the lifeboat jolly, and of course, a small barge hooked on to it with her boat-hook, in order to steal a tow out. We made no objection to this, but then another hooked on to that barge, and another to that, and so on, until it became evident that the painter of the jolly would not stand the strain. It was sufficient to point to the rope and shake our heads, and the first man let go. As the barges emerged into the river, up went their red sails, with great celerity, and off they went on the port tack up the river, each doing precisely the same thing in precisely the same place as its predecessor.

We swung out into the flowing tide, and went at full speed up the river, which presently grew narrower, and lost its town look, and became a country river.

Now that the tide had covered all its mud banks, and the water brimmed the grassy banks, it was a broad and pleasant stream, bordered by willows and poplars. Over the banks the country was flat, and the view was everywhere bounded by serrated groups and rows of poplars.

We constantly passed fine barges, with all canvas set to catch the light air, which barely rippled the smooth and swiftly-flowing tide. At frequent intervals, by the banks, we saw fishers at work. A large net, like a huge landing net, kept open and extended by umbrella supports, was suspended from a wooden crane over the river, and lowered into the water and raised again by means of a windlass. We asked the pilot what kind of fish were caught in these nets, to which he replied,

"Little bright fish, dat smell like cucumber." Smelts, without doubt.

The river is spanned by a railway bridge, at the pretty town of Tamise, but there was no delay in opening it. We admired the town itself very much, as we passed rapidly by. It was sunny overhead, with a blue sky paled into grey by a silvery haze, and the reflected light made the wide river surface a very delicate blue in tint, which brought into bright contrast the brilliant green of the lush marginal grasses, and the warm red of the sails on its bosom.

Here and there was the red roof of a homestead with a bullock cart resting under a group of trees, or a barge hoisting sail at some rude staithe.

St. Amand was so pretty that I tried to photograph it, but failed. I remember, however, quite distinctly its tall

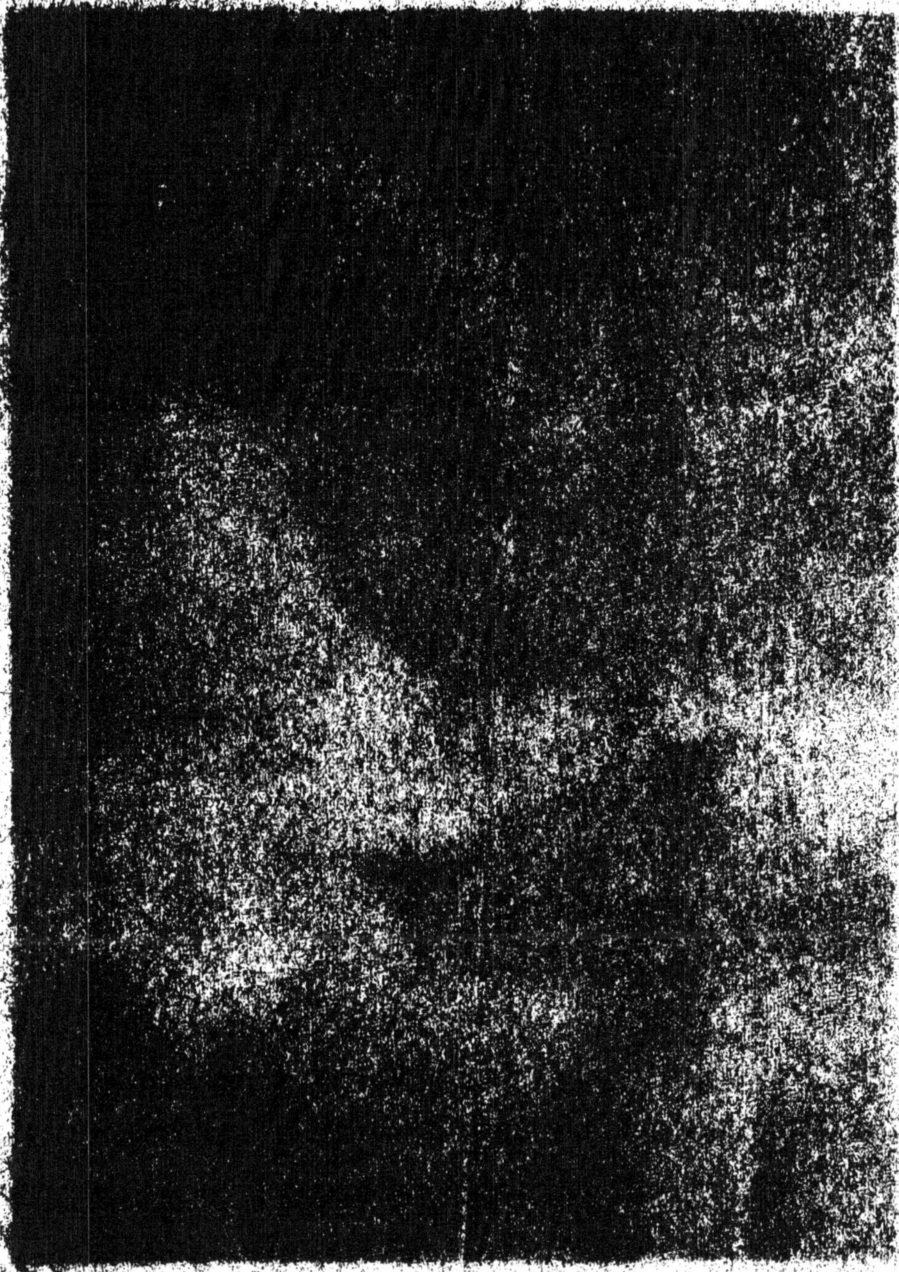

Engraved by Annan & Swan, London

ON THE SCHELDT

church spire, its red roofs, and its white walls, gleaming bright in the sunny haze, and with its green promontory jutting out into the river, mirrored faithfully in the shining water.

"Ah, this is pleasant," said Blake. "I do like the real country. I wish you fellows wouldn't take me to the big towns. They don't suit me at all, and I don't like them."

This was all very well, but no man enjoyed himself in a large town more than Blake did. But I agree with his theory.

I can call to mind most vividly the lovely picture St. Amand made, although it was but a glimpse as we passed rapidly by, but I have a difficulty in remembering much about Antwerp, except the images of the Virgin at the corners of the streets, the names of the streets written both in Flemish and French; and the detestably sly priests, who gazed furtively at us as they passed by. I took a great dislike to the priesthood of Belgium, as shown by the specimens walking about the streets. The possessors of such villanous faces as some of them had, ought to be hung without trial. They were a contrast indeed to the courteous, refined, and intelligent Roman Catholic priests whom I have met in England.

But away with the priests. We are afloat on a splendid

river, in the heart of the country, and there is a barge I will photograph. The illustration is a copy of this photograph, which was taken while the Atalanta and the barge were meeting each other at a joint speed of ten miles an hour at the least, the camera being held in my hand, and of course an instantaneous exposure being made. It certainly is a marvellous science.

As we approached Termonde (or Dendermonde), the river grew prettier. It had a very tortuous course, and at the bends there were bays and backwaters, which reminded us of English rivers. But subsequent experience showed that at ebb tide the steep mud banks are laid bare to such an extent as to take away all the beauty. But at high tide the mud is not even suggested. The banks, however, are somewhat artificial in appearance, inasmuch as the trees are planted with great regularity; a row of low willows on the margin, backed by a row of tall poplars, with frequently an intermediate row of other and more bushy trees. At a place called Grembergen we saw a number of the narrow, coffin-like barges being built. They are somewhat like the barges in use on English canals, but larger and more wall sided. They are, in fact, nothing but long, ugly boxes, with flat bottoms, and almost square ends.

Here is Termonde. We have not been long doing the

twenty-five miles from Antwerp. There is the bridge, a rickety-looking structure, about which men are employed in repairs, and looking so low at half-tide, that only a very small barge could get under with masts down.

We moored outside a Norwegian brig, just below the bridge, and went below to discuss our Atalanta stew, before going ashore.

We found Termonde to be an exceedingly quiet place, with absolutely no sign of any trade or business. The houses were dull and monotonous, and all painted grey or white. The streets were clean enough, and there were two quaint old buildings in the central square, but there was an utter lack of that interest in the buildings and people which is so abundant in Dutch towns. (I take it the reader is sufficiently well informed to know that we were then in Belgium.) One street, which had down its centre a slimy stagnant canal, was as dirty and as full of dirty people as any English slum, with the difference that these people, though dirty, were civil and respectful, and appeared to be industrious poor, having only the faults of poverty and dirt.

We strolled about the embankments, which were once fortifications, and dawdled on the bridge over the weedy moat, watching innumerable sickly-looking roach swimming in the clear patches, and then turned into a dingy *estaminet* for a cup of coffee and cognac, which was served to us in tall glasses, a Belgian fashion which makes the fragrant beverage look and almost taste like medicine. Then we turned into a shop where wooden shoes were exposed for sale. I bought three pairs for my children, and a gorgeously carved pair of boxwood shoes for my wife. Now I did think I knew the length of my wife's foot, but when I triumphantly produced the dainty *sabots*, I found she could pretty well get both feet into one of them.

CHAPTER XXVI.

TERMONDE TO GHENT.

DURING the afternoon we lowered the masts, a troublesome operation, which required care in the doing. The Atalanta lost sadly in good looks by the change; she was no more a yacht—only a steam launch.

The ebbing tide swept down like a mill race, and as steamers and barges arrived above the bridge, they had to let go their anchors and wait until the tide had fallen sufficiently to let them pass under, the barges, of course, lowering their masts. In a short time there were at least a dozen craft swaying at their anchors, within a space of two hundred yards above the bridge. The river here contracted considerably in breadth, and the rise and fall of the tide being very great, the current was extremely strong. We were surprised to find that none of the barges dragged their anchors, as some of them had swung to, close above the bridge.

The first vessel to drop under stern first was a long

steamer. Her crew threw us a rope to make fast, so that they might swing her, but the rope broke, and the fierce current bore her broadside down the stream, and she was quickly out of sight around a bend.

"We came best out of that," remarked Jack, as he gathered in several fathoms of new line.

The barges dropped through without any mishap; the empty ones, which were high out of the water having a tight fit of it.

The air was filled with a curious drift of some winged seed like thistledown. It had been falling gently all day, like the first beginning of a snow-storm. We enquired whence it came, but all that we could learn was that it was the seed of the "Canada wood," whatever tree that might be.

Turning into another *estaminet* during the evening in search of some amusement however mild, we had through our interpreter Dendy, a conversation with some of the natives, who assured us that although we might deem Termonde slow, it was nothing like so slow and dull as Ghent. This was not at all assuring, and we began to wish we had remained in Holland.

As we clambered in the dark over the brig and down her high sides on to the deck of a steam tug, which lay between her and the Atalanta—not a pleasant or easy operation, by the way, on a dark night, with channels of swift water underneath one—we saw that the tide had turned again, and that at the same hour in the morning there would be room for us to pass underneath the broken bridge.

Some time after we had turned in, Dendy, finding his cabin too hot, had gone on deck to cool, and he awoke us by calling out that the brig was coming away from her moorings. This brought us all out on deck, and we saw that the stern of the brig had swung out a little into the stream, her stern mooring ropes not being taut enough. This had the effect of steering us athwart the rushing tide, and being third vessel, we were well out in the tideway, and only twenty yards from the bridge. The great power of the tide on our broadside was trying our moorings to the utmost, and it seemed not unlikely that we might break away, and be driven across the arch, where we should be most surely sunk.

We got out all our extra ropes, and took every possible precaution, but were not by any means satisfied of their sufficiency.

"Never mind," said Jack, who always looked on the bright side of things, "if the ropes do break, it will be something for Mr. Davies to put in his book."

I know I slept with my ears open (a faculty the

skipper of a small yacht soon acquires, if he chances a bad anchorage) until the noise of the swirling water lessened, shewing that the tide had eased, and that all risk was over.

The next morning we crept cautiously at slack water through the narrow arch, and proceeded on our way up the river. The banks were high, with steep mud banks left bare by the tide. A tug was towing a number of laden barges, which stretched out behind in a long string. As the river was narrow and very sinuous, with shoal points, and eddies in the corresponding bays, the barges had their work cut out in steering, to avoid the shoals and the eddies. The Atalanta had a difficult job to pass them, as their serpentine course left but little room.

Slowly and carefully we reached past one and another, the pilot steering most skilfully, the wheel being kept in constant and rapid motion, to check the erratic impulses of the current, and the swell from the tug and barges. It was a very pretty and delicate bit of work. Once past the tug, we could steam ahead at any pace we liked, as there was deep water in the channel. In fact, we outran the tide, so that we were treated to the sight of the mud banks all the way up.

The day was quite an agreeable one, by way of change, inasmuch as it rained " cats and dogs," and there are few country Englishmen who do not tire of perpetual sun, and enjoy a rough day for a change. Clad in our oilies, we could keep the deck in the heaviest rain without discomfort, and there was a certain charm in travelling up the lonely river—lonely because the high banks shut out all view of the country beyond, and we met or passed very few barges.

Now and then we passed a house half hidden by trees; a man patiently babbing for eels, or winding at his smelt net; but of river life, such as there was on Dutch waterways, there was none. The peasants whom we saw looked extremely poor, haggard, and careworn, and their dwellings untidy, dirty, and poverty-stricken.

Dendy tried to take a brighter view than I did, and declared that if we could see over the dull river banks, we should see a smiling country, every inch of which was tilled, and made productive by the labour of a peasant proprietary. We actually fell to arguing, for the first and only time during the cruise.

I find on referring to my note-book, that I did not make a single note of our journey on Belgian waterways, from which it may be inferred that the country did not fit in with my personal idiosyncracies.

As we approached Ghent, the river grew very narrow, though still deep. We passed one or two good mansions with pleasant grounds, but as a rule, the houses were poor. The country churches which we passed were noticeable for the extreme height and narrowness of the buildings. The long, plain thin building gave one the impression that it was too high to be hollow, and that it was quite a solid, rather thick wall.

We passed through a rickety wooden drawbridge, which was decidedly curious in aspect, and passed a barge, which a poor hard-worked human beast was dolefully towing along, while his haggard wife, with a dirty baby at her lean brown breast, was steering it, and then stopped at Ghent.

It was a dirty, narrow, sewery hole, with coal-dust banks, and a high lock through which the yacht had to pass when the water rose sufficiently high. A lot of dirty little street boys danced on the bank, and amused themselves by slanging us, and singing some election ditties, (the election being just over). They even began to pelt us with mud, and were troublesome, until a violent thunderstorm drove them away.

When the thunderstorm was over, Dendy and I marched off to the post-office for letters, leaving the captain to take the Atalanta through the lock, and on to the Grand Basin.

It took us some little time to read our letters, and

answer those requiring an immediate reply, and, concluding that by this time the yacht would have reached the Basin, which was at the other end of the town, we made direct for it. But there was no yacht visible on the fine sheet of water, and no yacht had passed through the sluices and bridge leading to it. So we followed the canal by which she should have come—a narrow, dirty, evil-smelling, circuitous stream, which led us round the outskirts for a considerable distance. Not meeting her, I expressed my belief that she must have stuck hard and fast somewhere. But at last we came to the lock where we had left her, and there she was tightly packed in with a crowd of dingy barges. The lock was so full that no water was visible.

The sluice-gates, and the lock generally had none of the spruce neatness and efficiency of the Dutch lock, and as we had to wait some time before the water rose high enough, we continued to wish that we had stayed in Holland.

At last the gates were opened. The Atalanta was well ahead in the lock, and shoved ahead, without any regard for her paint, in order to gain priority at a subsequent lock. The barges sent out long slender lines, to which the women harnessed themselves like donkeys, and set to work towing, their bodies bent double with the strain. What a contrast between a healthy, comely English agricultural labourer's wife of forty, and these frowsy hags of the same age or less.

We steamed slowly along the narrow canal, and through another lock, where the dirty little street arabs of Ghent amused themselves by spitting upon us from the high walls. After cautiously creeping round a right-angled turn and through several bridges we gratefully emerged into the Grand Basin where it was very quiet, and there was plenty of room.

We moored to the quay, which was a good long way from the centre of the town, and gave Blake and Dendy a capital opportunity of trying their skill as pathfinders. Each of these gentlemen thought that he had the bump of locality, and that he could unerringly find his way about a strange town. I am bound to say that Dendy had a remarkable instinct in this direction. He would point to the east and say, "This is the way." Blake would point to the west and say, "No, this is the way; if you go that way Dendy, you will go out into the infinite"—a quotation from the captain's favourite poem,

"He went out into the infinite
By taking of the train."

Then Dendy would go his way and Blake his. I would follow Dendy, as a rule. Blake would presently turn up, owning that his route was not productive, but with undiminished confidence for next time.

Now Ghent is the most awkward place for a stranger to find his way about in, that was ever built. I did not pretend to decipher it, and Dendy fell from his high estate there, for he confidently led us several leagues out of our way. At least, we were so tired and hungry and cross, that it seemed fully that distance. He staked his reputation on the result and lost, and we could have eaten him.

The next day was Sunday, and a pleasant sunny day it was. I hurried over my breakfast in order to catch my letters at the *poste restante*, and having secured these, and— a blessed thing—an English newspaper, I had to wait an hour in the Place d'Armes for my companions.

It was very pleasant sitting outside a *café*, with my paper and a tall glass of cool beer before me, watching the groups of neatly-dressed people promenading in the large open square, under the shade of the limes. There were no well-dressed people in our sense of the term, but all were neat and clean, down to those who were plainly of the poorest. But it struck me that nobody looked happy. There was a turbulent, restless, discontented expression in the faces of most, particularly the poorer people, which was not pleasant to look upon. Doubtless the same spirit is present as in the historic days, when the citizens of Ghent were noted for their turbulence.

Presently Blake and Dendy arrived, proud of having found a new way, which they declared was more direct. We tried that way on our return at night, but it seemed the reverse of direct then.

Our next move was in search of some lace. Dendy and I had the previous evening visited the Beguinage, but were too late to be admitted, and as it was doubtful whether the Beguines would themselves sell their lace on Sunday, we had obtained the address of a depot in Ghent where it could be procured. To this we now bent our steps.

It was a private house, and we were somewhat diffident about knocking, in case there had been a mistake. Dendy, as interpreter, knocked, while Blake remained around the corner, ready to look as if Dendy did not belong to him, if occasion required.

It was all right, however, and we entered a room in which was a glass cabinet, containing fathoms of lace. A nice-looking middle-aged lady, who spoke French volubly, upon learning that we wished to buy presents for our wives, sweethearts, and daughters, speedily got out no end of the beautiful delicate fabric, with which she covered us and the table in festoons. It was lucky for us that we hadn't our particular young women with us, or they would have tempted us to our financial ruin.

Rude, uncultivated men that we were, we yet could feel the charms of that lace. It was long before we could make our choice, and one of us, whose knowledge of French measures was not exhaustive, astonished the dame by asking for a kilometre (1094 yards) instead of a metre (39 inches).

At last, happy in the thought that we had acceptable presents for our lady-loves, we sallied out, considerably poorer in pocket than when we went in. I am assured, however, that we made excellent bargains.

We then took the train to Bruges, passing through a flat agricultural country, cut up into small holdings, and each small holding subdivided into every variety of crop. Not an inch of ground was wasted, and the care and labour must have been enormous, ere such crops could be raised on such ground.

As will have been gathered, we thought very little of the Belgian peasantry as compared with the Dutch. Not only was there a painful contrast between the squalor and dirt of the country dwellings, and the too extreme cleanliness of their northern neighbours, but the Belgian peasant had a haggard and careworn appearance, very different indeed to the sturdy contented look of the

Hollander. The clothes of the former did not look worth eighteenpence, and it is very clear that he never had at any time a quarter of that value of food inside him.

The cause of this prevailing poverty was not far to seek. Belgium is a country of small holdings (of course I speak only of the agricultural districts), the majority being from five to ten and twenty acres. Under the influence of a genial climate, the country itself looks bright and smiling, but at what a cost! The ground is spade-tilled, and being light and sandy requires the most careful husbanding, and application of manure, the collecting of which is skilfully and laboriously managed. There is a rotation of five to seven successive crops, necessitating unremitting toil.

No English labourer has any conception of the slavery which the Belgian labourer's "interest in the soil" entails upon him, and no English labourer could live upon the hard fare upon which he is perforce content. With the great advantage of cheap water-carriage to markets (which we unfortunately have not in England), with the virtues of rigid economy, ascetic sobriety, abstention from marriage, a contented submission to fate, and the "constant exercise of industry, skill, and foresight," these peasant-farmers live from hand to mouth, having no savings, finding it difficult to pay a rental sufficient only to give the landlord two per cent. upon his capital, and in case of a sickness serious enough to stop the farm work, they are often compelled to sell off their stock to pay for medical attendance.

Some fifty years ago, a report was presented to Parliament by one George Nicholls, which fully bears out my own rapidly formed impressions. Shortly after such report, the late Mr. W. C. Chambers, of *Chambers's Journal* fame, visited Belgium. He then found the country in a more prosperous condition than it is now in, owing to the prevailing agricultural depression, but says (and I commend his wise remarks to all land-reformers and experimentalists), "The practice of executing all the operations of husbandry by the hand is utterly adverse to the cheap production of food, and cannot be tolerated in an advanced state of society. If land had been created to feed peasantry alone, the Belgian system would be entitled to unmeasured commendation. But such, it may be presumed, was not the case. The whole population of the country is as much interested in the soil as the mere labourers upon it, and hence the necessity for producing the largest quantity of food at the cheapest cost to the community at large. This is a point too much neglected in all discussions on the subject of agricultural labour, and should be fully borne in mind in estimating the condition of the peasantry and farmers of Belgium, or of any other country in similar circumstances."

It is to be hoped that this digression of serious matter in a book intended to be amusing only, will be pardoned, but the fact is we found so little to take up our attention in Belgium, that we got to talking politics, and as one of us was a red-hot Tory, another a mild Conservative, and the third a white-hot Radical, it may be imagined that our arguments were lively. The Home Rule debate was then drawing to a close, and while in Holland we were so much interested in our immediate surroundings that we hardly ever cared to speculate what the result of the division would be, in Belgium we became keen upon the point—a keenness we happily lost when our faces were turned Hollandwards.

We liked Bruges infinitely better than Ghent. It was quiet and dull, but still had a happier, brighter look than Ghent. Like the latter town, its interest is chiefly historic, but it is easier to clothe its mediæval buildings with romantic memories of its glorious past, than it is the dull white houses and crooked streets of Ghent.

When we entered the market-place, there was a rush of several cabs towards us, two of them coming into collision with each other; but we did not heed them, and entered the comfortable and unpretending Hotel Panier d'Or, where we ordered dinner (we were always hungry, and a good square meal was what the guide-books call a principal attraction, when we entered any fresh town.) While the meal was preparing, we strolled about the ancient streets, finding much to interest us as connoisseurs in gables and "antikishis."

We had a capital dinner, very well cooked, and we were waited upon by a very pretty girl, whom Dendy, by his superior French, monopolized in conversation, as he always did. We had our coffee outside, under the shade of an awning, and much enjoyed the soft, warm air, and the sight of the lofty belfry opposite, whence the sweet tinkle of the chimes floated down at regular intervals.

The hostess spoke a little English, and entered into conversation with us. She said she supposed we had come from England by the steamer, for the bank holiday to-morrow. Blake was awfully indignant that we should be taken for bank holiday young men, and he explained that we didn't know what bank holidays were, and that we had come from England on our own yacht. Then she asked if we could recommend an English nurse for her children—"she must be a very good girl." We suggested that she should advertise in the *Daily Telegraph*.

"Now," said Dendy, who was our sight-seeing conscience, "we must make a start to see the principal attractions, and we had better begin with the belfry."

"Oh, that's inaccessible—just after dinner. I would as soon try the Matterhorn," said one.

"Let Dendy go up alone, and we will take his word for the view," said the other.

But Dendy would not be gainsaid, and we toiled protestingly up the four hundred and eighty steps up to the bells, and then! why, the view was worth the journey up the Schelde, and the locks and narrow canals, to see.

The atmosphere was brilliantly clear, with not a touch of mist to the furthest distance. A large part of Flanders lay below us, every detail showing clearly in the bright sunshine. Bruges itself was microscopically clear, with its red roofs and clean white streets shining brightly. There was not a single trace of smoke from any chimney on that hot June afternoon. Over the flat and fertile plain, the eye could note for many a mile, with great distinctness, villages, groups of trees, lines of poplars, gleaming canals and vessels upon them, and fields mapped out in squares, with various coloured crops.

We were deeply impressed with the vastness of the

view, and looked long from one arch and another, drinking in the fresh summer breeze, exhilarating as wine, that at this elevation was so delightfully cool, and thinking perforce, of all that we had read of the stormy scenes which had been enacted in past centuries upon this fair plain of Flanders.

As Blake used to say in his post-cards to his friends, "words fail to describe" the pleasure we experienced in gazing from the belfry of Bruges, and Dendy had harder work to get us to descend than he had to induce us to make the ascent.

We were among the bells while the chimes played. Considering the distance they can be heard, the noise on the spot is not so great as might be imagined. The mechanism is most ingenious. A great drum is covered all over with square holes; in some of these are stuck pegs, which as the drum revolves (actuated by a spring or weight) impinge upon levers, which actuate hammers striking the bells, the connections being made by wires. There are a great many bells, and an immense number of hammers, the whole apparatus resembling a gigantic musical-box. Of course the tunes can be varied by shifting the pegs, and, I believe are so varied once a year.

After a descent from the belfry, we did the cathedral

and other sights, and sat half-an-hour in a pretty little park, watching some great carp rolling about in the small ponds.

At the station we met a large company of archers. They were evidently countrymen, dressed in a kind of uniform, and were armed with very fine bows. We had not time to watch where they went to, but I think I have read of a Dutch game of shooting at wooden birds on the top of a pole, with arrows, and a similar game may obtain in Belgium.

A fat and "leary" friar was standing on the platform, with bare sandalled feet, bare head, and rope girdle round his brown cloak. I won't vilify him by saying more than that there wasn't a single prepossessing feature in his face, but he gave us the impression that he was a ghoul from the past spying upon the present, and that he would presently go back and hatch some devilry, to be wreaked upon the irreverent present. He gave us a good hearty scowl as we passed, which was the only thing I saw to like about him.

On our return to Ghent we tried Blake and Dendy's short cut, with doubtful result. We found Rowland in trouble, having dropped a pocketful of silver overboard. He had put several florins in his waistcoat pocket, and in stooping over the bulwarks to draw a bucket of water, he had tilted the whole lot out. He had employed a man with a long-handled, landing-net kind of scoop to try and fish the money up, but the water was too deep, and they were unsuccessful. So the skipper had no pleasant memory of Ghent. He had found also that the provisions were not of the first quality, and he had caught the milkman coolly filling up his pails with water from a stand-pipe. We had noticed at the *café* that the milk and butter were very poor.

We filled our tanks up with water, and ordered a start for Monday morning, feeling that it is hardly worth while making a special visit to Ghent by water, unless, indeed, one took it on the way to or from Bruges and Ostend, and by the canal to Terneuzen, which we were now to take.

CHAPTER XXVII.

GHENT TO TERNEUZEN AND FLUSHING.

UPON leaving Ghent, we entered a pleasant broad canal, with bare but grassy banks, on which were here and there pretty villas. As we left Ghent far behind us, our spirits rose, and I began to hunt for my note-book.

It was again a fine warm day, and as there was not much to see but the long line of the high banks against the sky, a few schuyts, or an occasional fisherman in charge of as many as six rods, stuck out round him like quills upon a sleepy porcupine, we just lounged on deck, writing letters, and lazily nursing Motley, with the outside of which we were well acquainted. I had read up to this time exactly twenty pages of the inside. I think that an edition of Motley with two-thirds of the three-syllabled words struck out, would be very interesting.

Presently one of us stretched himself, and said, "I somehow feel as if I were entering Holland."

"We are just over the border, sir," answered the pilot.

"There is Sas du Gand, where we shall be searched by the Custom House officers."

We stopped at a neat waterside village, where the canal was closely shaded by trim trees. A brightly painted trek-schuyt was lying moored to the bank. These craft, which used to be the passenger boats drawn

SAS DU GAND.

by horses, have been completely knocked out of time by the steamers, and we did not see one actually in use.

An official came on board, took a cursory look round, especially examined (and confiscated) a glass of wine, and we were free to pass through a bridge and into a lock, the trim solidity of which, and its surroundings, told that Dutch order reigned around. One of the officials and another person asked for, and were granted, a passage to Terneuzen, by which we lost our bathe. We were about to stop in a secluded portion of the canal for a

SCHUYTS AT SAS DU GAND.

swim, when the official assured us that bathing there was *verboden,* I suppose because a road ran along the embankment

Without any incident, other than meeting a large seagoing steamer, we arrived at Terneuzen, twenty-three miles from Ghent, and tied up to the bank. While the captain and pilot went off in search of a coal merchant, I essayed to picture the group of quaint houses, windmills, bridge, vessels, and trees which made up an enticing view of Terneuzen. The reflections in the absolutely calm water were simply perfect in detail and brightness of

AT TERNEUZEN.

colour. That negative was a failure, owing to a fault in the plate, but others of the grassy, tree-crowned banks, with the schuyts, barges, and sea-going brigs and schooners moored to them, were more successful.

The canal branched into two arms, each communicating with a sluice, and with a wide basin at the junction.

This basin was partly occupied by timber floats and barges, and a man was fishing in a very ingenious manner. He had a stiff, flat-bottomed boat, with a spar rigged out over the side like a crane. From this was suspended a large flat net, kept extended by four cross-pieces of bent wood. This was hung by a rope

SHIPS AT TERNEUZEN.

connected with a windlass at the foot of the crane. The *modus operandi* was to lower the net, which was about fourteen yards in circumference, to the bottom of the canal, and after waiting five or ten minutes, to haul it rapidly up by the windlass. Often there was no result, but occasionally a small eel, or two or three small roach were seen struggling in the net, which was very small meshed. The fishermen then took hold of the edge of the net, tilting it towards him, and the small fry rolled into his boat. We frequently saw this mode of fishing in Holland, but there was never any catch that would satisfy a Norfolk angler.

It was pleasant to lounge on the sea face of Teneuzen, and watch the vessels and steamers coming in and going out. There was a good deal of life and bustle about the place, and many people were holiday-making. We saw two drunken sailors, and it had become such a rarity to see any person intoxicated, that it was noticeable.

We had a little excitement during the afternoon. A tjalk, which was being poled along, overpowered her crew, and drifted sideways into us with the wind. I had to haul my jolly ashore in a hurry, and we all had to fend off to the best of our ability. She got clear at last, without having done us any damage, save the breaking of one of the boathooks, which held us off the shore.

Strolling about in the cool of the evening, we came upon a delightful group; a comely woman with a baby and a good-looking girl. They were got up in the most killing style of the country, and we followed them about. I commenced to ingratiate myself by chucking the baby under the chin, and presently got into a most amusing conversation with them, which made us laugh heartily, because with all our efforts we could only mutually understand a few words. The women were dressed like this: thick linen caps richly embroidered, with voluminous lace-edged flaps over the shoulders; gold skull-caps or bands with large spiral corkscrew ornaments on each temple, and pendants hanging from the spirals; necklaces of five rows of coral beads, with gold clasps; over the chest and back a folded handkerchief (query *fichu*) of brightly flowered and striped material, raised high on each shoulder like epaulets, and confined at the waist by a belt with silver buckles; a plum-coloured dress, with an outer skirt of brown, open fore and aft, and short sleeves confined above the elbows by broad velvet bands. The hull, so to speak, was both naturally and artifically broad, so that as they walked it imparted a buoyant, balloon appearance to the owner. The plump, red arms, and the thick honest fingers, plentifully decked with rings, and the clear, ruddy, comely faces were all very pleasant to look upon. The baby was a bonny little thing, with tiny corkscrews on its temples, just like the mother's.

At night, each vessel hung out a light, and lanterns were even placed upon the timber rafts, in the bye waters of the canal.

The next day, Tuesday, was again beautifully fine, with a smart breeze. We entered the large lock in company with a few barges, a steam-tug, and an exceedingly smart open launch, with a Belgian crew, whose blaze of nautical splendour put our modest attire far into the shade We noticed the inevitable camera on board their launch. When we emerged into the Schelde, the launch, which had been bottling up its steam for the purpose, started off at full speed, and soon passed the Atalanta, which was jogging along easy, while we were hauling the boat up on the davits. The crew of the launch gave us a derisive laugh as they passed, no doubt thinking they were doing a very clever thing. They went up to Antwerp, and we turned westward for Flushing.

We were now in a broad sea channel, where white-crested blue waves leaped to the brisk wind. It was about fourteen miles across, and we ran it in two hours or thereabouts without incident. We gratefully hailed the broad sea channel, with its freedom and air, and waves, after the close river and canal work of the last few days. The worst of a steamer is, that there is so little incident in making passages, and there is no fun in steering one. That tedious duty is left to the pilot. We passengers rarely touched the wheel, whereas in a sailing craft, two of us would not have been happy except at the tiller.

On reaching Flushing, with its great passenger steamers and big ships, tugs, and pilot boats, we passed through the lock without delay, and steamed on with the intention of making Middleburg, which is about four miles from Flushing, and half way along the great ship canal, which runs across the island of Walcheren, from Flushing to Veere.

But our pilot consulted his pocket-book, and told us that there was a *kermis* or fair at East Souberg, which it would be worth our while to see. We hailed the idea, and the Atalanta was accordingly stopped opposite the village, which is midway between Flushing and Middleburg.

CHAPTER XXVIII.

A *KERMIS* AT SOUBERG.

WE sat for a while in the long grass of the steep embankment of the canal, luxuriating in the hot sunshine, like the butterflies and bees which fluttered and hummed about us, and watching the steamers from Flushing and Middleburg discharging their freights of holiday-makers.

A bridge crossed the canal close by, and over this the country folk were streaming, all in holiday array. Some were walking, but many were driving in their four-wheeled, varnished oak wagons, with the chariot hoods. These vehicles were often elegantly carved and gorgeously fitted, but the horses were not much to look at, and hardly matched the carriages. They were harnessed a long way in front of the conveyance, and the gap between the small, long-tailed horses and high wagon had a comical aspect. The wagons generally carried the *pater* and *mater*, and three or four daughters, the sons walking.

the damsels were dressed in bright, dark-green bodices, open back and front to show white or flowered muslin under-things; dark-green petticoats (twenty or thirty, if one might judge by the exterior size), and short purple overskirt; head and temple ornaments, sometimes plain silver, with silver knobs or squares at the temples, but often gold, with gold knobs, spirals, and pendants down the ruddy cheeks. A close-fitting linen cap under a yellow straw bonnet, the latter ornamented with four long streamers of broad and gay ribbons, completed the head-gear. Many of the girls, of apparently a superior class, wore gold bands right across the forehead, meeting those round the head.

Armed with all this bravery of attire, the girls trooped to the fair, with serious faces, quite full of the importance of the occasion—just like an English girl going to her first ball. The *kermis* is an annual institution in all Dutch towns and country districts. It is looked forward to for months by the girls, who, sober-minded and decorous enough all the rest of the year, look upon *kermis* week as their holiday of right, when they may dissipate after their fashion to their hearts' content, and too often to their subsequent regret. It is absolutely necessary for a girl to have a cavalier at the fair. She would be shamed in the sight of her more fortunate friends if she had not. If therefore she cannot command the services of one for love or favour, she will even go to the length of hiring one for the occasion.

Strict police supervision has removed many of the worse excesses of *kermis* time. The fights between men with knives, and the fights between women with *dubbeltjees* are things of the past. The *dubbeltjee* is a small thin silver coin, and when held between the knuckles of the middle fingers of the clenched hand, would inflict a nasty cut on a blow being struck on the face. The women used to thus arm themselves; and an aged friend of mine, who lived in Holland as a boy, has often seen sanguinary encounters between Dutch viragos.

Just the other side of the embankment, we saw half-a-dozen women with babies in a perambulator, and, anxious to secure them (in a picture), Dendy and I made a rush for them, nearly tumbling into a ditch by the way; but, alas! they made a rush from us, as if the lens were a blunderbus. With the next two groups—which are reproduced—we were more successful, owing to the exertions of our pilot, who acted as interpreter, and explained that our intentions were harmless.

Following the stream of people, we passed down a long street of little brightly-painted houses, shaded by small trees, and came to a large space planted with rows of trees, so that there was a complete roof of foliage overhead. In the shady avenues formed by these trees, the *kermis* was in full swing. A dense crowd of people, mostly young, jostled up and down, in slow moving groups. Curiously enough, the girls kept by themselves, and the young men by themselves. In the evening they

SOUBERG VILLAGE.

got mixed up, but at this early period of the day they took their pleasure separately, out of doors, although in the *slitterijs*, where the crystal wine (in other words, gin) was flowing, matters were different.

With few exceptions, the girls were all decked in their finest clothes and bravest ornaments of the distinctive country costume. The few exceptions who were dressed like English girls of the same class, had a very ordinary and insignificant appearance beside the others. Here and there, we came across groups of girls of apparently higher class than the generality, having gold ornaments and smarter ribbons. The girls walked arm-in-arm in

GROUP AT SOUBERG.

strings of half-a-dozen or so, patrolling up and down, and were very loth to unlock their red arms to make room for us.

The girls were sedate enough at this time, but the young men were all very lively. One indeed, but the only one, was being marched off by a couple of policemen.

In a cleared space, fenced off by a rope, a score of youths were dancing in the most uncouth fashion, without partners. Laughing gleefully, but idiotically, with flushed faces, long, lank hair under tight peaked caps, and capacious, slobbering, open mouths, they simply anticked slowly and laboriously until they stopped through exhaustion. A crowd of people stared stolidly at this unedifying spectacle.

The only game of any interest was the old English pastime of tilting at the ring. One of the avenues of trees was roped off at the sides to form a long lane. Across this, at a height of about eight feet, was a ring suspended on a rope. Half-a-dozen steeds, long-tailed horses, such as drew the country wagons, but in very good condition, were provided for the use of the gamesters, who, armed with lances quite of the regulation pattern, rode furiously down the avenue, and generally missed the ring. The crowd on each side of the barriers seemed to enjoy the sport immensely, and when a successful knight carried off the ring, their plaudits were loud and long. The prize seemed to be a bottle of gin.

I planted my camera in the middle of the avenue, and had no trouble in inducing the proprietor to suspend his game, while I photographed the champion tilter, with his lance in position, and his horse under the ring. Unfortunately, the number of faces crowded in the picture, and necessarily out of focus, render it unsuitable for reproduction.

We tried several groups of girls, but the swells among them would not trouble themselves to stand for us, and the others and the young men, were too eager to be in the group, so that the resulting negatives, though interesting, are not artistic. Photography was difficult, too, when the deep green shade was only fleckered by shafts and spots of sunlight, finding their way through interstices in the leafy canopy overhead.

Some North Sea pilots who had come from Flushing, remarked that as we were evidently taking types of the people, we could not do better than depict the pilots themselves, but we told them they looked too much like Englishmen. These North Sea Government pilots, of whom we afterwards saw a great many at Flushing, are terrific swells, in blue cloth and gold braid.

Another great diversion at the fair was chopping gingerbread, at which some of us had a try. Long, thin slips of gingerbread are placed on a wooden block, and the object is to cut these in two, longitudinally, with the fewest cuts of a hatchet, the loser, I suppose, paying. It is not by any means so easy as it looks, to get the cuts quite in a line.

From this exciting amusement, we turned to listen to two or three singers on a platform, singing doleful ditties, to which few people paid any attention. The boors themselves made noise enough, with their gleeful howling, to make them oblivious of the itinerant singers.

Under the trees, in a quieter part near the church, were many little tables and chairs, and here the older people had gathered, with their girls under their wings, and there was a good deal of tippling going on. Some of us ventured into a tavern or *slitterij*, where groups, who were a little "forrader" than others, worshipped both Venus and Bacchus, all in a perfectly innocent though indescribable way.

"The "fun of the fair" was largely made up to us by the observation of the primitive manners and habits of the natives in many ways, which, although perfectly natural and guileless, and clearly within the bounds of their peasant propriety, are not describable. Suffice it to say, that if you gathered together all the realistic pictures of the old Dutch painters, in their portrayal of peasant life, they were paralleled in those leafy avenues at Souberg *kermis*.

Having exhausted all my plates, and got rid of my camera, we could walk about the fair without attracting too much attention. We were inclined to say that this was the most interesting day of our cruise. Certainly, in one hour we saw more of the Dutch peasant than in all the rest of the cruise. No one cruising or travelling in Holland should omit to see a country *kermis* if possible. I say a country fair, because the large town fairs, such as at Amsterdam or Rotterdam, are too much ruled by the low town element. At a country village, you have the rustics, pure and simple, in the honest vigour of their physical enjoyments.

The *kermis* times are noted in the local almanacs, but at Whitsuntide they are very common. The servant lasses all expect a holiday during fair time, even if it lasts a week, and they frequently stay out for the week, nobody knows where.

We were told that if we came in the evening, we should find things far more lively, but we preferred to leave while the idyllic phase of the *kermis* was uppermost. Already there was a stream of prudent parents returning over the bridge, with their families of girls packed in the wagon behind them.

We only saw two mendicants; one blind and the other pretending to be a crippled sailor, with a large model of a man-of-war on the grass by his side. After, with some difficulty, gathering together the component parts of our crew, we re-embarked, and the Atalanta steamed to Middleburg, which was only two miles away.

An apt illustration of turning the sword into a ploughshare, was noticeable on the banks of this fine canal.

Mooring posts are always provided at short distances apart, so as to afford no excuse for vessels sticking their anchors into the banks. On this canal these posts are made of cannons, which are buried in the ground, with some three feet of the breech end protruding, making capital mooring posts.

SCARCELY had we moored to the quay-side at Middleburg ere the harbour-master came up. He was a big, pleasant, polite man, but he could not speak English or French. He showed us some rules and regulations made by the municipal authority at Middleburg, as to the dues for vessels mooring at the quay. These are separate from those affecting the canal, which are given in the appendix, and, being in Dutch, we took some little time in finding out that there was a fixed charge for pleasure yachts, and we accordingly had to pay three and fourpence for mooring there for one night. We walked with the harbour-master to his office, in a street some distance off, to get the necessary receipt, a piece of business which always took a long time in Holland, although the resulting bits of paper were very small.

Middleburg seemed a wonderfully nice town. On finding our way to the market square, we saw a charming town-hall, built in 1468, the face of it adorned with twenty-five statues of counts and countesses of Flanders and Zeeland.

MIDDLEBURG TOWN-HALL.

The *concierge* was on the steps of it, and directly we entered the large empty square he observed us, and beckoned and called to us vigorously, until he led us triumphantly indoors. I never saw such a fellow to talk. Although he knew we could not speak Dutch, he rattled us round from one object to the other, describing them most volubly, and quite satisfied with an occasional "Ja" in return.

As a museum of antiquities relating to the town, the place was most interesting. If, however, one of us lingered to inspect something which took his fancy, the man would seize him by the arm and hurry him on.

AT MIDDLEBURG.

We took a delight in dodging him, and harking back to another room, and he got very excited, because we would not listen to his breathless harangues. He talked as if he had a race against time, but he was the most amusing *concierge* we ever saw. A workman passing down the beautifully clean staircase spat upon one of the steps. The rage of our *concierge* was fearful to see. Clearly sacrilege of the deepest dye had been committed.

We much enjoyed rambling among the quaint streets of Middleburg, and by its shady canals, but were annoyed by a *commissaire*, who would come insinuatingly up, and begin to explain things. We didn't want him, and told him so, but it was of no use. He returned to the charge again and again. At last we used strong phrases to him in English, French, and Dutch, and he took off his hat politely, and said with a sweet smile, "Tank you, sares," and went. At the next corner he was at us again, and then we seriously made him understand that we would punch his head, and he bothered us no more until the next morning, when he waylaid Dendy.

We were struck with the great brass milk-cans of antique shape, and highly polished, which were being carried about by the milk-carts. They were of most graceful form, being globular, or urn-shaped, with long narrow necks, and immense handles at the side.

As it grew dusk, we could peep into the houses as we passed by, without being rude. The tea-things were spread; the blinds partly up, and the only light was the

QUAY AT MIDDLEBURG.

glimmer of a spirit-lamp, or glow of a turf under the urns on the table. With Dutch economy, lights are not forthcoming, until it is absolutely too dark to see without them.

About nine o'clock we strolled along a pretty lane to meet the people coming from Souberg. We passed some pleasant villas, with moats, summer-houses, and bridges. The lads and lasses coming from the fair were, however, most comical. In groups of twenty or thirty, arms interlinked, lad and lass alternately, they came dancing and singing along in the highest and most idiotic state of glee. They jumped with the rhythm of the tune, and the capacious short skirts of the girls made them look like a lot of balloons on the hop. They made a great noise, and seemed perfectly happy. We could hear similar joyous sounds from the other side of the canal, and over the bridge there was a continuous stream of people returning. They were all well behaved, though gleeful in the extreme.

By ten o'clock, however, the nice, clean, broad quay was perfectly quiet, and we had an undisturbed night. We heard from our crew that the more roystering spirits from the *kermis* kept up the fun to a late hour in certain drinking-places, but the streets were perfectly quiet.

In the morning I had a quiet stroll by myself with the

camera, and about ten o'clock we started for Zierickzee, in Schouwen. It was blowing half a gale of wind, but this did not affect us in the canal.

We soon reached Veere, where there are sluices communicating with the sea-channel of Veerschegat. We landed at Veere, which we found to be a quiet old-fashioned town. The small town-hall was the most charmingly quaint of any we had seen. Unfortunately, it was so closely surrounded by houses, that we could not take a photograph of it. We could not get sufficiently far back to include the building within the limits of the plate. But, rather than be entirely done, we took a distant view of its slender ship-crowned tower, as visible over the roof of a cottage.

There was a small but extremely interesting collection of local antiquities in the town-hall. A detailed description of the contents of these provincial Dutch museums, with explanations, would form a most interesting book, and I commend the hint to roving antiquarians.

Rowland was specially tickled with the thief-catchers, which were poles having spring collars at the end. These, thrust at the neck, arm, or leg of an offender, grasped him tightly, and the spikes fastened to the interior of the collar prevented escape.

The ancient harbour of Veere, with its crowd of

VEERE TOWN-HALL.

antiquated craft, its quay, deep in the shadow of many trees, and its old-world houses, was a picture of pictures, but the vigour of the wind, which rudely tossed masts, sails, nets, and branches—even the gables seemed to move—prevented our obtaining a presentable negative. A curious well, and a fine church, with its tower destroyed and windows mutilated, were inspected, and then we returned to the yacht.

Veere is of especial interest to Scotchmen, who, on account of the trade with Scotland which used to be carried on there (the Scotch bringing coals, for there is no turf in Walcheren), had many privileges there. They paid no duties, and had judges and tribunals of their own. Some thirty Scotch families were settled at Veere in 1700.

Passing through the lock, we entered the wide tidal channel, which separates North and South Beveland. We turned to the eastward for some eight or ten miles, along the Zaandkreek. Only a few schuyts were visible, and out of the low, green, distant shores on either hand, clumps of trees and the tall spire of a church indicated a village, while a few masts mixed up with the trees bore evidence that a small harbour was hidden away there.

As we passed by a village which shall be nameless,

our pilot remarked that the priest there was a very good man and kind to the poor, and on our making further enquiries it appeared that his kindness consisted in the foregoing of his fees when couples inclined to marry had no money. He would perform the ceremony for nothing, and the only condition he imposed was that he claimed a privilege, too feudal in its nature for modern times.

Emerging into the broad sea of the Ooster Schelde, we had a six miles exhilarating steam over to Zierickzee. There was a strong wind and considerable sea, over which the Atalanta bounded like a greyhound over a low wall, as we drove her fast, in order to be into the harbour before the change of tide brought it in opposition to the wind, when there would be a dangerous sea at the entrance.

It was grand to feel the salt spray stinging our faces, and to see our sharp stem cleaving the blue white-topped waves. It is this mingling of sea and canal, rough and smooth which makes much of the charm of cruising in Holland, as it affords a constant change and variety.

Once within the piers there was smooth water. The town was some distance up the straight channel of the harbour, and on reaching it we moored alongside the quay. As it is a tidal harbour and at low tide we should be aground, we took the necessary precautions to prevent

Engraved by Annan & Swan London

TOWN HALL ZIERICKSEE

the yacht heeling over, but when low water came she had made herself a snug mud berth, in which she sat upright.

A crowd of loafers speedily assembled on the quay, and Rowland asked them somewhat tartly, if they were out of work. One of them replied,

WATER-GATE AT ZIERICKZEE.

"Yes, we are. Just like the people in your country, willing to work and nothing to do."

The day was showery, but that did not stop us wandering about the streets of Zierickzee, some of which were wide and handsome, but the majority very narrow and picturesque. The town-hall, in a narrow street, forms one of the illustrations to this book, so that it will speak for itself, and a curious old water-port is the subject of a smaller picture.

Curiously enough there did not appear to be any *cafés* in the town, which must be desperately dull to live in. A ship's chandler having a shop on the quay, showed us punts and guns belonging to some Englishmen, who visit the place for the sake of wildfowling every winter. He said they paid their expenses by the sale of the fowl they killed. The sands to the westward are favourite feeding grounds, and also break the force of the sea in a westerly wind.

Now that the end of the cruise was approaching, we were inclined to hurry it on, and two of us were anxious to get back to our professional duties. As the weather seemed to become unsettled, we were anxious to allow ourselves plenty of time at Flushing, in order to be ready to start back across the North Sea at the first favourable opportunity. A sudden change of wind at night brought a clear sky, a bright moon, and every sign of fair weather, but before the dawn there was another change of wind, which brought up storms of rain.

CHAPTER XXX.

FLUSHING. THE END OF THE CRUISE.

THIS morning we were rather amused at Rowland's orders to a man on shore, who was to provide us meat for breakfast,—

"Get plenty of kidneys for three gentlemen, *all hearty.*"

He was quite right, for by this time we had developed excellent appetites.

It was a rough morning, raining hard, and blowing a gale of wind as we left the quay at Zeirickzee. As the wind would be abaft the beam when we cleared the harbour, we hoisted the sails to keep the vessel steady, and also drive her a little faster, and when the sheets were taut, she heeled over as she felt the gusts, like a sailing yacht. Of course, the sails were too small to need reefing, even in a gale.

As we neared the mouth of the harbour, it was apparent that there was a stiff sea on, and we were somewhat curious to see how the long, narrow, and sharp-bowed

Atalanta would behave in the foaming and boiling water just off the piers. We were clad in our oilies, and had battened down the engine-room as close as the engineer would stand it, in order to keep out the water that was sure to come aboard. I went below for my camera, in order to take an instantaneous shot at the waves as we dipped into them.

"Are you going to take a photograph of her as she goes down?" asked Dendy, who, like myself, was doubtful whether the proceeding was safe. I have gone merrily over much worse seas in my own little four-tonner, but I never can believe that steamers are as safe as sailing craft. As we cleared the piers, up went the Atalanta's bow on a steep wave, down into a steeper hollow, and as the next wave seemed to be going to make a clean sweep of everything, I exposed. Then turning quickly around, I took the white sea astern, with the receding harbour in the background—then the sea *took me*—very unfairly, so to speak, below the belt. It got under my oilies, up to my waist, filling my sea boots, and making me wet through and uncomfortable, besides sousing my camera.

The Atalanta behaved very much better than we expected. After the first astonished dive, she went fairly along, over a short tumbling sea, and with wind and steam both at high pressure, we drove at a fine rate over the open, and were not long in reaching the comparative shelter of the Zaandkreek.

Here we saw a Dutch yacht at anchor, the seas breaking in rapid succession against her bluff bows, and sending showers of spray over her.

How it did blow and rain, and it was so cold. I sheltered at times under the lee of the funnel, with my hands pressed against it for warmth. Most men who only occasionally follow out-door sports, find their hands to be the weakest points about them in hard weather. It is hard to protect one's hands from the cold, and yet retain their efficiency, and on many a frosty, sunless day's pike-fishing, I have had mine numbed, when the rest of my body was comfortably warm. When clothed in oilies, with the water running off the sleeves on to one's hands, and a cold wind blowing, they get very cold.

The blasts were becoming very stinging as we reached Veere, and once through the lock, we could go below. For myself, I was rather chilled through standing for a couple of hours in wet things, and was glad to change.

We reached Flushing without further incident, and moored to the quay next a gun-boat, one of whose crew was always on guard, with a drawn cutlass, on the quay. It was a nice quiet berth, but we were destined to become uncommonly sick of it. Flushing is in some respects a quaint and picturesque town, but it would not compare in this respect with many that we had seen, and I could not get up sufficient enthusiasm about it, to take a single photograph. Some of its tidal basins were desperately

THE ATALANTA IN VEERE LOCK.

unhealthy at low tide, and I had not been there a day before I became affected with some of the symptoms of "Walcheren fever."

On Friday it blew a hard gale, and the same on Saturday. The Schelde was full of large steamers, taking shelter, and it was clearly no time for the little Atalanta to put her nose outside. We wandered to and fro between the meteorological station and the pilots' handsome Institute, trying to obtain some crumb of comfort; but the pilots told us that the weather in the North Sea was exceptionally heavy, and the meteorologists told us that there was no sign of any improvement.

On Sunday we took a walk along the great sea dyke of Walcheren, which bristles with a *chevaux de frise* of posts to break the backwash of the waves. Each of these posts, which are not a yard apart, is said to cost seven florins, and the whole dyke at West Kapelle might have been made of solid copper for what it has cost from first to last. Along the windy dyke, groups of red-armed peasant girls were strolling, and separate groups of men, with the curious, brimless top hats of the Walcheren peasant, but they created in us but languid curiosity, so engrossed were we in observations of the flying scud, the ragged stormy clouds, and the falling barometer

The only things interesting to us were the smart pilot schooners which lay in the harbour. They were craft of most beautiful lines, and, needless to say, good sea boats. One of them was for sale, and would have made a handsome and commodious cruising yacht. I imagine she could be picked up fairly cheap, as there are more schooners than are wanted for the pilots.

Matters were now becoming desperate. I felt so ill and depressed with the unhealthy dankness about Flushing, that I felt I must not stay there another day, or I should lose the benefits of the cruise. Both Dendy and I were due back at business, and as there was no chance of the Atalanta being able to leave for some days, we decided to return to England by the Queenboro' boat that evening. The captain said he would stick to the ship, and we applauded his resolution. We thought, however, he protested too much.

The steamers from Flushing to Queenboro' are very fine paddle-steamers, and at ten o'clock at night we said good-bye to Blake, who required all our compliments upon his sense of duty, to induce him not to come with us even at the last moment.

Directly we got clear of the harbour, I lost the sense of continual sickness and depression which harassed me in Flushing, and became myself again. I should never stay at Flushing even a night again, if possible, but would push on to Middleburg, where there is nothing offensive, but, on the contrary, everything is strikingly fine and fresh. On no other part of the cruise did I experience anything but benefit, but of Flushing I have a horror. The others were affected in the same way, but not to the same degree.

As we opened out the sea it was blowing a three-quarter gale, and promised more. When the seas were breaking over the sponsons, and the decks ancle-deep in water I thought it time to go below, and being tired, slept well until the morning, when we entered the Thames. Going on deck, I asked a deck-hand if the passage had been a rough one. He stared at me as if to ask where I had been not to find that out without asking, and replied that it had been uncommonly rough. Yet I learned that half-way across, in the height of the gale, a small decked boat, said to be only sixteen feet in length, closely reefed, and with three men on board, passed close under our stern, and was apparently taking no harm. I should doubt her being quite so small as was represented, but there is no doubt that a small decked boat, properly constructed, is as safe in a gale and heavy sea as a corked bottle.

During the day, a telegram came from the captain,

"Can't stand being alone. I shall come across by big steamer to-night."

The Atalanta was delayed a week before the weather moderated sufficiently to permit her to cross. She had to put back once, and her skipper is not a man to be turned back by trifles. I was uncommonly glad to see her safe back in Lowestoft harbour, as I had been in a constant fidget about her during the week.

The only trouble we had with the customs was at Lowestoft, where the officers insisted upon my opening my boxes of photographic plates, which we did in a dark room kindly placed at our disposal by a local artist.

Seeing that owners, passengers, crew, and yacht were so well known at Lowestoft, this seemed to me to be an unnecessary trouble.

So ended the cruise of the Atalanta on Dutch waterways. We only wished we had spent more time on the Zuyder Zee and in Friesland, but these may be revisited another year, and if so, it will be in a sailing yacht. If the yacht were first sent over, three weeks would be ample time to do all that we did of Holland or more, even in a sailing vessel. Where the Atalanta steamed four hours a day, the sailing yacht might well do eight if necessary, and still leave time for sight-seeing.

At all events, it will be pleasant during the coming winter to plan out another cruise, and if it comes to pass, and the public happen to like this book, why, the log of the next one may also be told.

Some useful information will be found in the appendix. Perhaps, like the postscript to a lady's letter, it will be the most useful part of the book.

APPENDIX.

PILOTS.

The addresses of our two best pilots are

    K. de JONGE,

        No. 2, Buiter Wieringger Straat,

            AMSTERDAM.

For the Zuyder Zee, North Holland, and North Sea Canal.

    F. STORM,

        No. 18, Lunden Street,

            ANTWERP.

For anywhere South of Amsterdam, including the Rhine. He is a certificated Rhine pilot.

CHARTS.

ZUYDER ZEE. The English Admiralty Chart is corrected down to 1883, and may be relied upon. Five feet is the outside draught for safe navigation of the Zee.

HOLLAND. The best general Map showing the Waterways is a very clear and accurate one, on a scale of six miles to the inch. Published by Smulders and Company, The Hague.

BELGIUM. An equally good Map of Belgium, but on a somewhat larger scale, is published by L'Institut Cartographique Militaire. Both Maps may be procured of Philips and Son, Fleet Street.

ROUTE OF THE ATALANTA.

DATES.	PLACES.	MILES.	ROUTE.	SLUICES.	DUES.
May 23, 24	Lowestoft to Ymuiden	102 knots	North Sea	Ymuiden	Lock, 10s.
,, 25	Ymuiden to Amsterdam	15 miles	Canal and Y	Schellingwoude	No dues
,, 27	E	27 ,,	Y and Zuyder Zee		Harbour 75 cents
,, 28		12 ,,	Rail		
,, 29	orn to Urk	24 ,,	Zuyder Zee		
,, ,,	Urk to Kampen	15 ,,	Zuyder Zee and Yssel		
,, 30	Kampen to Zwolle	9 ,,	Rail		
,, 31	Kampen to Urk	15 ,,	Yssel and Zuyder Zee		
,, ,,	Urk to Stavoren	18 ,,	Zuyder Zee		H , , 2 cents
,, ,,	pen	6 ,,	Rail		
June 1		13 ,,	Zuyder Zee		H r, 60 cents
,, ,,	Medemblik to Twisk	4 ,,	gen		
,, 2	i p	36 ,,	Zuyder Zee and Texel Stroom		
,, 3	r to aar	24 ,,	h Holl d	Ni we iep	L
,, ,,		15 ,,	h Holl d	Pu	No
,, 4	d to Haarlem	24 ,,		aarlem	No lues
,, 5	H m to Rotterdam	48 ,,	Yssel &	Gousluis, Gouda	
,, 7	R t d he	18 ,,	Rail and Tram		

ROUTE OF THE ATALANTA. (Continued).

DATES.	PLACES.	MILES.	ROUTE.	SLUICES.	DUES.
June 8	Rotterdam to Dordrecht	12 miles	River Maas		No dues
,, ,,	Dordrech to Me dinge	45 ,,	Sea Gh of Holland-sche Diep, Keaten, Mas gat, E. Schelde	W me dinge, Hans-wee†	
,, 9	Me dinge to An werp	30 ,,	S. Beveland Canal & R. Schelde	An werp	Lock, gue der
,, ,,		25 ,,	River Schelde		
,, ,,		25 ,,	Ri	G t	50 ents
,, ,,		25 ,,			75 ents
,, ,,		23 ,,	l e	Fl	No des
,, ,,		18 ,,	al		s, 1
,, 16		5 ,,		Veere	
,, ,,		18 ,,			
,, 1		26 ,,	al		

N.B. *The dis* nces *are calculated from the chart.* *from the Captain's diary,*
nd *may perhaps include gratuities* n *some instances.*

CANAL REGULATIONS.

Resolution of February 5th, 1879, establishing the General Regulations of Police for the Netherlands Government Canals.

WE WILLEM III., BY THE GRACE OF GOD, KING OF THE NETHERLANDS, PRINCE OF ORANGE NASSAU, GRAND DUKE OF LUXEMBURG, ETC., ETC., ETC.

On the report of our Minister of Waterstaat, Trade and Industry, dated November 21st, 1878, let. H, section Trade and Industry;

Having considered Art. 190 of the Constitution and Art 577 of the Civil Code;

Having thought it desirable to establish general police regulations for the use, the navigation, and the conservation of the Government Canals;

Having taken into consideration the advice of Our Council of State dated January 21st, 1879, No. 18;

Having considered the further report of Our aforesaid Minister, of the 3rd inst., let. F., section Trade and Industry;

Have thought fit and resolved :

TITLE I.

GENERAL STIPULATIONS.

Art. 1.

These Regulations apply to all Government canals including their harbours and whatever belongs to them according to the special regulations and bye-laws, in so far as these are not contrary to the provisions of these General Regulations.

Art. 2.

Throughout these Regulations are designated :
By ships all sorts of vessels ;

By captains those who are in command of the ships or timberfloats, or who conduct the same;

By sailing ships are also understood steamers under sail and not under steam;

By steamers all ships under steam, whether carrying sail or not.

By special regulations are understood the general measures of internal Government, by which the application of these Regulations to the separate canals is regulated.

Art. 3.

These Regulations are to be printed in the Dutch, English, German, French, and Norwegian languages, and may be had on applying for them to the canal-officers and officials.

Any captain, navigating on a canal or making use of its harbours, must be provided with a copy of these Regulations and of the special regulations. He is bound to produce them, if required, to the waterstaat, canal, and police-officers.

TITLE II.

STIPULATIONS RESPECTING THE NAVIGATION.

§ 1. *Of Ships in General.*

Art. 4.

The special regulations fix for each canal the maximum of the allowed dimensions of the ships.

In the case of temporary shallows or low water the waterstaat or canal-officers may limit the depth of gauge allowed by the special regulations.

No ship of larger dimensions than those allowed by the two preceding clauses are permitted to navigate on the canals, except by leave of the Chief Engineer.

Art. 5.

In case of taxes being raised on a Government canal, no ship shall navigate on such a canal, or make use of its harbours, without having paid these dues to the official collectors.

The captain is bound to produce to the officers, charged with the collecting of these dues, the certificate of registry and other documents needed to fix the amount of his dues.

A receipt will be delivered to the captain, who is bound, whenever required, to show it to the official or officer entrusted with the enforcement of these Regulations, or charged with the collecting of these dues.

Art. 6.

Vessels with no fixed decks and of larger tonnage than 10 M³. must be provided with water-tight planks, boards, or sides, reaching at least 0.35 M. above the water.

Art. 7.

Without leave of the canal-officers, no ships moored abreast are allowed to navigate upon any canal or in its harbours, or to take up berths other than appointed for that purpose. Ships are also forbidden to lie or be adrift athwart the fairway.

Art. 8.

Any sea-going ship in a canal or its harbours is to hoist the colours of the nation to which she belongs, and keep them hoisted from sunrise to sunset. Ships caught by the ice in the canal are excepted.

Ships whose draught exceeds 4 meters, have to hoist a small foremast flag besides. Ships of less draught are forbidden to do so.

No merchant ship is allowed to hoist a pennant on any account whatever.

Art. 9.

Any captain, leaving his ship, shall appoint a capable person as his substitute on his responsibility. This prescription does not apply to ships of less than 10 M³. tonnage, or worked forward from the shore by means of poles.

No ship of more than 10 M³. tonnage may lie without any hands on board in a canal, without leave of the canal-officers.

The canal-officers are to seize and moor any ship having no one on board in charge, and drifting in a canal, at the expense of the captain or the owner.

Art. 10.

Ships overloaded, in a foundering state, or in the opinion of the canal-officers, insufficiently manned or rigged, shall on the first intimation of the officers, stop their course, and be removed according to the directions of the said officers.

Art. 11.

Except in outer-ports, opening on rivers, floods, roads, sea-harbours or other fairways, where anchoring is allowed, no anchors may hang overboard, unless a special leave be granted by the sluice or harbour-master to the captain, who is held responsible for the damages which may be caused.

On the cleats along the wales or on the fore-ends of the leeboards no protruding iron spikes or points may be fixed.

Art. 12.

In passing a canal no square or studding sails may be set.

Of square-rigged ships, whether navigating or moored, the yards must be braced on larboard along the ship. Of ships going out the yards must be topped on larboard, of ships going in on starboard. The jibboom and the flying jibboom must be hauled or taken in as far as possible.

River ships are to top their jibbooms on approaching the sluices.

When ships are discharging their cargoes entirely or partly, the harbour or sluice-master may direct their topgallant yards and topgallant masts to be taken down.

Art. 13.

It is forbidden to place a ship in or outside a canal or its harbour in such a way as to obstruct the passage into it or out of it. The captain of such a ship shall remove her on the first intimation of a canal-officer.

Art. 14.

It is forbidden, wherever canal banks serve as a high road, to have any spar, bowsprit, or other rigging projecting over the canal boards, and either to lower the sails or make them fall over at that side of the canal.

Art. 15.

It is forbidden to cut the tow-lines or ropes of other ships. Any ship, whose crew are found guilty of such offence, shall, without prejudice to the penalty incurred by the infringement of these Regulations, pass at the sluices only after the ship whose tow-lines or ropes have been cut.

Art. 16.

No ship may enter the outport of any canal, when during the day a red flag is hoisted, or during the night a red light is placed on one of the piers of that port, as a sign of the entrance being obstructed by ships or other causes.

Art. 17.

The opening of a sluice to let the water through is announced at least one hour before, during the day, by a blue flag, bearing the word "*spuijen*" in white letters, during the night by two superposed blue lights.

This signal being displayed, or the opening of the sluice for letting the water through having been given notice of by one of the canal-officers, ships in the canal are to be duly moored by ropes or chains, to prevent their running aground.

In this case the canal-officers are qualified to assign berths to the captains of the ships, and to direct them as to the manner of mooring their ships.

No sufficient number of berths being available, laden ships are to be accommodated first.

Art. 18.

On approaching a sluice or bridge, captains shall slacken the speed of their ships, that in case of need they may be stopped at 100 meters' distance from the sluice or bridge. At the fixed signs or posts the sails shall be lowered or clewed. The sluice or bridge men must be warned either by means of the steam-whistle, ship-bell, or fog-horn, or by shouting.

Captains shall make their ships stop, if by day a red ball or flag, or by night a red light, is displayed on the sluice or bridge, and if deemed necessary, cause them to be moored at the place pointed out by the sluice or bridge man.

The exact place of passing the bridge or sluice is indicated during the night by green lights.

Art. 19.

When several ships at the same time approach a sluice or bridge, the sluice or bridge man regulates the order of approaching, and the distance to be kept between them.

Art. 20.

Each ship is to pass the sluice in turn, according to the order of arrival.

When several ships approach the sluice from opposite directions, wanting to be let through, they pass by turns from either side, beginning with the ship approaching from that side where the water is on a level with that within the sluice. The sluicemen are authorised, for the sake of order, to distribute tickets, indicating the turn of each ship for being let through the sluice.

Art. 21.

The right to be let through first is granted to
1. Ships hoisting a pennant;
2. Government ships, serving exclusively for the conveyance of officers charged with the superintendence of the canal, or canal-officers.
3. Ships serving for the regular conveyance of persons, goods, or cattle, with their lighters and barges;
4. Ships loaded with fish; and
5. Ships loaded with easily flaming or explosive goods.

Ships loaded with gunpowder, fireworks, gun cotton, nitro-glycerine, or other such highly explosive materials are to pass, if possible, before all other ships, no other ship being allowed to come within the sluice at the same time.

Art. 22.

While passing the sluice, every ship within the sluice or in its proximity must be duly moored fore and aft at the place pointed out by the canal-officers.

Ships that are to pass or be let through, shall not approach the bridge or sluice until the canal-officer gives the sign to do so. If, to his idea, the ship whose turn it is, does not approach fast enough, he is qualified to make another ship pass first.

When the canal-officer means that a ship is not made to pass the sluice or bridge with sufficient speed, he is qualified to provide against this at the expense of the captain. While passing the sluices or bridges, captains must comply with the injunctions of the canal-officer.

Art. 23.

Of ships passing the sluices or bridges all sails should be lowered or clewed, and kept firmly so, until the ships have quite passed the sluice or bridge.

The hauling or winding ships in and out of sluices may only be performed by means of the contrivances placed there for that purpose.

In passing the sluices or bridges steamers and towed ships are not allowed more speed than is needed to steer them.

No ropes or chains are allowed to be dragged along when passing the sluices or bridges.

Art. 24.

In case the passage through a sluice or bridge on account of stormy weather, or of the water being let through the sluices, drawn off from the canal, or let into it, is inexpedient, the sluice or bridge man may refuse it.

It is forbidden to pass a sluice or bridge during the absence of the canal-officer, or in opposition to his orders.

Art. 25

Every time two ships consecutively have passed a bridge, the bridge, if necessary, is closed in behalf of the passengers and carriages.

Several ships tugged by the same steamer may pass together.

In passing a bridge, ships going down stream have got the preference above those going up stream.

Art. 26.

The stipulations concerning the passage of bridges are not applicable to railway bridges, in so far as special regulations have been established respecting them, or in so far as they do not agree with the stipulations of the general regulations for the railway service, established by Our Resolution of October 27th, 1875 (*Gazette* No. 183), or to be established later by us.

Art. 27.

Should any ship in a canal or its harbours be overtaken by the frosty weather in such a way that she cannot proceed on her voyage, the captain, on the intimation of a canal-officer, is bound to cause an opening of at least one meter in width to be made in the ice around the ship, and to be kept open. In case the captain should neglect this precaution, the canal-officers shall have it done at his expense.

The navigation on the canal, when the rivers are frozen up, may be prohibited by the King's Commissary.

Art. 28.

Frosty weather setting in, or contrary winds blowing steadily, any ship lying in the outer harbour shall, on the intimation of the harbour-master, either be hauled out to the roadstead, or be passed through the sluice into the inner port.

In this case, and also when, the water being frozen over in the canal, ships are let through the sluices into the inner basin, any ship in the canal shall, if necessary, tow further up according to the directions of the canal-officers.

If necessary, the canal-officers shall cause an opening to be made through the ice, at the expense of the ships to be hauled up, according to their tonnage.

Art. 29.

In transporting easily inflammable or explosive goods, captains, besides being subject to the laws and prescriptions on this head, shall submit to the special precautionary measures prescribed by the canal-officers.

Art. 30.

In the case of any article of a ship being lost in the canal, which floating or submerged might be dangerous to the navigation on the canal, the captain shall give immediate notice thereof to the first canal-officer he is to meet. The lost articles are fished up and removed at the expense of the captain, and on his refunding the costs, returned to their owners.

Captains shall take care that no lighters, rafts or beams, used by their ships, shall be found drifting about or unmoored.

Art. 31.

In case any ship runs aground, and her cargo has to be discharged in order to get her afloat, in the opinion of the canal-officers, the captain shall do the same without delay. In default whereof, the canal-officers shall direct it to be done at the expense of the captain.

The Engineer may allow the level of the canal to be raised as much as is needed to get the ship afloat.

Art. 32.

The captain of any sunken ship shall immediately take measures for lightening her, and at the same time inform the nearest canal-officer of the accident, who sends notice thereof to the Engineer. The captain is bound, directly after the accident, to place on or near the sunken ship a beacon, that always keeps above water, provided with a white flag during the day, and with a white light during the night. In default whereof the canal-officers shall have it done at his expense.

If they have not commenced raising the ship within 24 hours after the accident, an official report shall be drawn up.

Should the Engineer judge that the sunken ship obstructs the navigation, and no adequate measures have been taken by the captain to raise her, he, after the expiration of the said twenty-four hours, shall proceed authoritatively to raise the ship.

The raising shall also be effected by order of authority in the case of the sunken ship not obstructing the navigation, if the captain fails to raise the ship within the time appointed by the King's Commissary. Such a case is to be stated in a report drawn up by the Engineer.

As soon as they have proceeded to raise the ship by order of the authority, nobody, without any exception, shall be admitted to the ship and cargo without leave of the Engineer. The Engineer shall point out the berth the sunken ship when raised, is to take up.

The costs of raising the ship are to be refunded by the captain. Only upon payment of them ship and cargo shall be restored to the parties thereto entitled.

In the cases of the owner and the captain being unknown or being in default to pay these costs within a certain time to be fixed by the King's Commissary, they shall be recovered from the proceeds of the sale of the ship and cargo, after a valuation of the same by two experts to be appointed by the King's Commissary.

§ 2. *Special Stipulations for Steamers.*

Art. 33.

Special regulations will fix the maximum of speed at which steamers are allowed to proceed along the canal or in its harbours.

In behalf of the navigation and of the canal works the waterstaat or canal-officers are authorised to limit the rate of this speed for a time.

Without leave of the Chief Engineer, no ship shall proceed at a greater rate of speed than allowed in the two foregoing clauses.

Art. 34.

Neither the screw nor any other part of the steamer may project beyond the keel, unless the projecting part keeps within the ship's graded maximum of draught.

Art. 35.

The rests of the fires of the engines may not be thrown either into the canal and its harbours, or on the grounds belonging to them.

The captain is bound to show these rests to every canal-officer, when required, until they are discharged at the end of the voyage.

Art. 36.

Steamers are not allowed to proceed at a rate exceeding 75 meters in a minute:

1. When navigating between the fixed signs or posts on the sluices and bridges;
2. On approaching or passing dredging-machines and ships for which the swell might be dangerous, and which as a sign thereof are to show a blue flag by day and a blue light by night;
3. On approaching or passing canal works in the course of constructing, or only just constructed. These shall be indicated during the day by blue flags, during the night by blue lights, placed at both ends of the works.

In case of need, the canal-officers are qualified to order the captain to slacken even the speed designated above.

Art. 37.

Steamships carrying high-pressure engines, must be provided with an escape pipe outside the funnel for letting out the exhaust steam, or with a partition of wire-work in the smoke box. Such partitions must be found in all steamers whose boilers are heated by means of coke, peat, or wood.

§ 3. *Of Timber Floats.*

Art. 38.

Special regulations will specify for each canal the dimensions allowed to timber floats, and the rate of speed at which they may be towed.

Art. 4 (3) is applicable to this clause.

Timber floats must be fastened and joined at both ends, in such a way that they cannot obstruct the navigation, nor cause damage to other ships and timber floats or the canal works. The beams are not to be fastened crosswise, but in such a way that they may easily be counted.

The laths for fastening the beams may not project beyond the float.

Any timber float shall be provided with a board, placed along the float at the canal side, on both sides of which board the name and residence of the owner or captain are to be written or painted in legible letters, easily to be read from the canal banks.

Art. 39.

No ship shall discharge her cargo of timber in the canal or its harbours in order to convert the same into floats, unless the officer, whom it concerns, has given leave.

It is in no case allowed to discharge more beams at a time from any ship, than can be formed immediately into one float or more floats, a sufficient number of hands being on the spot.

Art. 40.

On the completion of a float it must immediately leave the spot of discharge and proceed farther on. If the place of destination is situated on the canal, the float, when arrived, must be taken to pieces and cleared out of the canal within two times twenty-four hours after its arrival.

No timber float shall stay in other place than those indicated by the special regulations, unless the canal-officers have given leave.

Art. 41.

A timber float of no more than twenty-five beams may be fastened to a ship, provided one man is on it to steer it.

Any other timber float shall be towed separately.

On any float, twenty-five meters long and less, at least two able-bodied men shall be present for the purpose of steering it.

Timber floats fastened to one another are considered to be one float.

Art. 42.

The masts or towing-poles on timber floats may not be higher than three meters above the water.

Art. 43.

During the night no timber floats may be transported along the canal, or stay in the harbours without leave of the harbour-master.

Art. 44.

Timber floats are only allowed to pass sluices and bridges after the ships present, unless they, in the case mentioned in Art. 41, clause 1, can be let through together with the ship.

Art. 45.

No timber float shall approach a preceding float within a distance of 500 meters.

Art. 46.

Saving the preceding stipulations, Art. 5, 7, 9, 10, 13, 15—20, and 22—30 of these Regulations also apply to timber floats.

§ 4. *Of Towing.*

Art. 47.

Saving the stipulations laid down in the special regulations, any one is permitted to tow with horses.

Art. 48.

The drivers must take care, as far as possible, to be careful to keep the lines tight, while towing across any ship or timber float, and to slip the same in due time, when not crossing above it.

They are bound to slip the line at the fixed signs or posts, to slacken their speed on approaching any sluice or bridge, and to comply with the injunctions of the canal-officers.

They shall warn the captain of everything calculated to obstruct the navigation.

Any ship moored at a tow-path shall, as far as possible, lower her masts, and assist the passing ships and floats in carrying over their tow-lines.

Art. 49.

It is forbidden to put more than two horses abreast to the tow-line.

Art. 50.

Any driver punished for the infringement of any of these Regulations, or being in a state of inebriation, may be refused the right of towing by the canal-officers.

Art. 51.

The largest number of ships to be towed by a steam-tug is fixed by special regulations.

Art. 52.

Any captain who wants to have his ship towed, shall inform the captain of the steam-tug of the exact draught of his ship, and take up the place assigned to him by the captain of the steam-tug among the other ships to be towed.

Art. 53.

No ships being towed are allowed to carry sail without leave of the captain of the steam-tug, and are bound to make sail or take in the sails, as soon as he thinks fit. On his injunction the ropes shall be veered or hauled on. In case of refusal he is qualified to loose or cut the ropes.

Art. 54.

The tow-ropes of ships being towed are to be loosed by their captains only by turns, and in such a manner that the hindmost ship looses first and the foremost ship looses last. Each time the captain of the steam-tug shall give the sign of loosing the ropes by striking the bell.

Art. 55.

For signalling, the captains of the ships in tow shall make use of a red flag with a white square centre.

The flag hoisted shall mean: All's well on board; the ship is ready to depart; the engine is to work at full speed.

The flag half lowered shall mean: The engine is to work at half speed.

The flag wholly lowered shall mean: Stop at once.

§ 5. *Of Piloting.*

Art. 56.

Any pilot on duty on board a ship navigating on the canal or in its harbours, shall with respect to the police ordinances for the canal comply with the orders of the canal-officers.

Art. 57.

Any pilot on duty on board a ship is bound to have with him a printed copy of these Regulations, and of the special regulations for the canal on which he is navigating. If necessary, he is obliged to acquaint the captain with the contents of the same.

Art. 58.

Any pilot on duty, being in a state of inebriation, may be retained by the canal-officers.

Art. 59.

In the case of any ship having caused damage to any of the canal works, or any infringement having been made on these Regulations, the pilot shall speedily give notice thereof to the harbour-master or the nearest canal-officer.

TITLE III.

STIPULATIONS RELATIVE TO THE USE OF THE CANALS AND THEIR APPURTENANCES.

Art. 60.

Any captain of a ship or timber float staying in any canal or in one of its harbours, shall submit to the orders of the canal-officers, relative to the berth of his ship, which berth may be shifted according to their directions.

Art. 61.

No ships are allowed to lie between the sign posts for stopping at either side of a sluice or bridge.

Art. 62.

Ships and timber floats staying at any place must be moored at the mooring poles or posts placed for that purpose.

On any ship approaching, if needed, all chains and ropes must be slipped in time and to such an extent that the passages be free.

Of ships lying alongside the tow-path, the masts must be lowered, if possible.

Art. 63.

In no canal any anchors may be brought out from any ship unless in the case of heavy currents, when the water is being let through the sluices. Where, however, no mooring poles or posts are found, river ships may use kedge anchors, wholly stuck in the ground and near the board.

Art. 64.

Ships shall take in or discharge cargo only at the spots designed for that purpose or pointed out by the canal-officers.

It is forbidden to deposit or discharge any goods on the banks of the canal, without leave of the harbour master.

Art. 65.

In loading or discharging any ship, no obstruction of the roads or berms may take place, nor any damage be done to the canal works.

The captains of ships lying close to each other, are obliged, for their common convenience, to allow the necessary space for the use of lighters and for hauling out.

Art. 66.

The captain of a ship lying at a landing place must allow another ship to lie alongside his ship, and to communicate across her with the shore, not, however, for the purpose of taking in or discharging cargo.

Art. 67.

Any ship having completed or discharged her cargo, shall immediately make room for any other ship. In case of want of room, several ships arriving at the same time, those coming to take in their cargoes have the preference above those coming to discharge.

Art. 68.

No ships or timber floats are allowed to settle in any canal or its harbours for the purpose of carrying on a trade, keeping inns or lodging places, or residing.

The Engineer may allow a lodging place to be kept aboard a ship in the case of canal works being in the course of erection.

Art. 69.

During the night no bells may be tolled on board any ship or timber float except in case of accident.

Art. 70.

Any captain on board of whose ship a fire bursts out, shall immediately cause the bell to be tolled, and the ship to be hauled out of the neighbourhood of other ships.

Art. 71.

On board any ship or float in the canal or in its harbours, no easily flaming or fell burning articles may be cooked, melted, or warmed without leave of the canal-officers.

It is forbidden to fire off cannon, guns, or pistols, or to let off fireworks on board the ships in the canal or its harbours.

Art. 72.

Captains wishing to leave the harbour with their ships shall give notice to the harbour master, who, if necessary, shall decide the order in which the ships and floats are to haul out.

TITLE IV.

STIPULATIONS FOR THE CONSERVATION OF THE CANALS AND THEIR APPURTENANCES.

Art. 73.

Except in cases of obtained rights it is forbidden without leave of the Minister:

1. To draw off water from any canal or water course belonging to it, or direct any new water courses into it, or change the direction of any water course already connected with it;

2. In, on, through, or along any canal, its harbours, berm ditches, berms, tow-paths, roads, and other grounds belonging to any canal, to effect any work, to erect or plant anything, to cut any trenches, to delve or dredge, to make any new drains or conduits, and either to change or to fill up wholly or partly existing ones;

The King's Commissary, however, may give leave to make, change, or remove any halting and landing place for embarking and discharging cargo, any steps, stairs, pier, horse, or foot-path, or railings.

3. Within the distance of five decimeters from the lines of separation between the canal grounds and the nearest private premises, to place hedges, and within the distance of two meters, measured in the same manner, to plant high trees, or to cut trenches.

Art. 74.

It is forbidden:

1. To damage or injure the canal works or whatever may be built, planted, or grown upon them, or despoil any part of them;

2. To obstruct or prevent the use of the passages and approaches to the canal works;

3. To throw, sink, turn off, or let float anything into the canal or the berm ditches, sluices or harbours, that might obstruct the passage, damage the ships, prevent the course of the water, or cause shallows;

4. To throw any dirt or rubbish along the canal or on the grounds belonging to it, and to hang or place there any objects without special leave of the Chief Engineer;

5. To cross any canal bridge or sluice doors before they are duly closed;

6. To open the bars or railings before a bridge without leave of the bridge-man;

7. To get on or into any canal work, to which the access is prohibited;

8. Unless at the positive request of the canal-officers to tilt, turn, open, or close a bridge, to open or to shut the sluice doors, to raise the flood gates or wears, or to perform other duties of the canal-officers;

9. To deposit on any of the usual places of embarkation or discharge, any goods not discharged from or destined to be loaded into ships, or to let goods lie after the period fixed by the canal-officers for embarking or removing the same.

Art. 75.

Except in cases of obtained rights, it is forbidden without special leave of the King's Commissary to ride or drive on any canal grounds, not destined as high roads for public use. This is only allowed to the carriages of the waterstaat and canal-officers, and to tow horses as far as relates to tow-paths.

Art. 76.

Except in the case of grounds being farmed out, and special stipulations in the contract granting permission, it is forbidden without leave of the King's Commissary to graze horses or cattle on any of the canal grounds.

All horses and cattle, in opposition to these stipulations and without any attendant, found grazing on any of the canal grounds, shall be stopped and pounded at the expense of the offenders.

TITLE V.

STIPULATIONS FOR THE ENFORCEMENT OF THESE REGULATIONS.

Art. 77.

In these General Regulations and in the special regulations are designated:

1. By "the Minister": the Minister charged with the execution of this Resolution;

2. By "the King's Commissary": the King's Commissary for the

province, in which the whole of the canal, or the part thereof referred to, is found;

3. By "Chief Engineer" and "Engineer": the chief engineer and engineer charged with the superintendence of the canal or the part thereof referred to;

4. By "Waterstaat Officers": the inspectors, chief engineers, engineers, sub-engineers, and surveyors of the waterstaat;

5. By "Canal-officers": the governmental harbour-masters, canal, sluice, bridge, ferry, and dyke men.

Art. 78

The enforcement of these General Regulations and the special regulations is entrusted to the governmental and local police, waterstaat, and canal-officers. At their request the chief magistrates of the localities situated along the canal, and all functionaries invested with authority are bound to support them.

The report of any infringement of these regulations, if not made upon the oath, taken on entering the service, must be confirmed upon oath within 48 hours after being drawn up, before the district judge within whose jurisdiction the infringement has been committed.

Such reports are then forwarded to the legal officer, charged with the prosecution thereof, and copies sent to the Chief Engineer.

Art. 79.

Any official and officer charged with the enforcement of these General and other special Regulations, are qualified to cause to be taken away, prevented or done, in case of need with the assistance of the legal force, at the expense of the offenders, whatever is done or left undone in opposition to the said regulations.

Art. 80.

All officials and officers entrusted with the enforcement of these Regulations are qualified to go on board any ship on any canal or in its harbours at any time.

The captains are bound to comply with all injunctions given them by the said officials and officers on behalf of the navigation.

They are held responsible for any damage done to the canal works caused by their own or their subordinates' fault, negligence, or imprudence, and also for the costs of the measures taken pursuant to Art. 79.

Art. 81.

Any officer and official shall, of all damages caused to the canal works they happen to observe, draw up a report, stating the condition of the damaged part before the accident, the circumstances attending it, the probable costs of repairing the damage, the person held responsible for the payment, and the sum that he is bound to refund. In fixing which sum the state of the works before the damage caused, shall be taken in account.

This report shall be sent to the Chief Engineer by intermediary of the Engineer, and a copy of it served on the captain of the ship that has caused the damage.

Art. 82.

The captain of the ship or timber float which has caused the damage, shall forthwith pay the amount of repairing costs, estimated in the report, to the official or officer, or give security for the money, without prejudice to his liability of paying so much more as the costs of repair shall prove to be. In default of which the ship shall be detained.

Art. 83.

In the case of the damage being caused by any ship or timber float towed, and her captain refusing to pay the amount of costs stated in the report or to give security for it, the captain of the steam-tug shall pay or give security, without prejudice to the costs being recoverable by him from the captain of such ship or timber float.

In this case the last clause of the preceding article shall also apply to the steam-tug.

Art. 84.

Captains may appeal from the injunctions of the canal-officers to the King's Commissary, immediate submission, however, to those injunctions being obligatory.

Art. 85.

Any infringement on these General Règulations and other special regulations of police, and any non-observance of the injunctions and directions of the officials and officers, entrusted under the provisions of these Regulations with the enforcement thereof, shall be punished in pursuance of the law of March 6th, 1818 (*Gazette* No. 12).

Art. 86.

These Regulations shall come into operation for the separate canal at the same time as the special regulations to be established for them.

Our Minister of Waterstaat, Trade and Industry is entrusted with the execution of this Resolution, which shall be inserted in the *Gazette*, and communicated to the Council of State.

The Hague, February 5th, 1879.

WILLEM.

The Minister of Waterstaat, Trade and Industry,

Tak van Poortvliet.

Given the Twenty-fourth of February, 1879.

The Minister of Justice,
H. J. Smidt.

Resolution of August 6th, 1880, establishing the Special Regulations of Police for the North-Holland Canal.

We William III., by the Grace of God, King of the Netherlands, Prince of Orange-Nassau, Grand-Duke of Luxemburg, etc., etc., etc.

On the report of our Minister at Waterstaat, Trade and Industry, dated July 2nd, 1880, No. 40, section Trade and Industry;

Having considered the General Regulations of Police for the Netherlands Government Canals, established by our Resolution of February 5th, 1879 (*Gazette* No. 30);

Having taken into consideration the advice of our Council of State, dated July 27th, 1880, No. 6;

Having considered the further report of our aforesaid Minister, dated August 3rd, 1880, No. 50, section Trade and Industry;

Have thought fit and resolved to establish the following Special Regulations of Police for the North-Holland Canal:

Art. 1.

By the North-Holland Canal is understood:

The canal from the Y, opposite *Amsterdam*, to the *Nieuwe-diep* harbour, including the Merchant's innerport (*koopvaardersbinnenhaven*), the outerport of the Merchant's sluice (*koopvaarderssluis*), the William's sluice harbours (*willemssluishavens*), and whatever works belong to them.

Art. 2.

These Regulations are to be printed in the Dutch, English, German, and Norwegian languages, and may be had on applying for them to the canal officers and officials.

Art. 3.

No ship having a draught exceeding 4.80 meters is allowed to enter into or to navigate on the canal or in its harbours.

A written leave, delivered by the Engineer, may permit the entrance of ships of greater draught, however not exceeding 5 meters, when the height of the water allows it.

Ships in distress, and ships bound from the sea harbour at *Nieuwediep* for the Railway port (*Spoorweghaven*) or the Merchant's innerport (*koopvaardersbinnenhaven*) at *Nieuwediep*, or vice versa, may be passed through the sluices with any draught, according to the depth of the outer or inner water, and the judgment of the harbour-master and the surveyor of the waterstaat.

Art. 4.

A seaship, running up behind another seaship, is not allowed to pass her, she being less than 1500 meters distance from a bridge or sluice to be passed.

Art. 5.

Without leave of the harbour-master or sluice-master, no ship or timberfloat lying in the outerports of the William's sluices (*Willemssluizen*) and the Merchant's sluice (*koopvaardersschutsluis*) is allowed to stay there longer than is needed for passing the sluice.

Art. 6.

The order of arrival, according to which the ships are to pass, designated in Art. 20 of the General Regulations, is determined at the Merchant's sluice (*koopvaardersschutsluis*) at *Nieuwediep* as follows:

For inward-bound ships by the order in which their captains will apply to the sluiceman for being passed. Captains of seaships may have the application made by their first mates, as their substitutes;

For outward-bound ships, coming from the canal, by their order of passing the handpost.

From the canal, out of the Inner port, and the Railway port, ships shall be passed by turns.

No ship coming in shall be admitted into the outer port or the sluice without her captain having shown the required ticket to the sluiceman.

In the case of ships, according to Art. 11 of the General Regulations, being allowed by a special leave, granted by the harbour or sluicemaster, to pass the sluice with one or more anchors hanging overboard, the same anchors are to be hung in the anchor chains in front of the hawse, and secured to the catheads above them.

Of such ships, having passed and going up the canal or arriving at the Merchant's innerport (*koopvaardersbinnenhaven*), the anchors shall be hoisted in at once.

Art. 7.

No sea ship shall be passed through a sluice from an hour after sunset till an hour before sunrise, unless a special leave be granted by the harbour-master or the surveyor of the waterstaat.

No ship shall be let through the Merchant's sluice (*koopvaardersschutsluis*) and the *Nieuwe Werk* sluice at Nieuwediep, as soon as the outer water has reached a height exceeding 0.65 meter above ordinary high water.

Art. 8.

Every ship, during the night let through a sluice or a bridge to be opened for that purpose, in addition to the canal and sluice dues fixed in the tariff, is to pay to the sluiceman or bridgeman:

From 9 o'clock in the evening till 5 o'clock in the morning:

For being let through a sluice	f. 0.20
For having a bridge opened	0.10

From sunset till 9 o'clock in the evening, and from 5 o'clock in the morning till sunrise:

For being let through a sluice   f. 0.10

For having a bridge opened   0.50

No payment is due for the opening of bridges built across sluices.

When two or more ships, belonging to the same person, and fastened to each other, pass the sluices and bridges, this retribution is only paid as for one ship.

For ships, serving for the regular conveyance of travellers, goods or cattle, on appointed days and hours, only one-half of this retribution is due.

Art. 9.

The maximum of speed, designated in Art. 33 of the General Regulations, is in a minute:

For steamers of more than	2.75 meters' draught	125	meters
,, no more ,,	2.75 ,,	150	,,
,, ,,	2.40	200	
,, ,,	2.00	250	

Art. 10.

The greatest length allowed to timber floats is 100 meters, provided they be constructed in such a way that they can be divided into parts of no more than 50 meters' length.

The greatest breadth allowed is 7.50 meters.

The rate of speed at which they are permitted to proceed is not to exceed 80 meters in a minute.

Art. 11.

Sea ships of 1100 M^3 and more are to be towed alone.

No steam-tug is allowed to tow more than two sea ships at a time, whose joint tonnage may not exceed 1550 M^3.

The number of river ships or lighters towed at a time is not to exceed ten.

The Chief Engineer is authorised to limit the number of river ships to be towed at a time.

Art. 12.

The maxium of speed at which ships may be towed, is in a minute of 150 meters, and from an hour after sunset till an hour before sunrise 100 meters, without prejudice to what is stipulated in Art. 9 about the rate of speed of steamers of more than 2.75 meters' draught.

Art. 13.

Any steam-tug, towing a timber float, on meeting a sailing or steam sea ship, or a sea ship towed, or a convoy of more than three ships towed, is bound to stop in due time and with the timber float to moor at the shore, until the ship or the convoy will have passed.

She shall act in the same way in the case of such a ship or convoy running up and wishing to pass the timber float towed.

Art. 14.

Saving the stipulations of Art. 64 of the General Regulations, ships and timber floats are forbidden to lie still or pass the night:

Against the west and south side of the canal, between the William's sluices (*Willemssluizen*) and the floating bridge at *Westgrafdijk*, and from 400 meters on the north of the double swing-bridge at Alkmaar to the bridge at the entrance of the Railway port (*spoorweghaven*) at *Helder*;

Against the east and north side, between the floating bridge at *Westgrafdijk* and 400 meters on the north of the double swing-bridge at Alkmaar.

Art. 15.

No ships laden with explosive or easily inflammable materials are allowed to lie during the night in the canal, except at the following places:

a. Against the east side of the canal, 800 meters on the north of the kilometer post 9, that is on the south of Ilpendham;

b. Against the north side, at the *Vinkenhop*, between *Spykerboor* and *Westgrafdijk*;

c. Along the wicker embankment in the *Alkmaar* lake near the island of *Saskerley*;

d. In the canal through the *Zype*, on the east side, between the *Jacob-Klaassen* sluice and the floating bridge in the *Burgerweg*.

Art. 16.

Ships lying in the Merchant's inner port (*koopvaardersbinnenhaven*) are exempted from the prescription in Art. 8 of the General Regulations of having to hoist the colours of the nation to which they belong, or, when having a draught exceeding 4 meters, to hoist a small foremast flag besides.

Art. 17.

In discharging or loading sand, ballast, corn, coals, or other similar articles, the captains must have a sail or cloth spread from the shore to the ship's deck, or from one ship to the other.

From an hour after sunset till an hour after sunrise it is only allowed to load or discharge sand, ballast, or cargo, with a written leave of the harbour-master, in such a manner and under such superintendence as shall be prescribed by the said officer at the expense of the captain.

Art. 18.

On board of every sea ship the captain must cause a regular watch to be kept by day as well as by night.

Art 19.

Relieving ropes, when used, are not allowed to be sustained otherwise than by the supports destined for that purpose.

The cables, chains, and ropes, used at the posts near the Merchant's sluice (*koopvaardersschutsluis*) for hauling ships into or out of that sluice, in deviation from Art. 62 of the General Regulations, need not be slipped unless the sluice-master directs them to be so.

A ship approaching, and not being able to pass behind these posts, is bound to stop at least 100 meters before such cables, chains, and ropes.

Our Minister of Waterstaat, Trade and Industry is entrusted with the execution of this resolution, which shall be inserted in the *Gazette*, and communicated to the Council of State.

The Hague, August 6th, 1880.

The Minister of Waterstaat, Trade and Industry,

G. J. C. KLERCK.

Given the Seventeenth of August, 1880.

The Minister of Justice,

A. E. J. MODDERMAN.

Resolution of May 28th, 1880, establishing the Special Regulations of Police for the Walcheren Canal. (Kanaal door Walcheren).

WE WILLIAM III., BY THE GRACE OF GOD, KING OF THE NETHERLANDS, PRINCE OF ORANGE NASSAU, GRAND-DUKE OF LUXEMBURG, ETC., ETC., ETC.

On the report of our Minister of Waterstaat, Trade and Industry, dated April 10th, 1880, No. 57, section Trade and Industry;

Having considered Art. 2 of the General Regulations of Police for the Netherlands Government Canals, established by Our Resolution of February 5th, 1879 (*Gazette* No. 30);

Having taken into consideration the advice of Our Council of State, dated May 4th, 1880, No. 22;

Having considered the further report of Our aforesaid Minister, dated May 24th, 1880, No. 49, section Trade and Industry;

Have thought fit and resolved to establish the following special Regulations of Police for the Canal through *Walcheren*.

Art. 1.

By the *Walcheren* Canal (Kanaal door *Walcheren*) are understood:

The canal from the *Wester-Schelde* at *Vlissingen* (Flushing), to the *Veergat* near *Veere*, its side cut to *Arnemuiden* and *Nieuwland*, the outer ports, the former *Marinehaven* at *Vlissingen*, including the works and grounds belonging to the harbours, the canal, and the harbour site at *Vlissingen*.

Art. 2.

These Regulations are to be printed in the Dutch, English, German, and Norwegian languages, and may be had on applying for them to the canal officers and officials.

Art 3.

The maximum of the allowed dimensions of ships, designated in Art. 4 of the General Regulations, is for those passing the double sluices at Vlissingen and Veere, and navigating on the canal between the sluices:

Of length	120.00 meters
,, breadth	19.75 ,,
,, draught of water	7.10

For passing the former *Marine sluice:*

Of length	120.00 meters
,, breadth	17.25 ,,
,, draught of water	6.00 ,,

For passing the connecting canal and the wet dock at Vlissingen:

Of length	120.00 meters
,, breadth	19.75 ,,
,, draught of water	6.00 ,,

For navigating on the side cut to *Arnemuiden* and *Nieuwland:*

Of length	50.00 meters
,, breadth	7.50 ,,
,, draught of water	3.75

Art. 4.

No ship shall be passed through any of the sluices when the outer water has reached a height exceeding 2.60 meters above Amsterdam watermark, or when its height is lower than 2.20 meters below Amsterdam water-mark, or in case of a still lower tide and the flood-gates being used, then 3 meters, and the ebb-gates being used, then 3.25 meters.

Art. 5.

No ship shall be passed until the captain has applied to the sluice-master and informed him of the name of the captain, the name or number, and the size in cubic meters of the ship, the places of departure and destination, and the kind of cargo, proved by documents if required.

Captains of sea ships are allowed to send their first mates as their substitutes.

Art. 6.

The bridges at Vlissingen and Middleburg shall be kept closed for 15 minutes before the departure of any train from the local station at Vlissingen and the station at Middleburg, and also for 10 minutes after the arrival of any train at these stations.

The bridge at Vlissingen shall also be kept closed during from 20 to 5 minutes before the time of starting of any train from the harbour station.

The time of the bridges being open is marked during the day by a white ball or a white board.

Art. 7.

On the responsibility of the captain, the harbour-master is authorised to allow a deviation from the prescriptions in Art. 12 and Art. 13, clause 1, of the General Regulations.

Art. 8.

When to the red flag or red light, mentioned in Art. 16 of the General Regulations, a green flag or green light is added, any ship having a draught of water not exceeding six meters, is permitted to enter the outer port at Vlissingen.

Art. 9.

For having the level of the canal raised or lowered, a request is to be sent to the King's Commissary, who, on the report of the Chief-Engineer, will dispose of the same.

Art. 10.

The maximum of speed, designated in Art. 33 of the General Regulations, is in a minute:

For steamers having a draught exceeding 2.75 meters   125 meters
       ,,   ,,   not   ,,   2.75   ,,   150 ,,
                         ,,   ,,   2.00   ,,   250 ,,

Art. 11.

The largest dimensions allowed to timber floats are of 100 meters in length, and 7.50 meters in breadth. The rate of speed at which they are permitted to proceed shall not exceed 75 meters in a minute.

Art. 12.

Only in case of urgent necessity, timber-floats are allowed to stay in the canal, and then only on the east side, in one of the wide spaces in the canal destined for the ships passing each other.

Art. 13.

The number of ships towed at a time by a steamer shall not exceed twelve.

Art. 14.

In the inner port at Vlissingen, including the widened canal between the sea-sluice and the next sluice, no ship without leave of the harbour-master shall have a fire lighted on board from 9 p.m. to 6 a.m., or a light burning from midnight till 6 o'clock in the morning, with the exception of one single light, that may be kept burning in a duly closed lantern.

Art. 15.

In the case of the quay for discharging goods (*loskade*), and the part of the canal superintended and kept in repair by the town of Middleburg, being implied in the General Regulations, and these Special Regulations for "governmental harbour-master," read "town harbour-master," and for "canal officers" read "the Middleburg municipal officers."

Art. 16.

The payment and security, designated in Art. 82 of the General Regulations, shall be made at the office of the collector of canal taxes, either at Middleburg, Vlissingen, or Veere.

Our Minister of Waterstaat, Trade and Industry is entrusted with the execution of this Resolution, which shall be inserted in the *Gazette*, and communicated to the Council of State.

WILLIAM.

The Minister of Waterstaat, Trade and Industry,

    G. J. C. KLERCK.

Given the Fifth of June, 1880.

The Minister of Justice,

    A. E. J. MODDERMAN.

THE SCENERY

OF THE

BROADS AND RIVERS

OF

𝔑orfolk and 𝔖uffolk.

TWENTY-FOUR PHOTO-ENGRAVINGS

BY

G CHRISTOPHER DAVIES

(Author of "Norfolk Broads and Rivers").

PRICE TWO GUINEAS.

OPINIONS OF THE PRESS.

The *Eastern Daily Press* says:—"I have just had the opportunity of inspecting a series of twenty-four photo-engravings by Mr. G. Christopher Davies, exhibiting the quiet loveliness of East Anglian waters. The effects are soft and beautiful. No works of art illustrating the picturesque with which I am acquainted have more charming specimens of nature's grace than these glimpses of land and water afford. I imagine every lover of nature and Norfolk will seek to possess a copy of these photos, which form a fine testimony to the taste and skill of Mr. Davies."

The *Norwich Mercury* says:—"Mr. G. Christopher Davies' photographs of Norfolk Broads and River Scenery have already been made a source of pleasure to a great many of the citizens of Norwich, at the same time that they have helped to benefit the funds of the Norfolk and Norwich Hospital and other charitable institutions. We cannot wonder, then, at the desire that has been often expressed to possess copies of these delicate artistic representations of scenery so familiar. The outcome has been this, that Mr. Davies has found it necessary to have the choicest of these pictures reproduced by a new process of photo engraving. We have seen a set of the proofs of the photo-engravings printed on India paper. They are beyond all praise for the beauty of reproduction and printing, the delicacy of the originals being maintained to the full. Such a charming set of local pictures has never before been available to the public, and we cannot doubt that they will be highly prized. A more beautiful gift for the next Christmas or New Year could not be desired."

The *Fishing Gazette* says:—"Mr. Davies is an enthusiastic angler and lover of nature, and a most charming writer."

Chambers's Journal says: "These rivers and broads form the distinguishing and characteristic feature of the modern scenery of East Anglia."

The *Daily Telegraph* says: "It will be enough if yachtsmen on other rivers, anglers of other streams, and lovers of nature would turn their attention to the rivers and broads of Norfolk and Suffolk, still isolated and comparatively unfrequented in spite of railways, to ensure that they will go there again and again."

LONDON: JARROLD AND SONS, 3, PATERNOSTER BUILDINGS.

Printed in Great Britain
by Amazon